SPECIAL MESSAGE TO READERS

THE ULVERSCROFT FOUNDATION
(registered UK charity number 264873)
was established in 1972 to provide funds for research, diagnosis and treatment of eye diseases. Examples of major projects funded by the Ulverscroft Foundation are:-

- The Children's Eye Unit at Moorfields Eye Hospital, London
- The Ulverscroft Children's Eye Unit at Great Ormond Street Hospital for Sick Children
- Funding research into eye diseases and treatment at the Department of Ophthalmology, University of Leicester
- The Ulverscroft Vision Research Group, Institute of Child Health
- Twin operating theatres at the Western Ophthalmic Hospital, London
- The Chair of Ophthalmology at the Royal Australian College of Ophthalmologists

You can help further the work of the Foundation by making a donation or leaving a legacy. Every contribution is gratefully received. If you would like to help support the Foundation or require further information, please contact:

THE ULVERSCROFT FOUNDATION
The Green, Bradgate Road, Anstey
Leicester LE7 7FU, England
Tel: (0116) 236 4325

website: www.foundation.ulverscroft.com

E. V. Thompson was born in London. After spending nine years in the Royal Navy, he served as a Vice Squad policeman in Bristol, became an investigator for British Overseas Airways (during which time he was seconded to the Hong Kong Police Narcotics Bureau), then headed Rhodesia's Department of Civil Aviation Security Section. While in Rhodesia, he published over 200 short stories before moving back to England to become a full-time, award-winning writer. His first novel, *Chase the Wind*, the opening book in the Retallick saga, won the Best Historical Novel Award, and since then more than thirty novels have won him thousands of admirers around the world. In 2011 E. V. Thompson was awarded an MBE for services to literature and to the Cornish community. He died peacefully at his Launceston home in 2012; *The Bonds of Earth* was his last book.

CHURCHYARD AND HAWKE

After suffering a serious beating whilst engaged in unofficial undercover work in the murky streets and taverns of London's 19th-century slums, Constable Tom Churchyard takes himself to Cornwall. Here, in spite of his injuries, he becomes right-hand man to Amos Hawke, now a senior Cornish policeman. His knowledge of the London rogues proves invaluable as Amos seeks to foil a gang of city thieves whose plan is to plunder the mansions of the Cornish gentry. When a brutal murder is committed during their investigations, it proves far more complex than it appeared at first glance . . .

E. V. THOMPSON

CHURCHYARD AND HAWKE

Complete and Unabridged

CHARNWOOD
Leicester

First published in Great Britain in 2009 by
Robert Hale Limited
London

First Charnwood Edition
published 2014
by arrangement with
Robert Hale Limited
London

A catalogue record for this book is available from the British Library.

ISBN 978–1–4448–2134–5

Published by
F. A. Thorpe (Publishing)
Anstey, Leicestershire

Set by Words & Graphics Ltd.
Anstey, Leicestershire
Printed and bound in Great Britain by
T. J. International Ltd., Padstow, Cornwall

This book is printed on acid-free paper

1

In his first floor office at the Bodmin headquarters of the Cornwall constabulary, Superintendent Amos Hawke became aware of raised voices coming from the police station inquiry office on the ground floor of the building. Frowning irritably at having his concentration broken, he waited for the commotion to cease, but it continued unabated.

There were three voices. One he recognized as belonging to Sergeant Hodge, the duty station officer, the second probably also belonged to a policeman, but the third was that of a young woman and she sounded upset.

Sounds from the inquiry office would not normally have been heard on the first floor, but Cornwall, indeed the whole of Britain, was in the grip of a heat-wave and it was being said that 1859 was the hottest summer anyone could remember. As a result, even though it was not yet noon, all windows in the police headquarters were open in the hope that a breeze would spring up and bring some relief to the perspiring policemen working inside who were obliged to carry out their duties wearing heavy, high-necked serge coats.

The noise from the inquiry office showed no sign of abating and with a sigh of resignation, Amos placed his pen on the ink-tray on his desk and stood up. Fastening the buttons at the neck of his coat and collecting his uniform cap from the hat-stand as he exited the office, he made his way downstairs.

He reached the corridor on the ground floor just as a young girl wearing cheap but tidy clothes was being led from the inquiry office to the front door between Sergeant Hodge and a constable, both of whom towered head and shoulders above her.

The girl was no longer protesting, but there were tears on her cheeks and, speaking to the sergeant, Amos demanded, 'What's going on, Sergeant Hodge, why is the young girl so upset?'

Before the police sergeant could reply, the girl wailed, 'They won't listen to me . . . they think I'm making things up.'

Over the girl's head, Sergeant Hodge gave Amos an exasperated look. After pointing to the girl he put a forefinger to his forehead and twisted his hand back and forth in a gesture suggesting there was 'something loose' in her brain, at the same time explaining, 'It's all right, sir, I've known Enid Merryn since she was small. In fact, it was me who got her work as a scullery maid up at Laneglos House, the big mansion off the Lostwithiel road. There's no harm in her but she has a vivid imagination and sometimes sees and hears things that aren't there.'

Struggling unsuccessfully to break free of the large policeman's arm, Enid retorted, '*You* may not see or hear everything I do, Alfie Hodge, but I knows Jem well enough when he speaks to me. I knows him only *too* well and I saw him yesterday evening.'

'Well, even if you *did* see him there's nothing we can do about it . . . '

To Amos, the sergeant said apologetically, 'This young man she's talking about worked up at Laneglos House until a few weeks ago. He wasn't there more than a couple of months but it was long enough for him to get to know young Enid a little too well and to steal money from her employers.'

'He took money from *me* too,' Enid declared, 'He promised to pay it back but then he ran off.'

Looking at Amos over the girl's head once more, Sergeant Hodge shook his head.

Ignoring the gesture, Amos asked, 'Why was this young man never arrested?'

'He likely would have been,' Sergeant Hodge replied, 'but Lady Hogg, up at the big house said the money involved was such a trifling sum it wasn't worth all the trouble it would have caused.'

'I should have been informed of this,' Amos said sharply, '*I* will decide whether or not someone should be arrested for breaking the law.'

Addressing the Laneglos scullery maid, he asked, 'This Jem . . . does he have a surname?'

Despite her earlier indignation at not being taken seriously, now Enid had the attention of a senior policeman she seemed to suffer from a sudden loss of confidence. 'Yes, and I know it . . . but I can't remember what it is.'

'Is he a local lad?' Amos put the question to her.

'No, he comes from London . . . where the

Queen lives. He's *seen* her, too, lots of times.'

Amos doubted whether her 'Jem' had actually seen Queen Victoria, but had boasted that he had, in order to impress this gullible young scullery-maid. He asked, 'I don't suppose Jem mentioned where it was he lived in London?'

'He did tell me, more than once. He said it was one of the smartest parts of London. It was called something like . . . Oxford, but it wasn't that, although I know it started with 'Ox . . . ' something or another.'

Amos tried unsuccessfully to think of a London district that began with 'Ox', before remembering that an 'H' at the beginning of any word was invariably ignored by Londoners from the poorer districts of London. 'I suppose it wasn't 'Hoxton' by any chance?' he suggested, mentioning one of the roughest slums in the East End of London.

Enid's face lit up immediately, 'That's it, 'Oxton', that's where Jem comes from.'

Before being taken on as a superintendent in the newly-formed Cornwall constabulary, Amos had been a detective in the Metropolitan Police's Scotland Yard and much of his work had been in the slum areas of London where crime thrived and law and order was despised. Of all these areas of narrow alleyways, dingy streets and jumbled houses, Hoxton was the worst. A high percentage of those arrested for the most violent crimes came from here and its residents were proud of the self-explanatory nickname 'Kill-copper Alley' which had been given to the area. If someone — anyone — from Hoxton was in

Cornwall, Amos wanted to know about it.

Speaking to the senior of the two men with Enid, he said, 'You may release Enid now, Sergeant Hodge. I would like to have a word with her in my office about this young Jem. Have a cup of tea sent up for her, will you?'

* * *

Enid Merryn seemed over-awed at being in Amos's office and in an effort to put her at ease, he asked general questions about her work at Laneglos House but even when a constable brought a cup of tea to the office for her she maintained her reserve — until Amos asked whether she had always lived in the Bodmin area.

'Oh no, sir,' she replied, 'I come from Porthpean, near Charlestown. My father was a fisherman there . . . but he died before I came to work up at Laneglos.'

'I know Porthpean well,' Amos said, glad to have found some common ground between them. 'My wife was the schoolmistress at Charlestown for many years. You might have known her . . . she was Talwyn Kernow then.'

'You married Miss Kernow, sir?' Enid's delight was unfeigned, 'I liked her very much. My pa paid for me to go to her school and she learned me to write my name — and to read . . . well, just a little. I wasn't very quick at learning, but she was always kind to me and I liked her lots. I would have liked to stay at her school, but when my pa was drowned we moved into St Austell to live with my grandma and Sergeant Hodge got me work as a scullery-maid at Laneglos — only he wasn't *Sergeant* Hodge then, he was a grocer who used to deliver to the big house and he spoke for me.'

The knowledge that she was talking to the husband of the woman who had once been her much-liked teacher succeeded in putting Enid at her ease and Amos was soon able to broach the subject of the mysterious 'Jem'. When he asked her once again if she knew his surname, she said immediately, 'Yes, sir, I've remembered now, it's 'Smith', he's Jem Smith . . . Jeremy Smith, really, but he said I should call him Jem.'

Even in the unlikely event that this was the young man's real name, there were hundreds of Smiths in the East End of London, many being of Gypsy origins. Amos knew he would get nowhere with this particular line of inquiry.

'How well did you come to know Jeremy when he was working at Laneglos?' he asked.

Enid's evident embarrassment gave Amos the answer even before she replied. Not meeting his eyes, she said, 'I thought he loved me . . . he said we would get married one day.'

'I see, but then he borrowed money from you and after stealing money from your employer he was dismissed?'

'No. When the money went missing he knew everyone would blame him because he wasn't from around here, so he just ran away. He didn't even say 'goodbye' to me.'

Enid became tearful yet again and Amos said hurriedly, 'Do *you* believe he stole the money?'

Enid hesitated for a long time before replying, 'No . . . at least, I didn't then. I loved him and thought he loved me, but when I saw him yesterday he wasn't the same, somehow.'

Tears were still trembling in her eyes and Amos asked gently, 'Where was he when you saw him, Enid . . . and what was he doing?'

'Miss Wicks, who's housekeeping up at Laneglos, sent me to fetch the candlesticks from the church, for cleaning. The church belongs to the house and is just behind it. When I was on my way there I saw something moving in the bushes. I thought it might have been a sheep got in there, or perhaps a dog, so I went to shoo it out. But it wasn't an animal, it was Jem and there was a man with him he said was his uncle. Instead of being pleased to see me Jem was angry, especially when I asked him if he'd come to give me back the money he'd borrowed. He was so nasty he made me cry.'

'Did he say what he was doing there?'

'No, but his uncle did. He said Jem hadn't meant to be angry with me. It was just that he was upset because he thought I was more interested in the money than I was about what he had been doing since he had to run away from Laneglos. His uncle said he and Jem had come all the way from London, 'specially to tell me they were going into a business . . . something or another.'

Here she paused, unable to find the word she was seeking and Amos prompted her, ' . . . venture? Was it a business *venture* he was talking about?'

Enid's face lit up and she said, 'That's right, that's what it was . . . a business venture. He made it sound very important and said it was going to make them a lot of money. When it did he said Jem would come back to Cornwall and give me twice as much money as I'd lent him because I was so kind to him when he was in need.'

'This 'uncle' told you that? Didn't Jem say anything?' Amos tried not to sound too sceptical.

'Yes . . . but he still seemed angry with me. He said I wasn't to tell anyone that he'd come all the way back to Cornwall to see me. If I did he said the police would come looking for him because of the money that had been taken from the big house and that even though he hadn't taken it you'd put him in prison and he wouldn't be able to give me back *my* money.'

'I see . . . yet you must have told someone of seeing him, or you wouldn't be here now — or did you think you ought to come anyway?'

Enid appeared uncomfortable now and she said, 'I didn't *mean* to say anything, but last night Lucy, one of the parlourmaids, was teasing me about Jem and she was being nasty to me. She said that because he'd got what he wanted from me I'd never see him again. She went on for so long that I got cross and told her she was wrong. That Jem *had* come back and I'd seen him only that day. She told Miss Wicks what I'd said and I was sent for this morning and told I had to come here and report that Jem — she called him Jeremy, of course — that he was trespassing on Laneglos land . . . but he *wasn't* trespassing, he'd only come back to speak to me. But it doesn't really matter, Sergeant Hodge didn't believe me anyway, so Jem shouldn't be cross with me.'

Amos was deeply disturbed by what this simple young servant had told him. If the mysterious 'Jem Smith' from Hoxton had returned to Laneglos and was skulking around the grounds with a so-called 'uncle' the chances were that they were planning to burgle the house.

'Did Jem or his uncle say anything more to you? Want to know who was staying at the house, perhaps?'

'No,' Enid shook her head, 'He asked me about some of the servants he'd known but a lot of his talk was about the summer ball that's being held in the great gallery at Laneglos next month. His uncle said Jem was worried that I might need to work too hard. They asked me how many people would be coming? What time it would end . . . ? All that sort of thing.'

Beaming through her tears at Amos, she added, 'Jem must have told his uncle lots about me or he wouldn't have known so much about what I do at Laneglos . . . so Jem really must love me, mustn't he?'

Ignoring her question, Amos asked, 'This uncle . . . does he have a name?'

'Of course! I mean, everyone has a name, don't they? But Jem never mentioned it.'

The sound of the town hall clock could be heard through the open window and, suddenly apprehensive, Enid asked, 'Can I go now, please?

Miss Wicks said I was to get back to the house as quick as I could and not dawdle.'

'Yes, you can go back to Laneglos. Tell Miss Wicks you've been a great help to me and I'll be coming up to the house to have a chat with her and Lady Hogg first thing tomorrow morning.'

Enid had been pleased when Amos had told her she had been a great help, but she was horrified when he said he would speak to her employer.

'I don't think Miss Wicks will be very pleased if Lady Hogg is bothered by what's happened, sir. She says it's her job to see the family aren't troubled by the goings-on of servants.'

Amos smiled, 'Very well, Enid, just tell her I've said you've been a great help to the police and very sensible. I'll be up at Laneglos to speak to *her*, just as soon as I can. If you see this Jeremy again in the meantime, be sure to tell Miss Wicks — but say nothing to him about the talk you've had with me, you understand?'

Enid nodded, she was in a hurry to get away but paused in the doorway to say, 'Thank you for listening to me, sir, and for believing me. I know I'm not very clever — but I don't tell lies.'

When she had left, Amos decided he liked the simple young scullery-maid. Not least because she had given him an excellent reason for putting boring paperwork to one side for a while and turning his attention to the work he enjoyed most. Pitting his wits against criminals.

2

After Enid had left the police station Amos was still thinking of what she had told him when there came a knock on the open door of his office and a tall, powerfully built man entered the room. On the right sleeve of his uniform coat he wore a badge depicting a silver crown, denoting that he was the force's sergeant major.

Responsible for training recruits to the recently-formed Cornwall constabulary, Sergeant Major Harvey Halloran was an ex-Royal Marines colour sergeant. He had served with Amos in the Crimean war and was his second-in-command when Amos was given the task of policing a small town captured from the Russians. Harvey was also an ex prize-fighting champion and Amos had been instrumental in having him appointed to his present post.

Because of this, and their association in the past, there was a close bond between the two men, although Harvey remained deferential in his manner towards the man who was once again his superior officer.

Saluting Amos smartly, he said, 'I hope you don't mind, Mr Hawke, sir, I've dismissed the recruits early because of the heat. One of them collapsed and I didn't want to lose the whole intake, so I brought the drill to a halt.'

'Well done, Harvey, we're having so much trouble recruiting suitable men I doubt if we're ever going to reach our complement. We can't afford to lose a single one of those we *have* taken on . . . but I'm glad you've come up to the office. I seem to remember you lived in Hoxton when we were both in London. Because of your association with prize-fighting you must have got to know many of the villains there — and it seems we might have had a visit from a couple of them . . . ' He went on to tell Harvey of the young Laneglos scullery-maid's visit to the police station and her story of the mysterious 'Jeremy Smith'.

When he ended, Harvey said, 'I doubt very much whether Smith is his real name even if Jeremy — or Jem — is, although I can think of half-a-dozen young ruffians by the name of 'Smith' who would fit the bill and Jem is a popular name in Hoxton, the name being that of a bare-fist fighter who was a local champion around twenty years ago. If we had a few more details I could write to a friend of mine, Tom Churchyard. He's stationed on the Met's 'K' Division, which takes in Hoxton. He's only a constable, but he knows just about every villain on his patch and should have been made a detective long ago. He's also an ex-Royal Marine, like you and me but, as I say, I'd need a bit more information to give him than a name that might, or might not, be his real one.'

Turning over in his mind what Harvey had said, Amos reached a decision, 'I have a nasty feeling about this,' he said, 'but, I agree, we need to know more about the young man in question and in view of the hot weather I think the recruits might welcome a break from drill for the rest of the day. Send them out on the beat with experienced constables and you and I will go along to Laneglos and see if we can learn a little more about this 'Jeremy Smith'.'

* * *

Before setting off for Laneglos, Amos had the duty station sergeant tell him all he knew of the big house and its residents.

Built in the 17th century, a short time before the outbreak of the English Civil War, it had a very large three storey façade with equally large wings set at right angles to it on either end. There was a cluster of outbuildings and stables to one side of the house and its own church some distance away at the rear. Laneglos had been in the Hogg family since the Restoration and the present owner was Viscount Edwin Hogg, one-time Member of Parliament and past Lord Lieutenant and Sheriff of Cornwall. In indifferent health for the last few years, he left the running of the great house to his second wife, whom he had married when she was a titled widow with grown up sons and daughters by her late husband, also a Viscount.

Hogg had a son and daughter by his first wife but both these children had married and moved away, although one day the son would inherit both his father's title and the estate.

Laneglos, one of the largest houses in the Duchy of Cornwall, was at the hub of the county's society. It had more than forty servants and gardeners all currently overseen by Laneglos's young but formidable acting housekeeper, Flora Wicks.

After making their way along a curving, tree-lined drive in a gig, one of a number supplied by the county for its police superintendents, Amos and Harvey arrived at the front door of the great house. When the horse and gig came to a halt, a groom was on hand immediately to take charge of the outfit.

After explaining their business the two policemen were escorted inside the house by a footman and taken to the housekeeper's sitting-room where Flora Wicks soon arrived to speak with them.

A tall, confident young woman in her twenties, Flora Wicks was surprisingly young for the important post she held. She was, in fact, employed by the Hogg family as the *assistant* housekeeper but the regular housekeeper, who had held the post for almost thirty years had been taken ill a few weeks before. She was now recovering slowly and in the meantime Flora Wicks was firmly in command of the household.

Flora was fully aware of her present status in the household of one of Cornwall's most influential families and Amos did not doubt that in spite of her lack of years she carried out her duties with the strictness and efficiency expected of her.

When Amos introduced himself and Harvey, the housekeeper said, 'Enid informed me you would be calling but although it was I who said she must come and speak with you, upon reflection I fear I might be wasting your time, Superintendent, Enid is a very imaginative young girl.'

'That may be so,' Amos replied, 'but I am not without experience of those who have inventive imaginations and I believe Enid is telling the truth about your late employee. Sergeant Major Halloran and I have come to Laneglos to learn what we can of this Jeremy Smith. It's probably not his real name but in conversation with Enid it seems he mentioned the district of London from whence he came. Sergeant Major Halloran is familiar with that particular area and many of the criminals who live there. We are hoping he may learn enough about this young man to identify him and form an opinion of what he might be planning — and I am convinced he is up to something. Would you have any of his references, or the names of the men or women from whom they come?'

'I *do* have a reference,' Flora admitted. Showing mild embarrassment, she added, 'Unfortunately it is worthless. When Smith applied for work at Laneglos he gave a reference purporting to come from a senior military man. I followed it up, of course, only to learn that the officer in question had closed down his London house on being posted to Bermuda. If it was a false reference then Smith must have learned of the officer's posting from one of the London newspapers and used it to his advantage.'

When Amos raised an eyebrow at the housekeeper's apparent breach of the basic principle of thoroughly checking references produced by prospective servants, she flushed and said defensively, 'Of course, in the circumstances I did not take it upon *myself* to accept the reference. I consulted Lady Hogg and her youngest son by her previous marriage, the Honourable Charles Delville, who happened to be at Laneglos at the time. The excellent reference was written in an educated hand on notepaper embellished with the crest of the officer's family and they both agreed we should accept it as being genuine.'

Nodding his head in acknowledgement that she was not entirely to blame for employing 'Smith', Amos said, 'I am beginning to think we might be dealing with some very resourceful criminals, Miss Wicks. I don't think your late footman was working alone and I doubt whether making off with a trifling amount of money was his main purpose in obtaining work at Laneglos. By his actions this young man might well have prejudiced a far more serious criminal plan, but in order to discover what such a plan might be, I need to learn more about him. Is there any one of your servants who was particularly friendly with him and who might be able to tell us something?'

The housekeeper shook her head, 'Only Enid — and I thoroughly disapproved of the friendship . . . ' A sudden thought came to her and she asked, 'Would it help if I showed you a photograph of Smith?'

Her question took Amos by surprise, 'You have a photograph of him?' Photography was still a comparatively new innovation and quite expensive. It was hardly something a servant could afford . . . but Flora Wicks explained.

'A photographer has being going around the great houses of Cornwall taking photographs of families and staff. Lady Hogg thought it would be nice to have one taken of all the household staff and servants. The result is hanging in the servants' sitting-room. I will have a maid fetch it. While we wait perhaps you and Mr Halloran would like a cup of tea . . . ?'

While the housekeeper was out of the room summoning a maid, Amos said, 'This is a stroke of luck, Harvey. If the photograph is a good likeness you should be able to send a description of this Jeremy Smith to your friend in London, together with any information we glean from the other servants.'

When Flora Wicks returned to the room carrying a framed photograph, she was accompanied by a maid bearing a tray on which were the promised tea and a plate of biscuits.

Harvey took the photograph from her while Amos moved a vase of flowers to one side in order that the maid could place the tray things on an occasional table. When the maid gave a hurried curtsy and hurried from the room, Flora Wicks said to Harvey, 'I will show you which of the servants in the photograph is Smith . . . '

'You don't need to,' Harvey replied, 'Unless I'm mistaken he's second from left in the back row.'

The housekeeper was momentarily too surprised to reply but Amos asked, 'You know him, Harvey?'

'Yes . . . but not as Jeremy Smith. He's Jimmy Banks, a young man who I believe served prison sentences for pickpocketing and theft when he was still a boy. It's common knowledge in Hoxton that he's been guilty of more crimes since then — although as far as I know nothing has been proven against him recently. Nevertheless, he's well on his way to maintaining the reputations of the rest of his family. His father was transported for robbery, at least two of his brothers have served prison sentences for burglary — and an uncle was hanged for murder.'

Lowering the photograph, Harvey said, 'You are right to be concerned about him. We can be absolutely certain Jimmy Banks wasn't working at Laneglos because he fancied a footman's life. He and his friends are up to something — and I think we need to find out what it is.'

The housekeeper's dignified air of authority had dissipated while Harvey was talking and now she groped for a chair that was behind her. Finding it, she sat down heavily and gasped, 'I am sorry, gentlemen . . . I feel suddenly faint!'

* * *

'I met one of your ex-pupils today, Talwyn, a rather simple young girl named Enid who used to live at Porthpean.'

Amos was speaking to his wife that evening in the kitchen of their home as she prepared the evening meal. They had been married for little more than a year and, after spending almost half of his twenty-nine years in the Royal Marines and a couple of years in bachelor lodgings when he was a Scotland Yard detective, the mundane details of domestic life were still very much a novelty to him. He also enjoyed watching Talwyn, whatever she was doing.

'You must be speaking of Enid Merryn. Yes, she is a simple girl, but she has a lovely gentle nature. She was only at the school for a year or so but I grew very fond of her. I hope she isn't in any trouble?'

'I hope so too,' Amos replied. He told her of his meeting with the Laneglos scullery-maid and of her involvement with Jimmy Banks, alias Jem Smith.

'Oh dear, poor Enid, she is such a warm little soul, she'd give her heart to any young man who said he loved her. If he's gone off with her savings and let her down she'll be heart-broken.'

'I fear it might be far more serious than a broken heart and a few stolen pounds,' Amos replied, gravely, 'I believe this young man might be in league with others who are planning some villainy against Laneglos House. He doesn't sound the type to desert the life he's been leading in London in order to work as a poorly paid footman in a Cornish country mansion — or go to the length of having a letter of reference forged in order to do so. The letter has been written by an educated man on headed notepaper. Such things aren't difficult to obtain in London, but they don't come cheap.'

'Do you think he and the others are planning to burgle Laneglos? They will need to be very bold, there are a great many staff employed there.'

'That's quite true,' Amos agreed, 'and the housekeeper told me her employer insists on having two armed gamekeepers patrolling the estate at night, that's why I believe something more than burglary is being planned. It seems the man who was with this young ex-footman when Enid surprised them in the Laneglos grounds yesterday was asking questions about a grand summer ball that's being held there in a couple of weeks time. Do you know anything about it?'

'Of course!' Talwyn stopped what she was doing in order to enlighten Amos. 'It's an annual charity event. I have never attended it myself but it is the social event of the year. Everyone who lays claim to being part of Cornish society will be there, showing off the latest fashions.'

' . . . And no doubt displaying their most expensive jewellery too,' Amos mused. 'It would make a tempting target for a gang of well organised thieves. I'll have a word with the Chief Constable tomorrow and see if he'll agree to me making a trip to London to find out all I can about young Jimmy Banks and his dubious friends.'

3

Four days after their visit to Laneglos, Amos travelled by train with Harvey Halloran to London. They crossed from Cornwall to Devon via the newly-opened railway bridge that now towered above the River Tamar, the waterway which formed a natural border between the two counties.

Amos had reported the happenings at Laneglos, together with his suspicion that a major crime was being planned, to the Cornwall Chief Constable. An ex-army man, the County's senior policeman was having a great many problems recruiting for his force, not least the opposition of many of the gentry at having such a force imposed upon them. He was alarmed at the prospect of a serious crime being perpetrated against one of Cornwall's most influential landowners and readily gave Amos permission to go to London to meet with Constable Churchyard of the Metropolitan Police taking Harvey with him, the drilling of new recruits being suspended for the immediate future.

Tom Churchyard met the two Cornish policemen at Paddington Station, in London. He was younger than Amos had expected, being no more than twenty-seven or twenty-eight years old, but en route to Scotland Yard where they were to have a meeting with a senior detective, Amos learned that Churchyard, like himself, had joined the Royal Marines as a young boy and seen action in a number of places in the world before leaving to join the Metropolitan Police three years before.

Brought up in the East End of London prior to joining the Royal Marines, he was immediately sent back to his birthplace to help keep order in the most lawless district of the whole of London.

Churchyard's knowledge of the area and the families who resided there gave him a distinct advantage over most of his colleagues and he quickly gained a reputation as the man to speak to if information was needed about any of the many criminals dwelling in the warren of dingy streets and alleyways of Hoxton.

The young policeman was tall and clean cut and, although he addressed the Cornish police superintendent as 'sir' and showed him the deference his rank demanded, his manner was in no way servile. Amos thought that despite his lowly origins Tom Churchyard considered himself the equal of anyone he was likely to meet with, whatever the other's station in life.

As an ex-member of the Metropolitan Police himself, Amos realized it was an attitude that would not please Tom Churchyard's superior officers. His knowledge of the notorious Hoxton area and the fact that he was exceptionally good at his work secured his place in the London force, but it was unlikely he would ever gain promotion.

Nevertheless, Amos took an instant liking to the young Constable and on the way to Scotland

Yard in a Hackney carriage, asked him how well he knew Jimmy Banks, alias Jem Smith.

'Well enough,' Churchyard replied, 'Although I've never arrested *him* I've taken most of his family in at one time or another. They're a thoroughly nasty lot who between them have been guilty of just about every crime in the book. Jimmy is a thief too — he could hardly be anything else with his background — but he's probably the best of a bad lot . . . '

Breaking off and showing signs of embarrassment, he added, ' . . . but if you don't mind, sir, I would rather wait until we get to Scotland Yard before going into detail about the Banks family and their accomplices. Detective Inspector Dyson is in charge of plain clothes police at Scotland Yard and has left word that he wants to be present when we discuss them.'

'So Dyson is still there!' Ames commented, 'I thought he might have moved on to less demanding work.'

Herbert Dyson had been a detective sergeant on one of the Metropolitan Districts when Amos had been at Scotland Yard. Amos liked neither the man, nor the methods he was rumoured to employ in order to secure convictions.

When Amos had been sent to Cornwall to investigate a number of brutal murders, including that of the officer who was then in charge of London's detectives, he had been made an acting detective inspector and it was expected he would take over the detective branch upon his return. Instead, the post had been given to Dyson — who was married to the daughter of one of the Metropolitan Police's Assistant Commissioners.

It gave Amos a moment of wry satisfaction that it was because of this he had accepted his present post with the Cornwall Constabulary. He now held a rank senior to that of Inspector Dyson . . . but Constable Churchyard was talking to him once more.

' . . . I was forgetting you were once a Metropolitan detective too, sir. I expect you and Inspector Dyson will have a lot to talk about.'

'I doubt it,' Amos said, 'we never worked together on any cases of importance.'

There was something in Amos's short reply that emboldened the young constable to say, 'I've heard many of those who *did* work with you in those days say it should be you heading the detective branch now.'

Amos shook his head, 'I am quite happy where I am — and I have no doubt Inspector Dyson is doing all that was expected of him when he was appointed.'

Tom Churchyard was a bright young man. He realized that Amos's reply was a diplomatic one and not an endorsement of Inspector Dyson's suitability for the post he held.

Equally non-committal, he said, 'I'm sure everyone at Scotland Yard would agree with you, sir.'

It was enough. Without saying a word against the officer in charge of the Metropolitan detectives, each man was made fully aware of the other's opinion of him.

* * *

Arriving at Scotland Yard, Amos and his two companions were shown into Inspector Dyson's spacious office on the ground floor and Amos thought ruefully that it was a far cry from the cramped attic office *he* had occupied when stationed here.

Dyson was not in the office and did not put in an appearance for another twenty minutes. When he did finally arrive he showed no sign of having been hurried and made only a cursory apology, saying, 'Sorry I'm late, Hawke, there was something that required my attention.'

It was quite apparent to Amos that the detective inspector had deliberately kept him waiting and that his mode of address was intended as a reminder that *he* had once been the senior of the two. However, the situation had changed and Amos thought he needed to make this clear to Dyson immediately.

Without any apparent rancour, he said easily, 'It's *Superintendent* Hawke now, *Inspector* Dyson and I have no wish to waste any more of your time than is absolutely necessary. Indeed, it's Constable Churchyard I have come to London to speak with. I think he might have information that can assist an investigation my force is carrying out, so if you'd rather I returned to 'K' Division with him . . . ?'

Dyson was aware of the justifiable rebuke implicit in Amos's words, but 'Superintendent' Hawke stuck in his throat. 'As the officer in charge of detectives it is important that I am aware of the activities of any criminals who reside in the Metropolitan Police area.' With a smirk, he added, 'Besides, next month I am to be promoted to superintendent and will be taking over 'K' Division, so I need to know anything likely to involve one of my officers there.'

Amos realized that Dyson's father-in-law had far more to do with the proposed promotion than Dyson's ability, but he made no comment that might alienate the detective chief any more than he had already. He needed all the help that Tom Churchyard was able to give to him.

In the event the meeting proved to be a frustrating one. The Hoxton constable was so vague in his replies to Amos's questions about the activities of Jimmy Banks, his relatives and their accomplices that Amos eventually brought the meeting to a close, expressing regret that Churchyard had been unable to provide as much information as he had been led to expect.

'Well, of course he is not a detective,' Dyson said smugly, 'but if Scotland Yard is able to be of assistance while I remain in charge you may make an application to me — via the Commissioner, of course.'

With this, Dyson ushered the two men from Cornwall out of his office, keeping Churchyard behind.

Walking away from Scotland Yard, Amos commented bitterly, 'We've had a wasted journey, Harvey. I thought Tom Churchyard would be able to tell us a great deal more than he did.'

'He should have done . . . and still might,'

Harvey said. 'When you and Inspector Dyson were leaving the office and I was saying goodbye to him he asked where we were staying. When I told him, he whispered he would come there as soon as he could get away from Scotland Yard.'

'Why the need for such secrecy? If he had something to tell us why didn't he speak when we were back there in the office?'

'I believe it's because he doesn't trust Dyson,' Harvey declared, 'Did you see how dismayed he looked when Dyson said he was to take over as superintendent of 'K' Division?'

'No, I had other things on my mind,' Amos replied. 'I don't like Dyson and never have. His methods of policing are not to my liking — but he's still a policeman and we are both pursuing the same ends.'

'Well, let's wait and see what Tom has to say when he comes to the hotel,' Harvey suggested.

4

The hotel where Amos and Harvey were staying overlooked St James's Park and was only a short distance from Scotland Yard. Nevertheless, they were kept waiting for half-an-hour before Tom Churchyard joined them there.

He explained that he had been detained by Inspector Dyson, who questioned him about what had been discussed between himself and the two Cornish policemen. Dyson seemed delighted that Amos had not gained the information for which he had come to London, adding his opinion that the Chief Constable of the Cornwall Constabulary should have requested the assistance of Scotland Yard and not sent Amos to London seeking information from a uniform policeman.

'I was not *sent* to London,' said Amos, 'I came with my Chief Constable's blessing to follow up my own enquiries . . . but you haven't come here to discuss any differences that may exist between Inspector Dyson and myself'

'Well . . . in a way I *have*,' the London Constable declared, 'I didn't tell you very much on the way to Scotland Yard because I'd been ordered not to. The order was given to me by my inspector, but it came from Dyson. When I queried the reason for it I was told that any information about London criminals should be given in the presence of a London detective.'

'It seems such an order was unnecessary,' Amos shrugged, 'You don't have any information that could be of use to me.'

Suddenly ill-at-ease, Churchyard said, 'That isn't strictly true, sir. I know Jimmy Banks well enough and I know those he goes around with — and what their specialities are.'

'Then why did you say nothing when we were at Scotland Yard?' Amos demanded.

Even more uncomfortable now, Tom Churchyard replied, 'If I speak honestly will you promise that nothing I say will get back to Inspector Dyson? I enjoy police work and I would be dismissed immediately. As it is, he's ordered me to go straight back to Hackney police station and have the station sergeant record the time I arrive, so I'll probably need to run most of the way when I leave here.'

'Inspector Dyson and I have very little in common, Churchyard. I doubt if he and I will ever meet again. Even if we did, I can't envisage sharing confidences with him.'

When the London constable still appeared uncertain, Harvey said, 'I'll vouch for that, Tom. You can speak your mind to Superintendent Hawke. When we were in the Marines together I said things to him that would have had me court-martialled and flogged had they been repeated to anyone else.'

Harvey's words succeeded in re-assuring Tom Churchyard. Hesitantly at first, but with increasing confidence, he said, 'Things don't always go the way they should when they're reported to Inspector Dyson. Villains who've been caught bang-to-rights never reach court, others who've done little — or perhaps nothing at all — go down, sometimes for a very long time. This isn't just hearsay, sir, I've had it happen to villains I've handed over to him.'

Silent for a long time, Amos frowned, 'These are serious allegations, Churchyard, have you spoken of them to anyone else?'

Tom Churchyard shook his head, 'I wouldn't dare. As you mentioned when we were talking about him earlier, he's the son-in-law of an Assistant Commissioner and I would lose more than the job I enjoy. I keep my mouth shut and do my best to keep out of his way.'

'That's not going to be easy when he takes over 'K' Division,' Amos pointed out.

'I know,' Tom Churchyard said, unhappily, 'I'm going to have to think of a reason for moving to another Division.'

Changing the subject, Amos said, 'You told me there was something you had kept back when we were all in Dyson's office, what is it?'

'It's about Jimmy Banks. With his family background there has never been any doubt that he'd get himself into trouble. He was born into a family where thieving is a way of life and he's never known anything else, but he's a small time thief and, quite frankly, has neither the gumption nor the brains to be anything else but until he disappeared from the scene some weeks ago he'd started keeping company with men who will either end their lives on the gallows, or be put away never to be seen again. He showed up again recently and since then has been swaggering around looking like a cat that's had the cream. Even more worrying, the more active villains have gone very quiet and are keeping their heads down. A rumour is going around that something big is being planned and it's got back to senior officers on the Division. I was asked to try to find out what's going on. I managed to corner someone who has given me good information in the past. He told me I shouldn't worry because, although something big *is* being planned and will involve the Banks family and others, it's not going to happen on 'K' Division — or even in London. He either couldn't, or wouldn't, tell more than that, but from what you've told me, I'd say trouble is coming *your* way and you're right to be worried about it.'

'I am *very* worried,' Amos said, 'The Cornwall constabulary is a new force and has a great many critics. My Chief Constable is anxious we should be seen to be making a big difference to crime in the county. All the information I have at the moment indicates that something is going to happen at or around the time of the county's summer ball. Everyone with any social standing in the county will be there, so if anything goes wrong it will be disastrous for the force. Is there any chance this informant would say more if he was offered money?'

'There would probably have been a very good chance,' Tom Churchyard said, adding apologetically, 'Unfortunately, he got drunk a couple of nights ago and chose the wrong man to pick a fight with. He was knifed and died on the pavement outside a side door of St Leonard's hospital, just around the corner from Hoxton.'

While he was talking, the London policeman had glanced at the clock on the wall of the hotel's lounge. Now he said, 'I really must get back to the station, or I am going to be in trouble.'

'Of course,' Amos said, sympathetically, 'but before you go . . . you have my address. If you learn anything more please let me know as a matter of urgency. I would be particularly pleased if you could give me names of anyone rumoured to be involved in whatever is going on, together with the type of crime they specialise in, or crimes in which they are known, or even *suspected* of being involved.'

'I'll do what I can,' Tom Churchyard promised and shook hands with both the Cornish policemen but as he was leaving, Amos said, 'There's one other thing, Tom . . . if you ever feel like a change of scenery, or find it impossible to work with Dyson, I can offer you a place in the Cornwall constabulary with the rank of sergeant and guaranteed promotion to inspector within two or three years. You'd find it interesting work because I would have you working with me as an 'investigation officer'. It would be a brand new post, created especially to exploit the talents I believe you possess.'

The offer took Tom Churchyard by surprise. Recovering quickly, he said, 'Thank you, sir . . . thank you very much. It's an offer I'll consider seriously, but first I'll try to gather the information you want to justify the faith you have in my ability.'

* * *

As the date for the Laneglos grand summer ball drew ever nearer, Amos became increasingly anxious at the lack of more information from Tom Churchyard. He wrote twice pleading with him to send whatever information he had gleaned, but received replies to neither.

In the meantime, Chief Constable Gilbert had been called to Laneglos on two occasions by Viscount Hogg. The septuagenarian peer owned the great house and was responsible for the success of the prestigious social occasion. He had not been told of the threat from London criminals, but was anxious there should be no untoward incident to mar the evening's enjoyment.

The chief constable came to Amos's office after his latest visit to the peer's home and the two senior policemen discussed the situation. They had a close working relationship and Gilbert had no hesitation in expressing his concern.

'I am seriously worried about the consequences of a major crime being committed during the Ball, Amos. A great many of those who will be present were highly critical of Cornwall having a police force in the first place and they resent every penny being spent on us. If a major incident takes place while they are at Laneglos they will seize upon it to prove their point. It might even cost both of us our jobs! Have we been able to learn any more from London?'

'I've written two letters to the constable who knows Jimmy Banks and some of the other criminals we believe are likely to be involved, but have had no reply,' Amos explained.

'Could the lack of information have anything to do with the detective chief you do not see eye-to-eye with?'

'It's possible,' Amos admitted.

'Well, time is not on our side, Amos, the ball is only a few days away and, as I have said, our credibility and that of the Cornwall Constabulary is under threat. Unless you can make a breakthrough very quickly I will be obliged to call upon the services of Scotland Yard, regardless of your relations with the man in charge there.'

* * *

The 'breakthrough' referred to by Chief Constable Gilbert came about the next evening.

Amos was at home with Talwyn, seated in the kitchen drinking tea, when, looking out of a window, she said, 'There's someone coming up the path, Amos . . . it looks as though he might have been in a fight.'

Leaping to his feet and looking through the same window, Amos saw a tall young man with his left arm in a sling and a face that was bruised and grazed. At first he thought it must be someone coming to the house to report an incidence of fighting — yet there was something familiar about the man.

Not until the unexpected visitor had almost reached the door did Amos recognize him . . . it was Tom Churchyard.

5

'Coming for a quick game of billiards before turning in, Tom?'

The speaker was leaning across the green cloth of the billiard table, peering down the length of a slightly warped wooden cue as Tom Churchyard passed through the recreation room, en route to the staircase that led to the upstairs cubicles which served as bedrooms in the Hackney police section house

'No, it's been a hard day, I think I'll turn in early. Who's duty sergeant tonight?'

'Sergeant Dogget . . . so you needn't worry about being disturbed.'

As he spoke the off-duty policeman played his shot. The white ball cannoned off the red and dropped into a corner pocket and Tom left the billiard room, relieved to know Dogget would be on duty in the section house that night. There were strict rules governing conduct in the barrack-like police quarters. One requirement was that all constables were to be present in the building by 10 p.m. unless on late shift and all lights were required to be extinguished by midnight.

The duty sergeant was instructed to check that these rules were being adhered to — but some sergeants carried out their duties more diligently than others. Sergeant Dogget was nearing retirement and spent his duty hours carefully avoiding anything that might involve him in extra work, or cause problems for himself. It suited Tom to have such a man on duty this particular night.

Far from having an early night, he intended taking advantage of an insecure window in a ground floor cloakroom after 'lights out' and heading for the beer-houses and dubious taverns to be found in the narrow alleyways of nearby Hoxton. Here he hoped to meet up with one of his informers who might be able to give him some useful information about what villainy the Banks family were planning to carry out in Cornwall.

* * *

A few minutes after midnight, Tom climbed through the insecure sash window of the darkened cloakroom and dropped to the ground in a small yard at the rear of the section house. Letting himself out through the yard gate he entered an alleyway that ran behind the premises.

Wearing old clothes that had been used on more than one occasion when carrying out surveillance duties he would not be out of place among those frequenting the area towards which he was heading. Nevertheless, he was aware of the increasing danger of being recognized by those he had arrested in the past.

Although it was the early hours of the morning, there were still many people abroad in the litter-strewn streets and alleyways of the

London slum and most of those who bumped against him were in varying states of intoxication.

There was no street lighting here. The naked flame from a pitch torch would have been dangerous, so old and rotten were the timbers of the overhanging upper rooms of the tightly packed and jumbled houses. Occasionally, the dull and uncertain yellow light from a candle stub escaped through a window pane that had not been blocked by a piece of rotting wood, or stuffed with a cloth to keep out rain, or the fetid, cold air.

Once, when passing by such a window, Tom tensed when someone called out to him in greeting. The call came from a drunken man who had recognized a familiar face but, fortunately, alcohol had confounded the recollection that Tom had once arrested him.

Before long Tom was in the foul-smelling heart of Hoxton. The stench, offensive to even the most insensitive nose, emanated from a variety of obnoxious causes, all detrimental to the health and well-being of those who lived here.

Occasionally, in the darkness Tom was accosted by a whining prostitute, too pox-raddled to show her face in the lighted streets where her younger sisters plied their age-old trade.

This was the area from which Tom had made his escape when he left to join the Royal Marines, many years before, and it held no terrors for him, although he would not have dared to show his face here alone in the uniform of a police constable.

Yet there was a certain jollity here in these night hours, albeit fuelled by cheap alcohol. He passed a number of smoke-filled beer-houses where discordant singing added to the general hubbub inside, before arriving at one that was in a small square and larger than the others. Pulling his cap down in a bid to shadow his face more, Tom entered the smoky and crowded interior and pushed his way between the drinkers, looking around him for a certain 'Nick Shelby', hoping the informer was not pursuing his nefarious 'trade' in a more salubrious area of London.

Shelby was an opportunist thief, stealing anything that its owner was careless enough to make available to him. Unlike many of Hoxton's criminals, Shelby was not a violent man. Slightly built and with a wasting lung disease, he would not have lasted long had he chosen to take up more violent crime — or had he chosen an honest way of life. He was tolerated by his peers only because he was basically as dishonest as they were — and because his father had been a highly regarded burglar until, pursued by servants, he fell to his death from the roof of a mansion he was robbing.

Tom had arrested Shelby on two occasions. For the first offence the petty thief had received three months imprisonment for stealing clothes from a washing-line. The next time their paths had crossed, Shelby had stolen an overcoat from a tavern similar to the one Tom was now visiting.

Seized by a passer-by, Shelby had been

handed over to Tom, but the coat's owner had declined to proceed with a prosecution, not wishing to have it known that he frequented such establishments.

However, Shelby had been convinced that Tom had persuaded the coat's owner not to prosecute and showed his gratitude by supplying him with occasional snippets of useful information about the predations of his fellow thieves.

Eventually, Tom located the petty-thief seated at a table talking to a youngish prostitute whom he believed to be supplementing the meagre income Shelby earned from his dishonest ways. His suspicions were confirmed when Shelby nudged his companion and nodded to where a prospective 'client' was showing an interest in her.

When the woman crossed to where the man was seated, Tom carried his drink across the room and sat down on the seat she had just vacated, saying, 'Hello, Nick, it looks as though you've found yourself a good little wage earner. Is she as generous with her money as she is with her favours?'

'I don't know what you're talking about, Mr Churchyard, me and Molly was just talking, friendly like, when I saw the punter eyeing her. I was enjoying her company, but she's a working-girl and has a living to earn so I told her he seemed interested and off she went. She might buy me a beer later on if she does well out of him, but that's all.'

'You don't need to make excuses to me, Nick, I'm not particularly interested right now. I thought you might be able to help me with information about something I *am* concerned about.'

Relieved, Shelby said, 'If I can help you in any way, I will, Mr Churchyard, you know that.'

'Good. Tell me what I want to know and I might even buy you another drink before Molly comes back.' Leaning closer to his companion, he said softly, 'There seems to be a lot going on involving Alfie Banks and the sort of villain we're not used to seeing in Hoxton. What can you tell me about it?'

The light was poor in the smoky tavern, but Tom could have sworn that the small-time thief paled at his question. Looking about him hurriedly, Shelby said, 'Now that ain't a fair question, Mr Churchyard — you know it ain't. If word was to get back to Alfie that I'd even mentioned his name when I was talking to you my life wouldn't be worth a dud ha'penny.'

'Word's not likely to get back to him, Nick . . . certainly not from me, but something is going on . . . something big, and I want to know what it is. You've got bigger ears than most around here, what have you heard?'

Looking about him again, and licking his lips nervously, Shelby said, 'You probably already know as much as I do, Mr Churchyard. There's something being planned, but Alfie and his mates are tight-lipped about it. All I *can* say is that it's not going to happen around here. The wife of one of Banks's mates was telling my ma that her old man was going to be out of 'The Smoke' for a few days but when he comes back she'd be able to pay back the couple of quid she borrowed from ma nigh on a year ago. I believe a couple more of Alfie's 'boys' have said they're going away for a day or two, as well.'

'When is this, Nick? When are they going to be out of London?'

'I believe it's towards the end of next week . . . but I'm not certain about that.'

Tom nodded his acceptance of the other man's statement, 'Fair enough . . . but you've mentioned there are a few men involved. I'd like names, Nick — not only of the Banks family, but of those who've been coming to Hoxton to talk with Alfie . . . '

The petty thief was about to protest, but Tom cut his protest short. ' . . . Before you say you don't know, you'll have heard rumours of some of those who've been seen around. I want their names.'

'You're putting me in a tight spot, Mr Churchyard. I've always helped you in the past when you've wanted something, you know I have, but this is *big* time. It's not only Alfie who'd be looking for me if word got out that I'd been talking to you about 'em. We're talking of men who'd top the likes of me as soon as spit.'

Aware that Shelby was really frightened, Tom said, 'Just give me names, Nick. I've got a good memory, so there's no need to write anything down. Even if I'm recognized in here, as far as anyone is concerned we could be discussing the weather. Once you've told me the names of those you know about I'll buy you a drink, then go off and leave you alone . . . '

Ten minutes later Tom made his way out of the tavern, leaving behind him a deeply troubled thief. He was aware now that Shelby's fear was fully justified. Some of the names he had given to him were of well-known criminals. A few were already known to him, others he knew only by the reputation they had made for themselves in the criminal world.

He was well-satisfied with what he had learned, even though he had not been given times or dates for whatever was going on. The diverse 'talents' of the criminals named by Shelby indicated that something well out of the ordinary was being planned and if, as seemed highly probable, the gang's target was to be Cornwall, Superintendent Amos Hawke was facing a major problem.

Tom was still thinking about Amos and what might be about to happen in Cornwall when he heard the sound of hurrying footsteps behind him, coming from a group of men. As they drew closer he stepped into the shallow recess provided by a doorway in order to allow them to pass.

Two men had passed by when those following stopped, apparently aware of his presence in the doorway. When one of them addressed him, saying, 'Constable Churchyard?' Tom knew he was in trouble. The mode of address, coming as it did, here in Hoxton, was ominous and he thought he recognized the voice of Alfie Banks, uncle of the young man Amos Hawke had come to London to enquire about.

Thinking quickly, he replied, 'Not me, mister.

It must have been that bloke that almost pushed me over when he ran by just now.'

To Tom's dismay, the man who had spoken to him chuckled, 'Nice try, Churchyard, but I'd recognize that voice anywhere — and you've been using it to ask too many questions about too many people. It doesn't go down well in Hoxton, you should know that.'

It was dark in the alleyway, but Tom realized there were probably five or six men around the doorway. He could not hope to take them all on . . . but neither could he remain where he was.

Hoping to take them by surprise, he lunged at Alfie Banks and slammed him back hard against one of his companions before leaping from the doorway. His intention was to flee along the alleyway in an attempt to escape from the Hoxton men.

He might have been successful had not one of the men who had accosted him been knocked to his knees when his escape bid was made. Tom tripped over him and, before he could climb to his feet and run a heavy boot caught him on the side of his temple. Temporarily dazed, he fell to the ground and as he struggled to regain his feet he was pummelled, kicked and finally stamped upon as he lay upon the ground, covering his face with his hands.

The attack seemed to last an age, although it could have only been a matter of minutes before the man who had previously spoken to him, said, 'All right, that's enough, we don't want to kill him . . . at least, not *this* time.'

When the attack ceased, Alfie Banks said to

Tom, 'You've been given just a warning this time, Churchyard, take it and be grateful — and don't come into Hoxton poking your nose into something that don't concern you. Nothing's going to happen on your patch, so mind your own business. Ask any more questions and you won't get off so lightly next time . . . in fact, you probably won't get off at all. You were born here, so you know why it's called 'Kill Copper Alley'. Don't make us prove a point, it's not worth it.'

As quickly as they had caught up with him the men had departed as anonymously as they had arrived, leaving Tom to climb painfully to his feet, aware that a wrist, stamped on by one of the booted men was probably broken.

Knowing too that there was no way he could keep his injuries a secret from the police force to which he belonged . . .

6

Leaving a startled Talwyn staring after him, Amos reached the front door in time to fling it open just as Tom Churchyard raised his sound arm to make his presence known.

'Churchyard . . . what's happened to you?'

'It's a long story, sir,' the young Londoner replied wearily, 'but I have news for you . . . some good, some bad.'

'That can wait for a few minutes. Come on inside, you look done-in.'

'Thank you, sir. I must admit I've felt better . . . '

Talwyn had come into the hallway behind Amos and was looking with some trepidation at the man Amos was inviting into their home.

Aware of her concern, as Amos guided their visitor to the sitting room, he explained, 'Talwyn, this is the man I have been waiting to hear from, Constable Tom Churchyard of the Metropolitan Police.'

'Ex-constable, sir,' Tom corrected him, 'I was dismissed by Superintendent Dyson yesterday. It was one of his first acts as Superintendent of 'K' Division and I think it probably gave him a great deal of pleasure.'

'You were dismissed . . . ? Why? Tell me what's been happening . . . have you managed to find out anything about Banks and his fellow ruffians?'

'It's all tied in together . . . but may I sit down, sir? I've walked all the way from the railway station, after travelling from London.'

'Of course, you look very weary . . . ' turning to his wife, Amos said, 'Talwyn, can you ask Katie to fetch Tom a cup of tea?'

Katie was the young village girl who helped out in the house as a maid-of-all-work.

'Of course, I'll go and find her.'

Talwyn was away for only a few minutes, by which time Amos had taken the visitor's coat and sat him down in a comfortable armchair — with a brandy to help revive him after his long journey.

When Talwyn settled herself on another chair, Amos said, 'First of all, Tom, tell us how you came by your injuries — and why Dyson dismissed you.'

Tom grimaced wryly, 'It's all to do with Jimmy Banks and the villains he's working with. As soon as I began making serious enquiries about them I realized something *really* big was being planned. They've been meeting up secretly and bringing in villains not usually associated with that part of London. Unfortunately, I wasn't always sent out on the patch which included Hoxton, so I needed to go there when I was off-duty — and that's when I ran into trouble . . . '

The arrival of the young maid with a tray on which was tea and portions of cake interrupted Tom's story and he admitted he had neither eaten nor drunk anything on that hot summer's day.

Amos allowed the unexpected visitor to eat some cake and did not prompt him to continue his story until a second cup of tea had been poured for him.

Resuming his report, Tom said, 'As you know, sir, police section houses have a strict rule about anyone not actually on duty being in by ten o'clock, with lights out at twelve. You'll also know that the type of men we're interested in don't keep those hours, so I used to come and go using a back window with a faulty lock and spend some of the night hours in Hoxton, either speaking to a couple of narks I know, or seeing who was meeting up with the Banks family. Unfortunately, word got around that I was asking questions about them. When I was walking along a dark alleyway behind the Britannia theatre I was jumped on by four or five men — one of them Alfie Banks, Jimmy's uncle — beaten and left half-conscious. Before they went away I was told to keep my nose out of what was none of my business, or next time I wouldn't get away so lightly — if I got away at all. Luckily, St Leonard's hospital was just around the corner so I went there. They patched me up but told me I had a fractured wrist. Of course, there was no way I could keep my injuries a secret and I was up before Dyson yesterday. I told him I'd gone out to keep an eye on some criminals I believed were up to no good, but I think he guessed what I was really doing. He said that any information about criminal activities should have been passed on to the detective branch and that I was there to *prevent* crime, not incite violence by my actions. He fined me two week's pay for being involved in a fight when I was off duty and dismissed me from the force for rendering myself unfit for duty by my own actions.'

Talwyn had been listening sympathetically as Tom's story unfolded. Now she said, 'You poor man! What will you do now . . . and where will you be spending the night?'

Shrugging his shoulders, Tom said, 'I was hoping you might be able to tell me of somewhere near at hand — but before I go I'd like to tell Superintendent Hawke all I've learned about the plans of the Banks brothers and their gang. It's the reason I've come to Cornwall and it's important — probably very important.'

'Then you'll stay here with us, at least until the summer ball is over,' Talwyn said firmly, 'but wait while I tell Katie to make one of the spare rooms ready for you before telling Amos what you know. I would like to hear it.'

When Tom appeared surprised that she should intend being present for what was essentially a police matter, Talwyn explained, 'You know the people who are planning something against Laneglos, Tom, and Amos is going to have to make plans to stop them — but I have lived here for most of my life and know Cornwall a lot better than he does, so I think we might all have something to contribute.'

7

By the time the housemaid had been given her instructions and Talwyn returned to the room, Amos had poured drinks for them all and Tom began relating what he knew.

'As you know, even before Harvey wrote to me I'd heard rumours that something big was being planned by Hoxton criminals, involving the Banks family and their pals, but it wasn't until I began looking into it for you that I realized it was likely to be *really* out of the ordinary, involving villains who would normally keep well clear of the thuggery associated with the Banks's.'

Interrupting Tom, Amos asked, 'Before you go any further, do you have any names of those involved?'

'Quite a few,' Tom affirmed, 'but apart from the Banks themselves I know only one or two by sight. Many of the others have been involved, or suspected of being involved in crimes but they specialise in the sort of villainy a uniform constable rarely gets to deal with, although there's a chance you will have come across some of them during your time at Scotland Yard. I have a list here of those who have been seen in the Hoxton area recently but it's by no means complete.'

As he was reaching awkwardly into an inside pocket of his coat, Amos asked, 'Is there any one

Hoxton man in particular these men are going to see?'

Locating two slightly crumpled sheets of paper, Tom pulled them free from the pocket and handed them to Amos, at the same time replying to his question, 'That's something of a mystery. I know they are meeting up with the Banks family and Alfie Banks is, loosely speaking, the one the family looks up to as their leader, but as far as I am aware he's never operated outside London and doesn't have the brains to organise something as big as this would appear to be.'

While Tom spoke, Amos was glancing through the list of names. Reaching the end of the second page, he looked up; and said, 'I *do* know one or two of the villains on the list and I've heard of others, but you are quite right, Tom, they are a diverse bunch who should have nothing but dishonesty in common with one another. I notice there are also a couple of women on the list. Have you learned anything about them?'

'I actually know one of them quite well. We grew up together. She was Dolly Brooks then and I believe she's distantly related to the Banks family. She had the looks to get her out of the East End and went on the stage. By the time she was twenty she was the mistress of some titled young buck and had changed her name to Adelaide Brokingdale — the name she uses now. She adopted the airs and graces to go with such a name too but eventually her lover's father became alarmed because his son was becoming *too* involved with her. He gave him the alternative of going off on the grand tour of Europe — or being disinherited. According to Dolly, her lover wanted to smuggle her out of England and take her with him but she has a very real terror of travelling on the water. It had already come between her and her career when her theatrical company went to America. Anyway, her lover had no option but to go to Europe without her. Dolly set herself up running a high class whorehouse in the posh part of London. Her establishment also became known as a place where women with enough money could obtain a discreet abortion. Unfortunately for Dolly, when the daughter of an otherwise respectable family died as a result, there was such a scandal that she went to prison. It wasn't long before someone with influence secured her release, but her so-called men 'friends' deserted her and she returned to the stage. But her glamour has faded somewhat and it would seem she's on the downward slope now and has turned to her family again.'

'You've done well, Tom, but I wish we knew exactly what it is her family are planning to do.'

'I was hoping to learn more on the night I was attacked,' Tom said, ruefully, 'but someone must have told the Banks family I was taking too great an interest in what they are doing. Even if I were to return to Hoxton now my narks would be too frightened to tell me anything.'

'I wouldn't hear of you going back to Hoxton,' Amos said, firmly, 'but I wonder whether it's worth contacting Scotland Yard now Dyson has gone, to see whether they've heard anything that might help me find out what's going on? Time is getting short if they are planning something at the county ball.'

Tom shook his head, 'The new man in charge is Inspector Tilling. He was a sergeant with Dyson and they are close friends. He came to the office at the Yard while I was still there, shortly after you and Harvey had left and agreed with Dyson that there was no sense stirring things up in Hoxton when whatever was going on wasn't happening on the Met's ground. Like Dyson, Tilling is ambitious. He wouldn't risk doing anything to upset an Assistant Commissioner's son-in-law.'

Amos reluctantly accepted that Tom was probably right and he said so, adding, 'You must come to my office with me tomorrow, Tom. I'll arrange a meeting with the Chief Constable and get Harvey in on it too. We'll see if between us we can work out what it is the Banks family and their friends are up to.'

* * *

Later that night, in the darkness of their bedroom, Amos and Talwyn were discussing the implications of the information Tom Churchyard had brought with him from London. Amos expressed his doubts about the ability of the inexperienced Cornwall constabulary to effectively deal with the influx of so many ruthless and experienced criminals.

'It sounds as though that is exactly why these criminals have chosen Cornwall as their target,'

Talwyn said, 'As you've said yourself, most other counties have had an organised police force for many years. This will probably be the last opportunity they have to get away with such a thing — and the only place where they are likely to succeed.'

'My duty is to see they *don't* succeed,' Amos pointed out, 'but just talking to you about what could happen has already given me an idea. There are so many doubts about the force being able to cope with whatever these villains intend doing at Laneglos that the obvious answer is to disrupt their plans before they get to the house.'

They were lying together in bed and Amos could not see her expression, when she said, 'It's all very well to say that's what you'll do, but you don't even know what it is they have planned, so how can you prevent them from doing it?'

'We'll certainly need to have luck on our side,' Amos agreed, 'and the first piece of luck will mean outguessing them — but that might not be as hard as it seems. The list Tom brought from London contains the names of villains who have been involved in almost every crime that's come before the London courts. They range from pickpocketing and robbery, to deception, sleight of hand, confidence tricks and all types of fraud. It's the men and women who carry out the last crimes I've mentioned who are going to be most difficult to detect. The best of them are adept at passing themselves off as gentry.'

'But . . . what can such men — and women — hope to achieve at a *ball?*' Talwyn was puzzled.

'I can think of a number of things,' Amos replied, 'At such large functions as a grand ball in a house like Laneglos there will be rooms set aside for smoking and drinking — and where men gather in such places they will wager — and discuss business matters. A clever villain would be able to rile a drunken man sufficiently for him to wager far more than he otherwise might on something the criminal has rigged. Others might pretend to be very knowledgeable about what is going on in the city and persuade someone with money to sign his name to something he believes will make him a healthy profit. But this is just scratching the surface of what *could* happen. There are a great many ways a clever rogue can part a rich man from his money — especially when drink is flowing freely. There will also be well-dressed pickpockets circulating among the guests, relieving men of gold watches and purses — but I suspect the main target will be the women, many of whom will no doubt be weighed down by a fortune in jewellery.'

'Surely no thief will be able to take jewellery from a woman in a crowded ballroom?' Talwyn's disbelief was evident in her voice.

'Some of the London thieves I know are so skilful they could probably rob them of the clothes they're wearing as well,' Amos retorted. He was aware he was exaggerating — but not by very much. 'What really worries me is that some of the men named on Tom's list are known to go out armed. With so many villains involved they could be planning to hold up the guests and take *everything* from them all. If that happens it's probable some guests will have drunk enough to try to stop them — and it could turn really nasty. I can't allow matters to reach that stage, Talwyn, I need to nip it in the bud.'

'It's an absolute nightmare!' Talwyn was aghast at the thought of what Amos had suggested could take place at the County's social event of the year and the realization of the danger *he* would be in, 'Do you *really* think that is what is being planned?'

'It could go even farther,' Amos replied, grimly. 'Some of the names on Tom's list are of well-known burglars, many of whom are wanted men. *They* won't risk being seen at the ball. If they are involved in this they will be breaking into the house and stripping it of everything of value while the other gang members are busy in the ballroom.'

For a long time Talwyn lay beside Amos in silence, then she said, 'The sheer scale of all this is almost unbelievable, Amos. Cornwall will have seen nothing like it since the French and Spaniards came pillaging the coastal towns and villages! It is a very, very frightening prospect . . . '

Then, the tone of her voice changing, she said, 'But there is nothing more that can be done about it tonight . . . Have you remembered that tomorrow is the first anniversary of the day we moved into this, our first home? I know you're going to be very busy . . . far too busy to celebrate, I fully understand that, but let's not waste tonight . . . '

Amos believed that *nothing* could take his

mind from thoughts of the imminent onslaught the London criminals had planned, but marriage was still a comparatively new experience for both of them — and Talwyn was a loving, caring and resourceful young woman . . .

8

Chief Constable Gilbert was so worried about the prospect of the Cornwall Summer Ball being taken over by London criminals that he readily agreed with Amos that he should try to thwart them in every way possible. After discussing the matter in his office, he said, 'You may call on the services of every man in the force if need be, Amos . . . but do you have any plans of how best to use them?'

'I think fifty constables should be adequate,' Amos replied, 'but they must be the best men we have and we'll need to depend to a great extent upon Sergeant Major Halloran — and Tom Churchyard.'

The ex-London constable had been introduced to the Chief Constable before going off with Harvey to sift through the list of London criminals believed to be on their way to Cornwall.

'Churchyard's fractured wrist is going to prevent him being of any great help,' Gilbert pointed out.

'On the contrary,' Amos said, 'His knowledge of the criminals involved will be invaluable. For that reason alone I would like him to be taken on as a sergeant — with immediate effect. I'll go further and forecast that within a couple of years you will be making him an inspector. We need men like him in the force.'

'We need recruits, certainly, especially those with police experience, but they need to be *able-bodied.* I would be pilloried by the Police Committee if I took on a disabled man — and as a sergeant!'

'With all due respect, sir, I don't think we can afford *not* to take him on. We are going to have to rely very heavily upon Churchyard's knowledge in order to identify the villains involved — and I am sure I don't need to remind you that he sustained his injury whilst obtaining information on behalf of the Cornwall constabulary.'

Amos could see that his reminder of the importance to the force of the success of the county ball had given the Chief Constable pause for thought and he added, 'The Committee have already approved the appointment of a sergeant clerk to assist me in my office and Churchyard is the ideal man for the post . . . after all, it is Churchyard's *left* wrist that's broken.'

Shrugging his shoulders in a resigned gesture of acquiescence, Gilbert said, 'Alright, Amos, you have convinced me . . . I hope I can do the same with the Police Committee. You had better keep him in plainclothes for the time being. We can't have an invalid going around in uniform.'

Amos was delighted. The arrangement would suit him well. The Police Committee had made it clear in the past that they would not agree to having a plainclothes detective section within the force, expressing an opinion that it would be tantamount to having the police 'spying' on the populace. This was Amos's means of obtaining his own way by subterfuge. He intended that

Tom Churchyard would remain in plainclothes for the foreseeable future — even when his wrist had healed.

* * *

'If none of those we're looking for get off this train I shall begin to worry?'

Tom spoke the words to Amos as they sat in the station-master's office at Bodmin Road railway station waiting for the arrival of the 6.15p.m. train from London. The Grand Ball at Laneglos was only forty-eight hours away but, as yet, there had been no sighting in Cornwall of any of the London criminals and he was worried he might have been fed false information about the plans of the Hoxton criminals. It was not unknown for them to deliberately mislead policemen in order to divert attention from their real intentions.

'I'll save my worrying until after tomorrow's train,' Amos lied, 'None of them will want to spend more time than is absolutely necessary in Cornwall, so they will leave it until the last minute to arrive . . . ' He broke off to say, ' . . . but here's the train now!'

The Great Western locomotive, dribbling dark smoke from a tall crenulated smoke-stack had come into view along the curving line from the east, heading a line of chocolate-and-cream coloured carriages.

As the locomotive slowed alongside the platform and the block brakes of the train screeched in complaint, the fireman on the open footplate, his face blackened by smoke and perspiring heavily, waved off the small boys who were running to keep pace with the engine, while the driver tugged at levers and opened and closed valves to bring the train to a halt.

Seven passengers alighted from the train and, laying a hand on Amos's arm, Tom said excitedly, 'There's Dolly Brooks . . . The woman wearing the leghorn hat.'

Looking to where a tall, slim and attractive woman was being handed from the train, Amos exclaimed, 'And I recognize the man she's with! The last time I saw him he was standing in the dock at Marylebone magistrates' court. He was charged with a comparatively minor fraud under the name of Shannon . . . Conrad Shannon. He is a very plausible rogue. So plausible that he convinced the magistrate of his innocence and as a result got away with it. I heard afterwards that Shannon was only one of many names he's used during a lifetime of fraud, deception and forgery. He has been in prison more than once.'

Dolly Brooks had linked arms with Shannon and the pair were walking towards the station exit followed by a porter carrying a suitcase he had lifted from the carriage compartment they had just left.

'What do we do about them?' Tom asked.

Amos had cast an eye swiftly over the other passengers. Satisfied they were country men and women who had probably travelled no farther than from Plymouth on the train, he said, 'We'll see whether they are being met by anyone. If they are not . . . we arrest them.'

* * *

Outside the railway station the majority of Cornish passengers boarded a waiting horse-drawn bus, others choosing to walk the mile or so distance to Bodmin town. Dolly and her companion paused for a moment before being directed to a waiting hire-carriage by the porter carrying their baggage.

The porter handed the portmanteau to the driver of the carriage and the couple from London were about to board the vehicle when the two policemen accosted them. It was Tom who spoke first. Addressing the woman, he said, 'You're a long way from home, Dolly, to what do we owe the pleasure of your presence in Cornwall?'

Startled, Dolly regained her composure very quickly. Drawing herself up to her full height and speaking in a cultured voice, she said haughtily, 'I don't think we have met before and my name is not Dolly. You have apparently mistaken me for someone else.'

Shaking his head and assuming a sad expression, Tom replied, 'You may have changed your name and lost your Hoxton accent but we have known each other too long for there to be any mistake, Dolly. I repeat, what are you doing here, in Cornwall?'

Amos thought he had detected a brief moment of alarm on the face of Dolly's escort when Tom first spoke to her but now, aware he was talking to a man with an arm in a sling, the man said arrogantly, 'My companion has told you she does not know you — and has no wish to do so. It is none of your business but her name is Adelaide, not Dolly, and we have come from London to attend a ball being held by Viscount Hogg. Now, if you will kindly excuse us . . . '

He was about to hand Dolly into the carriage when Amos spoke, 'One moment, sir, perhaps my colleague should have introduced himself. He is Sergeant Churchyard of the Cornwall constabulary — and I am Superintendent Hawke. Your name is . . . ?'

'I have no wish to know either your names, or your ranks but you can be quite certain I will bring your behaviour to the attention of your Chief Constable . . . I presume he will be attending the ball at Laneglos?'

'Possibly,' Amos agreed, 'but you haven't answered my question . . . Your name, if you please?'

'This is unwarranted harassment,' blustered the man, 'I am Sir Richard Donahue. As I am employed at the Treasury in London it is possible I am known to your Chief Constable.'

'It is possible he will *know* you,' Amos admitted, ' . . . as indeed do I, but I seem to remember that when I last saw you, you were standing in the dock in Marylebone magistrates court, calling yourself Conrad Shannon — and some of my colleagues there could remember a number of other names you had adopted in the past. I think you and Dolly — or Adelaide — had better come with us to the police station in Bodmin and sort out exactly who we all are . . . '

9

Looking through a barred aperture in the solid oak door of the police cell, Tom Churchyard saw Dolly Brooks lying on the built-in wooden bench which, together with a bucket in a corner of the diminutive and Spartan room, formed the only furnishings. A rolled up coat served as a pillow and Dolly was lying looking up at the white-washed ceiling, meditating on the events which had led to her incarceration.

Tom entered the cell carefully balancing in his good hand a tray on which was a bowl of watery vegetable soup, a hunk of bread, cheese and a mug of weak tea.

Turning her head, Dolly said, 'Oh, it's you!'

'That's right, Doll,' Tom said cheerfully, 'Personal service, 'specially for you.'

'You can poke your 'personal service'. Just let me out of this bleedin' hole.' Sitting up stiffly, she added, 'I've done nothing wrong.'

The refined accent in evidence at Bodmin Road railway station had gone and she had reverted to the dialect of the area from which both she and Tom originated.

Still cheerful, Tom placed the tray on the plank bench beside her, saying, 'I believe you, Doll . . . and so does Superintendent Hawke, but that's only because we picked up you and 'Sir Richard' before you'd had time to do what you'd come to Cornwall for.'

'Oh? And what is it I'm supposed to have come here to do?'

Seating himself on the bench with the tray between them, Tom replied, 'Now, that's exactly what Superintendent Hawke and me have been wondering. As I told him, knowing you as well as I do, there are so *many* things you're good at. There were times I've known you go into a shop as skinny as an orphan — and come out looking eight months gone, with half the shopkeeper's stock stuffed up your jumper. I've also heard you bragging that you could go 'up west', collide with half-a-dozen rich men and have their watches and purses while they were still peering down inside your bodice and assuring you there was no need for you to apologize.'

Smiling benignly at her, Tom continued, 'Of course, there was much more, Doll . . . like the shilling-a-time knee-tremblers in the alleyway by the school for young gents at St Pauls . . . '

'All right, you've made your point — and stop calling me 'Doll'! It's a scullery-maid's name and whatever else I may have been I've never been a drudge . . . but to go back to my original question, I've done nothing, so why are you keeping me in here? It ain't right.'

'The problem is, Doll, you don't need to *do* anything at all, it's what your friends and relatives get up to that's likely to land you in trouble. You see, there's a crime — a very serious one — known as 'conspiracy'. That's when a lot of villains get together and decide they're going to break the law. Now, once the law is broken all those who conspired to do it are equally guilty

— *whether they were at the scene or not when it was committed* — and they'll be given the same punishment as those who carried it out.'

'But . . . that's not fair!' At first indignant, Dolly realized she had almost admitted she was aware something was planned and she added quickly, 'Anyway, I don't know of anything that's going on.'

'I'm afraid that won't wash, Doll. We already know that something's been planned and we know where and when it's going to happen. What's more, we've found evidence on your 'Sir Richard' that incriminates both of you. Evidence that proves your intention of being at the scene of the crime together with the others involved. I'm very much afraid that it's Newgate again for you — only this time it will be for very many years with no one to get you out.'

There was an element of truth in what Tom had told her. They had found two tickets for the Laneglos Grand County Ball in the possession of Conrad Shannon, the name in which Dolly's companion had been entered in the Police Station's custody book, despite his insistence that he was Sir Richard Donahue.

Whether this was sufficient to convict the pair of conspiracy was uncertain, but Tom's claim certainly scared Dolly. With unfeigned horror she pleaded, 'You can't have me sent back to Newgate, Tom . . . I couldn't take it. I'd top myself if I had to stay in there for very long, I swear I would. Take pity on me Tom . . . for old time's sake!'

Tom was aware that Dolly had been an actress

— and a very good one, with a wide repertoire of feigned emotions. She was also a convicted criminal. He had no illusions about her inherent dishonesty but he had known her before her conviction and was aware her upbringing and life itself had drawn her into ways that came naturally to so many of her contemporaries.

'There *is* a way you can stay out of prison, Doll, and probably keep many of your friends and family out too. I don't carry enough rank to make a decision on it myself, but Superintendent Hawke does. I can't promise he'll even *want* to help you, but I'll discuss it with him.'

'Bless you, Tom. You always were the best of our bunch. If you hadn't gone off to sea when you did, you and me might have got together and I'd have been a different woman . . . just for you.'

Tom could have reminded her that, young though she was at the time, she had set out on her course in life long before he left Hoxton. Nevertheless he felt that at least *some* of her tears might be genuine. However, Amos had already left the police station. Discussion about her future would need to wait until the next morning.

* * *

When Tom gave details of his interview with Dolly to his superior officer the next day, Amos said, 'Well, we certainly have enough evidence to bring them both before a magistrate right now, Tom. The stationmaster at Bodmin road railway station has just been to see me. It seems that two of the tickets handed in from the London train were very clever forgeries. They were for the journey from London — and Dolly and Shannon were the only passengers to have travelled the whole way. All the other passengers had boarded the train at Plymouth. Nevertheless, if Dolly is willing to tell us exactly what is being planned and we are able to nip it in the bud I would be quite happy to send her back to London without charging her.'

Smiling, he added, 'I would even be willing to pay for a genuine ticket for her out of my own pocket. Shall we go and have a word with her now?'

'It might be better if you go alone. She believes that because we were once kids together in Hoxton she can get away with far too much with me. She'll probably say more to you if you are hard on her and are blunt about the consequences of not telling us what we want to know.'

'That makes sense,' Amos agreed. 'All right, I'll bring her out of her cell and see what I can learn. In the meantime I would like you to go to Laneglos to speak to the housekeeper, a Miss Wicks. As well as the forged railway tickets taken from Shannon, he had a couple of tickets to the County Ball. I believe they may be forged too. If they are it's highly possible that all the tickets being carried by the Hoxton villains are forged. It could be a means of identifying anyone who gives us the slip at the station and succeeds in getting as far as Laneglos . . . so it is very important to us to know, one way or the other.'

10

When Amos entered the cell Dolly was sitting up on the wooden bench and had eaten all the food she had been given for breakfast. The tray, on which was an empty mug and plate had been pushed beneath the bench. There was a strong smell of urine from the bucket in a corner of the room and, wrinkling his nose in distaste, Amos spoke to the constable who had unlocked the door to allow him into the cell. 'I'm taking the prisoner up to my office to question her. While we're there have the tray removed and the bucket emptied — and send some tea up to my office, we could be talking for quite a while.'

Beckoning for Dolly to follow him, he led the way from the basement cells and up two flights of stairs to his first floor office. Once there he seated himself behind his desk and waved Dolly to a padded seat opposite him.

Dolly sat down gratefully and in a display of bravado she was far from feeling, she said, 'Can I take this chair back down to the cell with me. That wooden bench is playing merry 'ell with my bum!'

Amos smiled, accepting her cockney humour. In contrast to her travelling companion she had abandoned her pretence of affluent respectability and settled for being Dolly Brooks, of Hoxton.

He was shuffling through a heap of papers on his desk when a tray of tea arrived and was placed on the desk between him and Dolly. Addressing her, he said, 'You can pour for both of us — and I'll have two sugars.'

As she poured he was aware she was trying very hard not to allow her hands to shake. Waiting until she had taken a couple of sips of tea and was peering anxiously at him over the rim of the cup, he sat back in his chair and said, 'I believe Sergeant Churchyard has warned you of the trouble you are in? I hope you have thought about it very seriously?'

'What is there to think about? I've not *done* anything . . . not that it's likely to make any difference. If you've made up your mind to send me to prison there's nothing I can do about it, but whatever story you make up about me the truth is that I've *done* nothing wrong.'

'That's perfectly true, Dolly,' Amos took Dolly by surprise by agreeing with her, 'You *haven't* done anything and as long as nothing happens at the Laneglos summer ball I will be very happy to release you and send you back to London.'

Dolly's moment of hope vanished as he added, 'On the other hand, if something *does* happen, I have enough evidence to charge you and Shannon with conspiracy and as well as receiving the same punishment as those we arrest at Laneglos you will both serve even longer sentences because there are additional charges of forgery against you. I'm afraid you'd be an old lady before you got out of Newgate, Dolly — even if you survive that long. You'll have lost all your looks and, quite frankly, you could look forward to a bleak old age.'

Trying hard to hide the very real fear she felt at the thought of being returned to the horror of life in Newgate prison, Dolly asked, 'Are you enjoying telling me this, or are you hoping I'll break down and tell you about all the others involved in this so-called 'conspiracy'? If that's what you're expecting then you can think again. Even if something is going to happen — and I'm *not* saying it is — you'll learn nothing about it from me, I'm no copper's nark.'

'Well, you're going to have time to think about it, Dolly . . . but not *much* time. From what Sergeant Churchyard has told me about you I believe you're a brighter than average woman, so when you've thought about everything I believe you'll realize that by telling me all you know you'll actually save yourself *and* these friends and relatives of yours from going to prison. I *know* something has been planned to happen at the County Ball and I intend having enough constables on the spot to deal with it and arrest those responsible — *all* of them, but I'm paid to *prevent* crime and that's exactly what I am trying to do here. It's to everyone's advantage that I succeed. If I can find those involved and warn them off before a crime is committed it won't be worth my while taking a conspiracy case to court. In that event I'd not only open the cell door and set you free, but let Tom Churchyard drive you to the railway station in my carriage.'

Dolly found the possibility of being able to avoid a very lengthy stay in Newgate prison tempting — *very* tempting — but she remained suspicious. Expressing her thoughts, she said, 'I don't believe you, you're a copper. Once you've learned all there is to know you'll arrest everyone you can lay your hands on and haul 'em up before a beak just to show how clever you are.'

Amos shook his head, 'I don't need to prove myself to anyone, Dolly. I have the top job in the Cornish constabulary, answering only to the Chief Constable. If I can prevent anything untoward from happening at the social event of the year it will only be what's expected of me — and most of those there will never even know about it. On the other hand, if something *does* go wrong it will ruin the evening and I'll be heavily criticised, even if I succeed in arresting everyone involved and have them all sent to prison. So by preventing anything from happening we'll all be winners. If your friends try to pull off a job they're going to fail and you and they — and me — will all be losers — but *I* won't be going to jail!'

With an exaggerated gesture of apparent resignation, Amos added, 'But if you won't help me, then so be it. I see you've finished your tea, I'll have you taken back to your cell now. A police cell isn't the most comfortable place in the world but make the most of it while you can, it's a damned sight better than Newgate!'

* * *

'They look very like the tickets we have been selling . . . yet I am not absolutely certain. If you wait here I will go and fetch a ticket from Lady Hogg's desk and we can compare them.'

Flora Wicks was talking to Tom in the housekeeper's sitting-room at Laneglos, which the housemaids kept neat and tidy as part of their duties, housekeepers having a privileged status in the households of such large country mansions.

When she returned to the room, Flora placed the genuine ticket she was carrying upon the table alongside the two Tom had brought to the house. As they both leaned over to peer at them their heads were close together and, inconsequentially, Tom was made aware that her hair must have been recently washed, using an expensive soap, probably a gift from the family for whom she worked.

Eventually, the housekeeper straightened up and, turning to Tom, said excitedly, 'It *is* a forgery . . . but a very good one!'

'Are you sure . . . *absolutely* sure? I'd be hard put to tell them apart.'

'I don't doubt it, so would most people but I helped Lady Hogg to design the tickets so I know what I am talking about. The colour on the forgery is very slightly paler than on the original . . . although it is not easy to spot immediately. I noticed it only because Lady Hogg and I had a slight difference of opinion about it.'

'Oh . . . and who won?'

'Lady Hogg of course!' Flora smiled, 'After all, it is *her* ball — hers and Lord Hogg's . . . but that is not the only difference. Take this magnifying glass and compare the dates. The forger used a slightly different type-face for numbers, the eight and the nine are both different to those on the original.'

With the aid of the magnifying glass the differences were readily discernible but it would otherwise have required a very keen eye to spot them.

'May I keep the genuine ticket to point out the difference to Superintendent Hawke?'

'Of course, but what is all this about? Why should anyone want to forge a ticket just to get into a ball?'

A sudden thought came to her and she asked, 'Does this have anything to do with the footman who worked here using a false name?'

Tom hesitated for only a moment. There was a need for secrecy and Amos had tried to keep news from the organisers of the ball of what was possibly being planned by the Hoxton criminals, but secrecy could be carried too far.

'I'm not at all sure I should be saying anything to you at this stage but you're entitled to an explanation. If I tell you, will you keep it to yourself?'

Now it was Flora's turn to make a decision and she said, 'I can only give you such a promise if you tell me something that doesn't directly affect Laneglos or Lord and Lady Hogg. After all, they are my employers and my first loyalty must be to them.'

'I fully understand that,' Tom conceded, 'and if what we are trying to do is successful then nothing untoward will happen to disrupt the ball and no one need know what has gone on. I promise that if we are in any doubt you will be informed immediately . . . Will you accept that?'

After only a moment's hesitation Flora nodded. Suggesting she should first sit down, Tom gave her the outline of what was believed to have been planned by the Hoxton criminals and told her of the arrest of Dolly and Shannon. He added that actual details were decidedly sketchy at the moment but now they could prove the tickets in their possession were forgeries, he hoped they might be able to learn more.

He had tried hard not to alarm her but when he ended his explanation Flora was visibly shaken. She asked, 'How many of these criminals are there — and what do you *think* they will try to do?'

'We are not absolutely certain of the exact numbers at the moment. As I have said, we already have two of them in the cells in Bodmin and are keeping watch on all trains and roads into Cornwall. What we are hoping to do is identify them as they arrive, put them in police cells until after the ball, then send them back to London.'

'But there are so many people coming and going all the time . . . how will you recognize them?'

'Three members of the Cornwall constabulary — including me — know many of the villains believed to be involved and we have the names of most of the others. We are hoping that any we miss will be scared off when they learn that we are aware of what has been planned and are arresting those involved. Just in case we miss any of them we might possibly put constables on the door at Laneglos to check all tickets now we know we can recognize the forgeries . . . but that would result in a certain amount of unpleasantness and we'll avoid it if at all possible. If it does prove necessary then Lord and Lady Hogg will certainly be told what is happening, but I'd rather you said nothing to them before then.'

Flora had recovered her composure now and Tom added, 'You've been a great help, Miss Wicks. I promise I'll let you know if there is the slightest possibility of anything happening to disrupt the ball at Laneglos but now I had better get back to Bodmin and give Superintendent Hawke the good news about the tickets. Hopefully, when the two people we have in custody realize we've discovered they are forgeries they'll tell us all we want to know.'

'Thank you for letting me into your confidence, Constable. I will say nothing to my employers . . . for now, but I expect you to inform me *immediately* should the situation change.'

After Tom had given his promise, Flora walked with him to the main entrance door to the house. She fell silent along the way but when he said goodbye and turned to go she suddenly asked, 'Is there any possibility these criminals could arrive in Cornwall by boat?'

Taken by surprise by the question, Tom said, 'It's not impossible, but highly unlikely. I don't think there's a regular service between London and any of the Cornish ports.'

'Perhaps not a passenger service . . . but boats arrive regularly in Looe, coming from London carrying salt and other goods and returning to

London with a cargo of fish.'

She had mentioned a Cornish port which was only about twelve miles south of Laneglos. Tom knew nothing of the port but there was something in her voice that made him ask, 'Is there any particular reason why you've asked the question?'

'Yes. We have fish delivered fresh from Looe once a week. I meet the fish merchant and check what he's brought us before paying him. He's a great one for spreading gossip and when he called earlier this morning he was telling me that a boat came in last night with a number of Londoners on board — and it sounds as though they are a rough lot. After their boat arrived they went out in the town drinking and got into a fight with some fishermen at one of the inns, causing a great deal of damage. Afterwards one of them returned to the inn where the fight took place, apologized to the landlord and paid him for the damage caused, saying they wanted no trouble. He said they would be in Looe until the week-end but promised there would be no more fighting. The fish merchant said he couldn't think what they had come down here for in the first place. They were certainly not seamen or fishermen and were a very mixed bunch. Oh yes, he also said there was a woman on board . . . '

11

When Tom returned to the Bodmin Police headquarters and passed on details of what the Looe fishmonger had told the Laneglos house-keeper, Amos was alarmed. 'I never considered the possibility of them coming to Cornwall by sea, although I *should* have, especially when we picked up Dolly and Shannon at the station — and only those two. I ought to have tied it in with what you told me about her fear of travelling by sea. It explains a lot . . . but not everything. We still don't know exactly *what* has been planned. If we search this boat and the men on board we'll probably find more forged tickets but we're going to need more than that to justify a conspiracy charge.'

'Were you able to find out anything from Dolly?' Tom put the question to Amos.

'Nothing, although I think I scared her at the thought of being put away in Newgate again, possibly for the remainder of her life. Now we have something of a more immediate nature with which to frighten her, we'll go down to speak to her again before we plan what to do about this boatload of Londoners and we can't afford to waste any more time — it's the ball tomorrow night!'

* * *

The police station cells were dark and gloomy, with nothing to occupy the occupants and Dolly was lying fully clothed on the uncomfortable plank bench which doubled as a bed, but she was not asleep and sat up, startled, when the cell door opened and Amos and Tom entered.

When she recognized them she sank back again, saying, 'Oh, it's you. Don't you have homes to go to?'

'We like to keep our customers informed of what's going on, Dolly,' Amos said cheerfully, 'It's good news too and with any luck you could be out of here very soon.'

Dolly sat up once more and looked from Amos to Tom and back again, her expression one of disbelief, 'You mean it . . . ? You're not going to charge me with anything . . . I'll be free to go back to London?'

'It's not quite as simple as that,' Amos said, 'We thought we'd re-unite you with friends and family first, they're on a boat down at Looe. I haven't got cell space for everyone but I'd like you to be together so I can keep an eye on you, so I thought we might send you down there to join them. Once you're all together we'll have the boat taken out and anchored a mile or so offshore with a coastguard cutter nearby to keep an eye on you. You'll only be there until the county ball is over — it will be no more than three or four days at the most. Then, if nothing untoward has happened you'll all be able to sail back to London together.'

As Amos had been talking the colour had gradually drained from Dolly's face and now she said, 'Oh no . . . You're not getting me on any boat — and you can't make me, neither.'

'You'll be all right, Doll,' Tom said, easily, 'I believe there's another woman on board to keep you company and you'll be among friends and relations. I don't think the weather is going to be any too good, but I understand the boat's quite seaworthy . . . it must be, it's just made the trip from London.'

'If I'd wanted their company I'd have come to Cornwall on the boat with the rest of 'em,' Dolly retorted, 'but you know how I feel about going on the sea, Tom, everyone in Hoxton knows. If it hadn't been for that I'd have gone over to Europe years ago with the toff who was looking after me and be leading a very different life to the one I've got now. No . . . I'll stay here and take my chances with whatever's going to happen.'

Secretly delighted that she had confirmed that the boat now at Looe *had* brought the Hoxton criminals to Cornwall, Amos nevertheless feigned indifference, 'I'm sorry, Dolly, but you're going to have to put up with whatever I decide for you. I've got so many men out trying to find out exactly what it is that's about to happen that I can't spare an extra man on duty each shift just to take care of you.'

'But it's *not* just me, you have Shannon to look after too!'

It was the first time that Dolly had used 'Sir Richard Donahue's' real name, but Amos made no comment on this, either. Instead, he said, 'He will be appearing before a magistrate later. We found a number of share certificates in his baggage and I've no doubt they're forged, so he'll be charged with forgery and deception, then moved to Bodmin gaol. No, Dolly, you've given me no reason why I should treat you differently to any other prisoner. Putting you on the boat with the others will make things easier for me. I'll make arrangements for your baggage to be taken there with you.'

Dolly directed a silent plea to Tom, but he remained impassive. For many moments she looked from one to the other, hoping in vain for some sign that their resolve might weaken. Then her shoulders slumped, her face crumpled and, conceding defeat, she said, bitterly, 'I should know better than to expect a copper to show any finer feelings towards me, you're all bastards. All right, what is it you want from me?'

Once Dolly Brooks had made up her mind to co-operate with Amos, she held nothing back. She was taken upstairs to the Superintendent's office and by the time she was returned to her cell more than an hour later she had told Amos and Tom the names of all those she knew to be involved in the plot to profit criminally by the Cornwall grand summer ball, together with her part in the proceedings — and the sheer scale and audacity of the plot was breathtaking.

At the ball there would be two confidence tricksters, purporting to be from a well-known City stockbroker, armed with the share certificates and Exchequer bonds forged by Shannon. With apparent reluctance they would let it be known they had come to Cornwall to finalise a lucrative deal with a well-known peer of the realm who could not be named. Unfortunately, the peer was on a Continental tour and although he had arranged to be in Cornwall in time to attend the ball and pay for the shares, for reasons unknown he had failed to put in an appearance and they were unable to clinch the deal with him.

As it happened there *was* a senior and financially shrewd Cornish peer currently holidaying on the Continent, one who was well-known — and envied — by many of those who would be attending the ball.

In view of the absent peer's business acumen the stockbrokers' men had no doubts the shares and bonds would return a substantial profit for a potential buyer. This view would be confirmed, with suitable professional reluctance by 'Sir Richard Donahue', a very senior official from the Treasury, who just happened to be at the ball.

As a result it was expected that cheques, bankers' drafts and promissory notes would be exchanged for the false bonds and share certificates and the former cashed as soon as banks opened for business on the Monday following the ball.

Meanwhile the two London women would be working their charms on various men, helping themselves to purses and other valuables while singling out the women displaying the most expensive jewellery. Should any of these leave the ball early, word would be passed to waiting villains outside and their coaches waylaid when some distance from the great house.

The final act at Laneglos would be played out when the ball came to an end. In the general mêlée of departing guests it would be the turn of the London pickpockets. Some of the world's greatest exponents in the world of their nefarious art, they would expertly relieve female guests of their jewels before disappearing into the night with the richest pickings they had ever lifted.

But even this was not all. The true reason for the assembly of such diverse criminals became clear when Dolly revealed that, while all this was going on some of the Hoxton villains who specialised in burglary would be raiding at least six mansions owned by those attending the ball. She was unable to tell Amos and Tom which homes were to be targeted because she had not been included in the planning of this particular activity. However, she understood this too was intended to provide the perpetrators with more booty than they had ever stolen before.

It was this particular aspect of the London criminals' assault on Cornwall that gave Amos the gravest concern. Talking to Tom in the superintendent's office when Dolly had been returned to her cell, he said, 'I don't know how we can possibly counter this one, Tom. There will be somewhere between two hundred and fifty and three hundred guests at the ball, coming from perhaps as many as a hundred homes scattered all across Cornwall. With the constables we are going to need at Laneglos to ensure nothing goes wrong there we won't be left with enough men to visit even half those houses — and it's the Hoxton men who'll be involved in the housebreaking. Knowing them as we do, it would be dangerous to send less than half-a-dozen constables to any house that's being burgled. Our only hope is that we succeed in catching them on board the boat at Looe and are able to keep them there until Sunday, at least.'

'The scale of the whole plan is breathtaking,' Tom commented, thoughtfully, 'and the more I learn about it, the less inclined I am to believe it's all been planned by Alfie Banks. He's a crafty criminal — but not a *clever* one.'

'I agree with you . . . I think Dolly does too, but I believe her when she says she doesn't know who is behind the whole plan — and we certainly won't get anything from Alfie, even if we succeed in arresting him. At the moment he's committed no crime in Cornwall — and he's smart enough to be aware of that!'

'Do you think we'll find anything on the boat that might incriminate him.'

'Perhaps . . . but time is running out for us. We'll raid the boat as early as can be arranged in the morning and hope we make some kind of break through — but it needs to happen quickly. The ball takes place tomorrow night.'

12

By the morning of the day of the ball, Amos had succeeded in assembling thirty constables to carry out the raid on the London boat docked at Looe. Among them were a number of recently recruited men who were still undergoing training at the Bodmin police headquarters. Amos hoped enthusiasm would make up for their inexperience.

The constables carried only their regulation batons but he, Tom, Harvey and three inspectors were armed with handguns, Amos warning the policemen that these were only to be used in the most extreme circumstances.

It was mid-morning when three over-crowded carriages carrying the policemen trundled into Looe and headed for the harbour. The tide was in and it was swiftly ascertained that the London paddle-steamer, *Mermaid,* was moored alongside the quay, riding high in the water at a berth close to the mouth of the tidal river from which the fishing town drew its name.

During the night Amos had sent a constable ahead of the police party with an urgent letter for Looe's Chief Coastguard officer and he was waiting for them in the yard of the coastguard station with a small party of his officers. He confirmed that a manned coastguard boat was in position on the river, its crew ready to play a part in whatever ensued.

The senior coastguard also reported that since receiving Amos's message observations had been kept on *Mermaid,* during which time a number of men had left the vessel. Unfortunately there had been insufficient coastguard officers available to follow any except the last two, both of whom were at present buying fresh provisions in the small fishing town and were being watched by one of his men.

Two constables, accompanied by a coastguard, set off to arrest these two and Amos wasted no time taking the rest of his constables to *Mermaid's* berth and boarding the vessel immediately.

The men — and one woman — on board were taken completely by surprise and offered no resistance to the Cornish policemen. Within a matter of minutes they had all been handcuffed and mustered on the upper deck, many loudly demanding to know what they were supposed to have done to warrant such treatment.

There was a brief flurry of excitement when one man attempted to elude the policemen by diving fully clothed into the river. He was promptly hauled on board the coastguard boat and swiftly returned to the *Mermaid* and handed over to Amos and his men.

He was recognized by Tom as an escaped fraudster from a London prison. His presence on the *Mermaid* gave the lie to the protests of his fellow passengers that they were respectable men and women who had come from London merely in order to enjoy a brief holiday in Cornwall. Their credibility was further eroded when a search of their possessions revealed a number of forged tickets to the Laneglos Ball.

The raid on the *Mermaid* had been successful in that most of the men on the list of names given to Amos by Dolly had been accounted for. With the arrest of Dolly and Shannon it removed the threat posed to the Cornish gentry at their Laneglos gathering — but among those *not* accounted for were the known Hoxton ruffians. In their number were many of the Banks family. The majority were convicted burglars and it was logical to presume these were the villains planning to burgle the homes of gentry attending the ball.

It proved that Dolly had told them the truth . . . but Amos was still deeply concerned. She had been unable to give any details of where the missing men might have gone, or their intended targets. Amos realized his work was far from over.

The disgruntled passengers and crew on board the *Mermaid* refused to throw any light on the whereabouts of the missing men, the crew members saying only that some passengers had left the vessel, claiming they knew neither their names, nor how many were involved.

As Tom was quick to point out to Amos, the crew members came from the London docklands where many workers and seamen were from the same district of the city as the Banks family. They were unlikely to give any information about them to the police, even if they knew.

'That's true, Tom,' Amos said, 'but we both know the Banks family and those who work with them are violent men and most are professional burglars, I'm seriously worried about having them at large in Cornwall. The only advantage we have is that they aren't yet aware that we know what is being planned by them. They will expect to be able to bring the proceeds of their burglaries back to the *Mermaid* and set sail for London before we realize what has happened.'

'You don't think they might come back to the boat before carrying out the burglaries, learn what's happened and abandon their plans, making their way back to London as best they can?' Tom asked.

Amos shook his head, 'I don't think so. If any of them *do* come back here we'll have men waiting on the quay to arrest them, but I believe they'll have gone off to check out the places they intend burgling tonight and remain close to those houses until nightfall . . . and we have no idea which houses they are!'

When Tom could suggest no answer to the problem Amos said, 'Well, we'll just have to do the best we can. We've taken the names of everyone on board. We'll take the escaped prisoner back to Bodmin with us and inform London that he's here. Then I'll have someone go through the wanted files to see if anyone else on board is mentioned. Meanwhile the *Mermaid* can be towed out of Looe and anchored a mile offshore with a coastguard boat remaining nearby to keep an eye on it until the ball is over. That should keep those on board out of mischief. I'll put constables to watch this berth just in case anyone returns looking for the

Mermaid and in the meantime give some thought to what we can do about those we *haven't* managed to catch.'

⋆ ⋆ ⋆

'Do you think I might get any ideas if I went back to Laneglos and spoke to the housekeeper there?' Tom put the question to Amos as they rode back to Bodmin in one of the coaches.

Despite the seriousness of the present situation, Amos smiled, 'I think you've already formed a number of ideas as a result of your *last* visit to Miss Wicks. Keep calling in on her and *she'll* be the one to get ideas.' He was only half-joking. Tom had mentioned the Laneglos housekeeper on more than one occasion since his return from his visit to the great house.

Trying unsuccessfully to hide his embarrassment, Tom said, 'I'm merely trying to be constructive, Sir. Miss Wicks is a very intelligent woman and well acquainted with the Cornish gentry, she could give us some idea of who might be likely targets for Alfie Banks and the others.'

'True.' Amos admitted, 'It's clutching at straws but we've nothing else to go on. We'll be passing close to Laneglos, so you can be dropped off and I'll send someone from Bodmin with a horse for you to get back to headquarters with whatever you learn — but remember, time is not on our side. Ask particularly about those going to Laneglos from houses within, say . . . twenty to thirty miles of Looe. Concentrate on houses that are close enough to enable our villains to burgle them and get back to where they think the *Mermaid* is in time to set sail for London at dawn — with special emphasis on any which are likely to be of particular interest to the Banks's and their friends.'

13

Laneglos was a hive of activity when Tom arrived at the great house. Tradesmen's vehicles were much in evidence on the long driveway; gardeners putting final touches to the floral displays at the front of the house and raking and re-raking the granite chippings of paths and carriageways; servants putting a final sparkle on windows and carrying out a hundred other tasks on this, the house's busiest day of the year.

Flora Wicks was in the impressive entrance hall, directing staff with the authority of a general, while from the great gallery where the ball would be taking place, an unseen orchestra in rehearsal made stop-and-go progress with a Strauss waltz as its conductor imposed his own interpretation upon a piece of music that was essential for any event such as that taking place this evening.

Despite all that was happening around her, the Laneglos housekeeper managed a smile for Tom and greeted him with, 'Hello, I did not expect to see you before this evening, if then.'

'I'm sorry to interrupt you when I can see you are very busy, but something has come up that I need to discuss with you. Can we go somewhere a little more private?'

Flora's glance went to a tall, grandfather clock standing in the hall, 'It's time I had something to eat and there will be no time for a proper lunch today, I'll have some sandwiches made and sent to my sitting-room . . . have you eaten?'

'There has been no time. I was on my way back to headquarters from Looe when Superintendent Hawke suggested I call on you.'

'Then I'll order drinks and sandwiches for two.'

Once in the housekeeper's sitting-room, Tom sank gratefully into an armchair. The carriage used by the police to travel to and from Looe had not been built with comfort as a high priority, its springing insufficient to counter the state of Cornish roads.

While waiting for food and drink to be brought to them, Tom informed Flora of what had occurred at Looe. She was greatly relieved to learn he and his colleagues had succeeded in removing the threat to the guests attending the ball at Laneglos, but was deeply concerned about the threat posed to the homes of guests by the London criminals who remained at large.

When Tom explained his reason for coming to the house, she frowned thoughtfully, 'That's something I would prefer to have time to think about . . . but I realize that isn't possible and one or two places come to mind immediately as being particularly vulnerable. One is Astell Manor, the home of Sir Nicholas and Lady Trethewy. They have fallen on hard times in recent years and reduced their staff to a minimum, those remaining being almost as old as their employers. It is a fairly small manor house but full of treasures of all kinds and despite their circumstances the Trethewys will not part with a thing. They never miss a county ball and are particular friends of Viscount Hogg. Their home is no more than ten miles from Looe and close to Lostwithiel . . . in fact there are a number of fine homes in that area . . . '

Flora went on to tell Tom of all the houses she felt to be at risk from the criminals who had not been accounted for and he entered the details in his pocketbook with growing concern. There were far more than could be adequately guarded against burglars. Any policemen sent out to check on them would need to have a great deal of luck on their side.

Flora was racking her mind to think of more vulnerable houses when the door to the housekeeper's lounge was flung open and a tall, sharp-featured man entered the room. Scowling at Flora, he demanded, 'What is the meaning of this? You are meant to be out there supervising the staff, not skulking in your quarters entertaining a man. Does my mother know what you are up to?'

Before Flora could reply, Tom closed his pocketbook and, standing up, said, 'Miss Wicks has been helping me with details of the security arrangements in place for the ball tonight. You will be entertaining some very important people and we are anxious nothing should go wrong.'

Turning his attention to Tom, the sharp-featured man said, 'Who are the *we* of whom you talk . . . and what has anything that happens at Laneglos to do with you? You are obviously not a policeman — unless the constabulary are now so desperate that they are using invalids to do their work.'

'The 'we' *are* the Cornish constabulary, sir. I am Sergeant Churchyard and was sent here by Superintendent Hawke of Bodmin police headquarters — but you have the advantage of me, I don't think we have met before?'

Speaking for the first time since the man had burst into the room, Flora explained, 'This is the Honourable Charles Delville, Sergeant Churchyard. He is a son of Lady Hogg.'

Turning to speak to the Honourable Delville, she said, 'When the sergeant arrived and asked to speak to me I was about to take a break to have a sandwich for lunch. I took the opportunity to combine the two.'

'Why was I not informed about this? Do you usually take it upon yourself to give details of what goes on at Laneglos to strangers?' Delville addressed Flora, but it was Tom who replied.

'I have been to the house before, so am not exactly a stranger,' he said, 'and I learned on my first visit that Lady Hogg does not wish the family to be troubled by inquiries that can be dealt with by her staff. *That* is the reason I asked for Miss Wicks when I came to the house. She has been able to satisfy me that the Cornwall constabulary has nothing to worry about, so I trust you will have a splendid ball, sir.'

Delville looked from one to the other of the two people facing him, before saying, 'Of *course* there is nothing to concern you or your constabulary, so you may now leave the house — and I suggest you return to your duties, Flora.

There is still much to be done before tonight.'

With this he turned and left the room as abruptly as he had entered. When he had gone, Tom apologized to Flora, 'I'm sorry I brought that on, but . . . is he always like that? If he is it must make working here very difficult for you.'

'He hasn't *always* been like that with me and, to be perfectly honest I prefer him this way,' she said enigmatically, 'Anyway, he is an infrequent visitor to Laneglos. He comes visiting if there is a particularly important function, but doesn't usually involve himself with helping to organise things. I wish he had stayed out of this one, he has been more of a hindrance than a help . . . but you don't want to listen to the gossip and complaints of household staff. Thank you for putting my mind to rest about what might have happened tonight, Sergeant Churchyard, I wish you success with catching the rest of the London criminals.'

'Thank you for your help . . . and I would much prefer you to call me 'Tom'. As for tonight . . . Everything should be all right, but we will have two constables on the door and more patrolling the grounds. I will probably be here too. In addition, I believe the Chief Constable and a couple of our Superintendents will be guests at the ball. Should you have any problems we will all be on hand to help you.'

When Tom left Laneglos, he passed the Honourable Charles Delville who was standing in the entrance hall berating a footman. Tom had no doubt the irascible young man had seen him, but he gave no acknowledgement of the fact.

It was not until he was walking along the driveway from the house that he remembered what Flora had said about Delville not *always* having being so bad-tempered with her. He decided the young nobleman was most probably a womaniser who had been unsuccessful in charming the attractive young housekeeper.

He found the thought surprisingly pleasing.

14

Conrad Shannon, alias Sir Richard Donahue appeared at the Bodmin magistrates' court that afternoon and was remanded in custody to Bodmin gaol on a charge of forging a railway ticket and defrauding the Great Western Railway. There had been no time to prove whether or not the share certificates found in his possession were forgeries.

He protested his innocence and insisted he was Sir Richard Donahue of the government's treasury department, but his pleas failed to impress the Cornish magistrate.

Meanwhile, Amos had briefed the Chief Constable on the events of the previous twenty-four hours and the police chief was well-satisfied with all that was being done to protect those attending that evening's charity ball. Like Amos, he too was concerned that none of the Hoxton criminals had been among those found on the boat but even as the two were speaking news was received that an astute police inspector in Liskeard, a town approximately halfway between Looe and Bodmin, had discovered that some 'London men' had hired four vehicles there, namely two wagonettes; a light one-horse phaeton and a luggage van.

The information from the hirer of the vehicles was that the men had paid for their hire until Sunday evening, telling him the vehicles were to be used by a holidaying party who had 'come to Cornwall by boat' and wanted the vehicles to take them on a picnic to Bodmin moor. They had wanted a further vehicle, saying they were a party of ten and would be taking a great many picnic baskets and blankets, etc., but the hirer had no more spare vehicles and had referred them to the stables of Webb's hotel in town, where they occasionally had a horse and wagonette for hire.

The news gave Amos no clues about the houses that were to be targeted by the criminals, but it would seem to indicate there were ten men involved, and the number of vehicles they were trying to hire probably meant they intended burgling at least five premises.

Briefing his inspectors and sergeants later that afternoon, Amos said, 'Send all the constables you have out in pairs to examine as many of the houses as is possible, concentrating on those singled out as being particularly vulnerable, or which are known to contain items of great value. Initially, try to check out the houses without being observed. Remember we are dealing with professional criminals who would shift their attention to another house if they believe their intended target is being watched. They are also no strangers to violence, so take no chances, I want none of my constables to suffer serious injury at their hands.'

Later, speaking to Tom, he said, 'You and Harvey will be at Laneglos, I want you to keep a low profile but have men watching the nearby roads, as well as observing those entering the house. I think we've effectively scotched their plans for operating at the ball, but we can't afford to take any chances. I intend to detail armed and mounted men to follow any coach that leaves before the ball is over. By all accounts it won't end until after dawn — and Lord and Lady Hogg will be providing breakfast, so by the time the bulk of the guests leave it will be well after daybreak and people will be abroad, so I don't think anything is likely to happen then, but it's going to be a long night for all of us.'

'Where are you going to be?' Tom asked.

'Here, there . . . and everywhere,' came the reply. 'I shall initially base myself on Looe. I am hoping the missing Hoxton roughs won't have returned there after hiring their various vehicles for fear of attracting undue attention, so they will expect the boat to be still alongside when they arrive with whatever they've taken from any house they've burgled. I'd like to think we might actually catch them in the act but that's being too optimistic, so we need to be ready for them when they return to Looe.'

Tom gave Amos a wistful smile, 'It sounds as though you're in for an exciting night, sir. I'd like to be with you, but . . . ' He held up his broken wrist in a gesture of unspoken explanation.

'Never mind,' Amos returned the smile, 'No doubt you'll find something — or someone — to add interest to the hours you spend at Laneglos.'

* * *

Amos waited until the ball was underway before setting off on horseback for Looe. The system at Laneglos was working well, guests being warmly greeted by Flora Wicks while Tom stood discreetly nearby. She asked only to see the tickets of those she did not know by sight and did it in such a way that they were unaware it was anything other than the norm.

She had found no forged tickets by the time Amos left Laneglos and it seemed the ball might pass off without incident. It meant he could concentrate his attention on the missing London criminals — and he did not have long to wait for events to unfold.

Calling at Liskeard, he found the officers at the police station in a state of high excitement. Carrying out an inspection of a nearby manor house where the owners had gone to the Laneglos ball they had come across a horse drawing a hired wagonette tied to a tree in the grounds. Investigating further they surprised two London men at the rear of the house, apparently checking the security of the windows.

Both men had been armed with bludgeons but only one attempted to use his weapon and it proved no match for the truncheons wielded with excited enthusiasm by the two constables. The other London man offered no resistance and both he and his companion had just been brought to the Liskeard police station.

Amos immediately recognized the older of the two who was heavily bruised and bleeding from a cut on the side of his head. Addressing him jovially, he said, 'Hello, Stan! It's nice to meet old acquaintances — especially in such circumstances as these. What are you doing so far from home? Not that I really need to ask, you'll no doubt be following your usual occupation?'

Startled, the battered prisoner, said, 'Mr Hawke! What you doing 'ere, I thought you'd left the job?'

'No, I left London but I'm still very much a working copper.' Turning to one of the constables who had arrested the man he had referred to as 'Stan', he asked, 'What name did he give to you, Constable?'

'He said he was Frederick Smith, a merchant seaman who'd left London for the good of his health and come here looking for work. It was when I went to search him that he pulled out a bludgeon and laid about him with it.'

'Well he seems to have come off worse but he can still be charged with being found by night armed with an offensive weapon and assault on a constable — but charge him under his real name of Stanley Finch and have him remanded in custody, he has a long record and is officially registered as an 'incorrigible rogue'. As for being a seaman, the only ship he's spent time on was a prison hulk moored at Woolwich . . . at least, it was until he came to Cornwall on the *Mermaid*, isn't that right, Stan?'

'Why bother asking me stupid questions?' was Finch's surly reply, 'You seem to have all the answers.'

'More than you realize,' Amos replied, 'For instance, I know that even if you'd managed to burgle that house you'd have been stuck with all the stuff you took. You'd have gone back to Looe, only to learn that the *Mermaid* is now anchored under guard a mile out to sea — with most of those who came here with you still on board.'

Heartened by the London thief's expression of stunned disbelief, Amos said, easily, 'That's the trouble with your line of work, Stan, you just can't trust anyone not to talk about what you're up to . . . especially when you're working with someone like Alfie Banks.'

'Alfie won't have told you anything,' the criminal retorted, 'He knows how to hold his tongue, same as I do.'

Delighted that Stanley Finch had unwittingly confirmed beyond doubt Alfie Banks's part in the criminals' activities in Cornwall, Amos said, 'Unfortunately, staying silent isn't going to help anyone this time, Stan. As well as the charges you're facing at the moment I intend bringing conspiracy charges against you and the rest of the Hoxton gang. As far as I know you've never been charged with conspiracy before, so I'll explain what it means. Basically, I know that you, and all those who've come to Cornwall with you, have conspired together to commit all sorts of crimes . . . so many that I'm impressed . . . I really am. The problem you and your companions are facing is that you'll all be charged with *whatever* crimes are committed here in Cornwall tonight, and you'll suffer the same punishment as those who carry them out — even if you're in custody when they happen — because you've all *conspired* together to commit them. In other words, if someone succeeds in burgling a house — you'll be charged with it too. A highway robbery . . . and that will also go on the charge sheet. You'd better hope that no one gets carried away and kills one of his victims or the hangman will go home a rich man!'

Stanley Finch was a hardened criminal and well versed in the ways of policemen. His young companion was not. While Amos was explaining the offence of conspiracy his eyes had widened and his expression became one of sheer terror when murder was mentioned. Amos had seen this and he said to the constables who had arrested the two Hoxton men, 'Take them away and lodge them in the cells . . . separate cells. Let them have a few quiet hours on their own to think over what I've said.'

When they had been led away, Amos spoke to the Inspector in charge of the Liskeard police station. 'Your two constables did very well, but I think we might do better yet. Am I right in thinking you were once in the Hampshire police?'

When the inspector nodded, Amos said, 'Then you'll have had some experience in dealing with villains. Give the young one a couple of hours to stew over what I've said, before going down to have a word with him. Make certain he appreciates the seriousness of his situation . . . then try to find out if he knows what other houses are being targeted tonight . . . and what Alfie Banks is up to and where he might be arrested. If Alfie is the ringleader in all this I have a great many questions I would like to put to him. Now, I'll leave you to enjoy what little peace and quiet you're likely to have tonight and head for Looe. On the way I intend calling in on Astell Manor, which I believe is a likely target for our villains. I would like to take a couple of your constables with me, preferably men who know the manor in question.'

'I have one who is just the man you need,' the inspector replied, 'He used to be a gardener at Astell Manor. He knows the house and grounds as well as anyone you could hope to find.'

15

A three-quarter moon hanging high in the sky over the sea to the south of Cornwall was reflected in the sluggish waters of the East Looe river as Amos rode his horse along the river bank. Ahead of him were two Liskeard constables, using a pony and trap borrowed from a local magistrate who had been apprised of the events of the night.

When the small party reached the entrance to Astell Manor, the ex-gardener guided them to a copse just inside the grounds of the ancient house. Here they secured the two horses before quietly making their way to the manor via extensive shrub-embroidered lawns.

There were lamps burning beyond drawn curtains in two of the downstairs rooms even though it was now past midnight and the house's elderly residents were away, attending the Laneglos ball. Suddenly, all three policemen came to a halt as the front door of the small mansion opened. In the shaft of yellow light escaping from the doorway a man emerged carrying a number of items bundled inside what appeared to be a sheet, or perhaps a tablecloth. He carried his burden to a luggage van parked in the shadows beside the house and, placing it inside, returned to the house once more.

'That must be one of the men we're after — and we've caught them red-handed!' One of the constables whispered, excitedly.

'We have,' Amos agreed, 'but we don't want to lose them. Is there another door through which they might be able to escape?'

'There's a door leading to the kitchen garden, at the back of the house.' This from the ex-Astell gardener.

'Then make your way there quietly and, if it's open slip inside the house . . . but do nothing until you hear us inside.'

' . . . And if it's closed?' The constable sounded disappointed at not taking a more positive part in the capture of the burglars.

'Stay there and ensure nobody escapes that way . . . remember we are dealing with professionals. The fact that the lamps are on means they will have dealt with whoever is in the house and will almost certainly have given themselves a means of escape should someone surprise them, although they won't be expecting *us*. Do you know how many staff are likely to be in the house?'

'Probably only two,' was the reply. 'Their groom-cum-gardener will have taken Sir Nicholas and Lady Trethewy to Laneglos and neither of the maids live in. That leaves only the footman and the housekeeper who are both almost as old as Sir Nicholas and Lady Trethewy themselves.'

'Let's hope they didn't try to put up a fight,' Amos said, grimly, 'They wouldn't have stood much of a chance against two healthy and determined burglars, but get on your way to the back of the house. We'll stay here until one of the burglars brings something else out to the van, then follow him when he goes back inside.'

Amos and the constable remaining with him needed to wait for only a couple of minutes before a second burglar came out with a bundle similar in size to the first one, but this time it jangled as though it contained metallic objects and Amos thought they would probably be of silver.

When the burglar re-entered the manor-house Amos nudged his companion and, quickly covering the thirty or so paces to the partly-opened door, they went inside. It was unfortunate that as they entered the hall, one of the burglars was coming down the stairs carrying a pillow-case full of objects slung over one shoulder.

Startled to see them, he recovered quickly, shouting, 'Coppers . . . Get out quick!' to his unseen accomplice. Then, swinging the laden pillow-case from his shoulder he hurled it at Amos and the constable before leaping down the remaining three stairs to the hall and bolting through an inner doorway, heading away from the hallway.

The pillow-case caught the constable on the shoulder and knocked him off-balance, but Amos succeeded in dodging it and sprinted in pursuit of the burglar who was apparently heading for the back door. He fervently hoped the second constable had followed the instructions that had been given to him.

He had. What was more, after entering the house he had sensibly closed the kitchen door behind him and slipped the bolt into place. He was now standing before the door, baton in hand.

The burglar who had seen Amos and the other constable ran into the kitchen expecting the door to be already open and was halfway across the room before realizing his mistake. There were a number of kitchen knives hanging on hooks from a shelf on a huge kitchen dresser and the burglar snatched at a wide-bladed chopping knife but the constable was ahead of him in both thought and deed. Even as the loop attached to the handle of the sharp-bladed knife cleared the hook, the constable's truncheon struck the burglar violently across the back of his hand, causing him to cry out in pain and drop the would-be weapon.

Staggering back, the burglar collided with Amos who had rushed into the kitchen behind him and both fell to the floor. Before the intruder could rise to his feet the resourceful constable had dropped down on top of him and with a knee in his back twisted his arms behind him. Ignoring the burglar's cries that the truncheon blow had broken bones in his hand, he deftly handcuffed him.

Meanwhile, there was the sound of a commotion coming from the hallway Amos had just left. Running back to the scene he saw the second constable grappling with the other intruder. As he arrived the burglar threw the constable heavily against a mahogany side-table and ran for the open front door. Before he could reach it Amos brought him to the floor with a flying tackle. The two men grappled on the floor, both throwing punches whenever possible until the constable recovered from his heavy fall and joined the fray, making the outcome inevitable.

When the constable who had showed such initiative in the kitchen brought his still bitterly complaining prisoner into the hall both prisoners were ordered to sit on the floor with their handcuffed wrists behind them.

'Nice work,' Amos said to the two constables. 'One of you stay here with these two — and don't let them get up from the floor. The other can come with me and find out what they've done with the old couple who were looking after the house.'

'I'll stay with them,' said the constable who had been struck with the bag of booty. Drawing his truncheon, he added, 'My shoulder's still painful, so if they so much as twitch I'm liable to pay them back — with interest.'

Satisfied the two burglars would not escape Amos lit two small table lamps. Taking the other constable with him, he set off in search of the two aged servants known to have been in the house.

The elderly housekeeper was the first to be located. She was in bed in an attic room, with the bedclothes drawn up to her chin and when the two policemen entered the room she looked terrified.

Identifying themselves, Amos said, 'The two men who broke into the house are handcuffed and in custody downstairs, but how are you?'

'I'll be better when someone's untied me and I'm able to get up out of this bed,' said the woman, who gave her name as Nan Hodge.

The constable with Amos moved to pull back the bedclothes but the women said, 'Just take the clothes down far enough to untie my arms, I'll do the rest, I've had enough humiliation for one night. The way them two men left me wasn't decent although they thought it highly amusing . . . but have you found Harold . . . Mister Hockin, he's the footman?'

'Not yet, where is he?'

'At the end of the passage . . . least, that's where his room is, but I think he heard me hollering when them two burglars came into me. When one 'em went out I heard Harold shouting and it sounded as though there was a bit of a fight. I haven't heard a sound from him since then.'

Amos and the constable exchanged meaningful glances. Both burglars had proved themselves to be violent men. If an elderly servant had tried to prevent them from robbing the house . . .

'Stay here and do what you can to help the housekeeper. I'll see if I can find the footman.'

The door at the end of the passageway was closed and Amos opened it cautiously, fearful of what he might find inside. The room was smaller than that of the housekeeper and bedclothes were thrown back in disarray, but even when he held the lamp high, Amos could see nothing of the man who was meant to occupy the room . . . then he saw blood on the pillow.

Advancing into the room, Amos heard a faint sound. It seemed to come from the other side of the bed. Advancing farther into the room, he walked around the bed and saw a man wearing a nightgown lying on the floor. He was bound and gagged with a scarf tied about the lower part of his face.

As Amos hurried towards him he trod on a light-coloured nightcap. This too was stained with blood. Fearing the worst he brought the lamp down closer to the still figure. Much to his relief, the eyes flickered open and gazed angrily up at Amos.

Amos loosened the scarf and the man spat out a handkerchief before saying shakily, 'Whatever it is you want to know, I'm not telling you — and if I'd been twenty years younger you'd never have got the better of me like this, two of you or not . . . '

'It's all right, Mister Hockin, I'm Superintendent Hawke of the Cornwall constabulary. We have the two burglars downstairs, I'll untie you now . . . but there seems to be a lot of blood around, are you hurt . . . ?' While he was speaking Amos placed the lamp upon a small bedside cabinet and in its light could see bruising around one of the old man's eyes and blood on his face.

Amos found it necessary to identify himself once again and it was not until he began untying the injured man that he succeeded in convincing the aged footman he was *not* one of the criminals who had attacked him.

When realization came, Harold Hockin's first concern was for the housekeeper. 'What have they done with Nan? Is she all right?' The footman sat up and put a hand to his ear and

Amos saw it had been torn during his fight with the burglar and was the source of much of the blood. He was relieved it was nothing more serious, as it might well have been.

'She's unhurt, but she's worried about you. When you feel like it we'll go along and reassure her that you're not seriously harmed.'

'I'll not let her see me in my nightshirt,' the old man said, indignantly, 'Clear out of my room for a few minutes and give me time to get dressed, then we'll go along and speak to her before having a look around to see what they two rogues have been up to. It's the first time we've ever had anything like this happen at Astell and Sir Nicholas isn't going to be happy about it. It's a great pity the government changed the law when it did, no one got the benefit of it except them who go about robbing honest folk. When I was a boy they'd have been hung for this . . . and it would have been a good riddance to both of 'em.'

16

By the time Amos departed from the ball at Laneglos, the vast majority of guests had arrived and were in the great gallery where the dancing was taking place. Nevertheless, there were a few latecomers. Among these were two men, both probably in their late twenties, whom Flora did not recognize.

Behaving impeccably, she introduced herself with a friendly smile and explained that she was checking the tickets of those she had not seen at the house in order to use the opportunity to acquaint them with what was happening and where they could locate the various facilities they might require during the course of the evening.

The two men seemed grateful for her help and one of them had even begun flirting with her mildly when the Honourable Charles Delville appeared upon the scene. He apparently obviously knew both the men well and was livid that Flora had felt it necessary to check their identities.

'What do you think you are doing?' He demanded. 'These two gentlemen are personal friends of mine. You have no right whatsoever to stop and question them in this way. You will hear more of this . . . '

His outburst startled Flora. The two men were also taken aback by his verbal attack upon the housekeeper. Coming to her defence, one of them said, 'Steady on, old man, the young lady is merely being helpful . . . very helpful as it happens. She realized it was our first visit to your beautiful home and was acquainting us where everything we needed could be found.'

Refusing to be placated, the Honourable Charles snapped, 'It was quite unnecessary. I will tell you all you need to know about Laneglos and you have not come here to dance the night away.'

'Quite right, old chap,' agreed the second of the two men, 'We are here to relieve you of your money . . . I hope you have not lost it all before our arrival?'

'I have enough,' their host retorted, 'and tonight I intend relieving you of *your* money, so I trust you have brought ample with you.'

Clapping a hand on his shoulder, at the same time winking surreptitiously at Flora, the young man who had defended the housekeeper's actions said, 'If you succeed in doing that it will be the first time, dear boy, but lead on — and perhaps we can collect something to drink along the way. Your Cornish roads must be among the dustiest in the land.'

'Think yourself lucky there has not been any rain,' The Honourable Charles replied, some of his aggression ebbing away, 'Cornwall can also offer a traveller some of the deepest mud.'

The three men went on their way inside the house with an air of conviviality that was in sharp contrast to the Honourable Charles's manner when he had been talking to the Laneglos housekeeper.

Aware that the arrogant young man's outburst

had shaken Flora, Tom left the corner where he had been discreetly observing the new arrivals. Coming to stand beside her, he said, 'That's the second time I've heard him carry on like that, is it the way your employers usually speak to you?'

'Fortunately he is not one of my employers,' Flora replied, 'If he was I would have left Laneglos a long time ago. As I told you when you last met him, the Honourable Charles is Lady Hogg's youngest child by her first husband. Her other children are living abroad and now the Honourable Charles is living in London we don't often see him at Laneglos, thank goodness.'

Aware she was being less than loyal to the family by whom she was employed, Flora added, 'But he's been drinking . . . and drink affects some worse than others.'

'So I've noticed,' Tom commented, 'but having too much to drink is no more of an excuse for being rude and boorish than it is for committing a crime.'

'Well, if it makes him happy for a while, then so be it. I don't think he is going to have a very enjoyable night. The two men are here to play cards with him and it sounds as though they are used to winning. I am not surprised. The Honourable Charles's valet came to Laneglos with him and he is more talkative than a personal servant should be. He told the butler that Charles gambles far more money than he can afford. It seems he has also told the valet he might soon have to dispense with his services because he can't afford to retain him . . . but I am doing exactly the same as his valet! *I* should not be gossiping about the family to anyone.'

'I doubt if the Honourable Charles has such high principles,' Tom said, 'When I first met him I recall you saying something about his behaviour towards the women servants. That is certainly not the behaviour expected from a gentleman.'

'Did I say that? Well, I wasn't telling you anything that isn't common knowledge far beyond Laneglos. There has been more than one young servant girl leave Laneglos in tears because of him — and most have wished they had left much sooner.'

'It would seem that *Honourable* is something of a misnomer for the son of your employer,' Tom suggested, 'From what I've seen and heard of him he seems to be a thoroughly nasty character.'

'He is not my *favourite* man,' Flora admitted, 'but I would rather we changed the subject now . . . It would seem you and Superintendent Hawke have succeeded in keeping all the London criminals away from the ball. You must be well satisfied with yourselves.'

'We've done pretty well,' Tom admitted, 'but neither of us will be fully satisfied until we are able to account for every one of them and know we have prevented them committing any crimes in Cornwall.'

'I am sure you will succeed,' Flora said, 'Superintendent Hawke is very well thought of in Cornwall. When he first came down here from London a couple of years ago he solved some very nasty murders. That's how he met his wife. She was the daughter of one of the murdered men, a schoolteacher . . . but I am sure you already know all about that?'

'Not really,' Tom admitted, 'In fact I know very little about Amos Hawke, except that he was a very good detective when he was at Scotland Yard . . . and I heard about him before then, when we were both in the Royal Marines, he was commissioned in the field for bravery and put in charge of policing a captured town during the Crimean War.'

'You were in the Royal Marines?' Flora expressed surprise, she had thought that Tom had probably always been a policeman, 'You couldn't have been in for very long . . . I mean, you are not very old now and must have been a policeman for some time before coming to Cornwall.'

Tom smiled, 'I was a Marine for ten years . . . but I *was* only thirteen when I joined — much the same age as Amos Hawke was when he became a marine, I believe. Then I spent four years in the Metropolitan Police before coming here. When I came to Laneglos and met you for the first time I'd only just become a Cornish policeman.'

'You mean you were taken on as a policeman by Superintendent Hawke even though you have a broken wrist?' Flora expressed her surprise.

'That's right, but before then he needed my help to identify the London villains, and I got my wrist broken — and took a beating — from the Hoxton mob because I was asking too many questions about them on his behalf.'

Flora shuddered, 'And on behalf of Laneglos too. The Honourable Charles should be thanking you, not complaining because you are here.'

'I somehow don't think he is in the habit of showing gratitude,' Tom commented, 'but Amos Hawke appreciates what I've done on his behalf and that's the important thing — at least, as far as my career is concerned.'

'I appreciate it too,' Flora said, adding, 'and when all this is over and what has happened is out in the open, I will make quite certain Lord and Lady Hogg are aware of everything you have done for them.'

Tom felt that whatever her employers might say about his part in preventing their ball from becoming a disaster could not equal the pleasure he felt at receiving such praise from Flora herself.

17

It was a night of mixed fortunes for Amos and the Cornwall constabulary, but the general consensus was that the forces of law and order had prevailed.

In addition to the criminals arrested near Liskeard and at Astell Manor, two more were taken when they returned to Looe expecting to embark on the *Mermaid* with goods stolen from a house farther along the coast. An overly ambitious attempt by another pair of Hoxton criminals to burgle Boconnoc, one of the most closely guarded mansions in Cornwall, ended abruptly when they were challenged in the grounds by a patrolling gamekeeper. One of the would-be burglars drew a pistol and fired at him, but the shot went wide. The gamekeeper promptly returned his fire with a sporting rifle, severely wounding the trespasser.

The wounded man's companion bolted and was now being hunted down in thick woodland by police and Boconnoc employees. Coming from the city and unused to the type of country he was in, it was not expected the Londoner would be at large for very much longer.

Meanwhile, the younger of the two men captured near Liskeard earlier in the night and seen by Amos had proved so frightened of the fate forecast for him that he had broken down and told the Inspector questioning him all he knew — which included the names of all the men involved in the Cornish burgling spree.

When dawn arrived one of the hired wagonettes was found abandoned in a field by the side of the road about a mile from Looe, loaded with property stolen from a country mansion. There was no sign of the horse that had been hired to pull it, or the men who had been riding in it but Amos believed the vehicle might have been used by Alfie Banks and that he and an accomplice — most likely his nephew, Jimmy — had escaped together on the missing horse.

A more experienced criminal than many of those who had come from London with him, Alfie would have sent his companion on to Looe to check all was well before driving in to the small town with his stolen goods. The accomplice would have come back to report the presence of the police and the absence of the *Mermaid* from its mooring and the two London men would no doubt have made a hurried departure from the vicinity.

If the information of the frightened informer was to be believed, there were now only three London villains still unaccounted for, including the one being hunted on the Boconnoc estate but the hunt would be continued throughout the day, which meant there would be little sleep for Amos and his men.

* * *

The man who had fled in the Boconnoc woods was soon captured — by the same gamekeeper who had shot his companion — and the would-be burglar showed considerable relief when he was handed over to the custody of the police.

This left only two of the criminals unaccounted for . . . Alfie and Jimmy Banks. Amos was particularly keen to capture the man who was the leader of the Hoxton gang but by the end of the day he scaled down the search. His constables were exhausted as a result of their activities over the past twenty-four hours and he was reluctantly forced to the conclusion that the two men he was hunting had succeeded in finding their way out of Cornwall.

Chief Constable Gilbert did not share Amos's disappointment. He was delighted with the success of his force. Although they had not prevented the houses of some of those attending the ball from being burgled, all the stolen property had been recovered.

Congratulating Amos in his office later that day, he dismissed the fact that Alfie and Jimmy Banks seemed to have made good their escape, saying, 'I will have a warrant issued for their arrests and send details to the Commissioner of the Metropolitan Police. Cornwall's magistrates are well-pleased with the results achieved by our force, Amos. We have even received praise from some of those who were most sceptical about Cornwall having an organised constabulary. You have done well. Extremely well.'

* * *

That evening Amos and Talwyn held a small celebratory party at their home to thank Tom Churchyard and Harvey Halloran for their part in ensuring the fledgling constabulary's success against the London criminals.

The small party broke up early because all three men were tired as a result of their activities during the previous night and, as Talwyn was preparing for bed, she said, 'You must be very well pleased with your policemen, Amos, they did all that was expected of them.'

'They did far more,' Amos said, proudly, 'There will be a number of promotions as a result. I am particularly pleased with Tom. Even Chief Constable Gilbert agreed that I was right to insist we take him into the force — even though he is suffering from a fractured wrist.'

'He seems to get along well with Flora Hicks at Laneglos,' Talwyn commented, 'Did you notice how he was singing her praises during the course of the evening?'

'It's been obvious to me since their very first meeting that they are mutually attracted to each other. I sincerely hope something comes from it, they are well suited to each other and Tom deserves to have someone like Flora in his life. He has never known what it is to have a happy and settled home life.'

Talwyn was aware that Amos's own early life had been very similar to Tom's. After an unhappy and unsettled childhood he too had joined the Royal Marines as a drummer boy at the age of thirteen and served as a fighting man during the Crimean War. Leaving the Royal

Marines when he was still a young man, he had become a detective at London's Scotland Yard but it was not until he and Talwyn had met that he had learned what it was to enjoy a happy and settled home life.

Smiling at him, she said, 'You are just an old romantic, Amos.'

'If I am, it's what you and marriage have made of me. I like both Tom and Harvey very much and would like them to enjoy as happy a life as you and I have together but, as you said, today I should be very proud of all the men under my command. My only disappointment is that we have not caught Alfie and learned where the idea came from to put together such an ambitious plan to rob the rich people of Cornwall.'

'The fact that you haven't caught him means he is cleverer than you gave him credit for,' Talwyn said, 'Perhaps there was no one else involved and that he thought up the whole idea himself?'

Amos shook his head, 'No, Alfie is a crafty and wily criminal, but he lacks the intelligence and ability to plan something on this scale. Besides, he needed to have an accomplice here who is familiar with Cornwall and its great houses. There has to be someone else involved.'

'You already know that his nephew worked at Laneglos and Edith told you that when she last met him, the man he referred to as his 'uncle' was with him, so neither are complete strangers to the area.'

'That's quite true . . . but I still believe there is

an accomplice we haven't yet identified.'

'Well, you have played your part — and played it well, but you look the way you must feel . . . dog tired. Come to bed now and have a good night's sleep. You have earned it.'

18

Talwyn's hope that her husband would enjoy a long night's sleep was not fulfilled. At 6.30 the next morning they were awakened by a constable from the Bodmin police headquarters hammering heavily upon the door of their cottage. He brought Amos some very disturbing news. Laneglos House had been burgled during the night and much of the family silver and a quantity of other valuables stolen.

The constable was unable to provide any more details, but the incident was considered of sufficient importance for the duty inspector to send him to inform Amos right away.

* * *

'Do you think it's a coincidence that Laneglos has been burgled so soon after the other mansions?' Tom put the question to Amos as they rode together to Laneglos in the pony and trap. The young Londoner had been woken with some difficulty, having been in a very deep sleep and he still looked bleary-eyed, his face having not yet caught up with the remainder of his body.

'I don't know. It might be a part of the original plan and would explain why Alfie lay low yesterday. Or it could be a determination on his part to rescue something from what has been a disastrous trip to Cornwall for him. Either way, I should have anticipated that something like this might happen. Alfie would have known that the servants and the family at Laneglos would be very tired after the ball and he's taken advantage of it . . . but hopefully we'll learn more when we reach the house and find out *exactly* what has happened.'

They were met at Laneglos by Flora who had been up for a couple of hours and looked tired, but she had already set the staff to work tidying rooms that had been ransacked. She told Amos and Tom that the robbery had been discovered by a junior housemaid whose early morning task was to clean out the fireplaces and lay those that would be lit before the family came down to breakfast. She had found Downton, the under-butler, bound, gagged and bleeding in the pantry — where he slept in order to protect the household silver kept here!

'Mr Norris — he's the butler — is furious with Downton. His instructions were to always keep the pantry door locked so that no one can get to the silver.'

'Did he not do that?'

'No . . . but I can't say I blame him. There is no window in the pantry. If he stayed inside with the door locked the chances are he would suffocate. I have suggested more than once that a small grille should be cut into the door, but Mr Norris always dismisses the idea. *He* slept in a locked pantry when he was an under-butler and sees no reason why Downton should not do the same.'

Accompanied by Flora and a silently disapproving butler, Amos and Tom interviewed Downton. The under-butler had a bandage that went over his head and around his chin with a pad placed on a scalp wound. Another linen strip about his forehead held the first bandage in place, and he was feeling extremely sorry for himself.

When Amos asked whether he had recognized either of his assailants, Downton replied, 'Oh yes, one of them was that young footman from London who worked here for a while . . . Jeremy Smith.'

Amos and Tom exchanged glances and Tom asked, 'Are you quite sure? Were you able to get a look at the other one?'

'I got a good look at both of them,' the injured man replied, 'They weren't shy about showing themselves, probably because I was unconscious for half the time they were in the pantry, but they were using a lantern and I saw them all right.' He went on to describe a man who Tom said matched the description of Alfie Banks.

When Amos asked how the burglars had managed to get into the house, Flora looked grim, 'I think young Enid Merryn, the scullery-maid, might be able to give you the answer to that. She should have been the first up this morning, to light the kitchen fires, but they were not lit. Someone had drawn the bolts on the inside of the kitchen door at some time during the night — and now Enid cannot be found.'

Her reply took Amos by surprise, 'Are you

quite certain she is involved? I realized when I spoke to her that she is a somewhat simple girl, but she struck me as being honest and very happy to be working at Laneglos.'

'She is . . . or *used* to be. I noticed a change in her attitude at about the time she became involved with the footman we knew as 'Jeremy'. She was more secretive and less eager to please than before. I am afraid everything points to her involvement in this sorry affair.'

Speaking for the first time, the disapproving butler said, 'There is something else. Whoever broke in had a knowledge of where everything is kept at Laneglos — and not just in the house. A groom has discovered a pony missing from the stables and it has just been reported that a small wagonette has gone too. The burglars must have made off with them.'

'Did the coachman hear nothing?' This from Flora, who explained, 'He sleeps over the stables and should have heard anything that went on there.'

'The coachman was not in his rooms last night,' said the butler, 'Lady Hogg sent him to Bude to take the Dowager Lady Peruppa home. He stayed there overnight to rest the horses. The burglars must have known that too. It seems everything fell into place for them, had the coachman been there he would certainly have heard them, I believe he is a very light sleeper.'

While the butler was speaking, Amos had been thinking and now he asked to inspect the kitchen door that had been found open. He and Tom were taken to the kitchen by Flora where Amos inspected the two bolts that should have been securing the door when the robbery took place. There were two, one at the top of the door, the other at the bottom. He checked them without saying anything, keeping his thoughts to himself.

On the way back from the kitchen they were in the main hallway when they met with Lady Hogg who was accompanied by her youngest son. The Honourable Charles Delville immediately launched into a scornful verbal attack upon the two policemen.

'It seems the burglary at Laneglos has taken the county constabulary by surprise, Superintendent. It is a great pity the policemen who were available in such great numbers harassing family friends at the summer ball were not on hand to take action when there was a need for them.'

Amos had not been told what had occurred between Tom and the Honourable Charles on the night in question but before he could reply Tom spoke up, 'Oh, I don't think your friends felt in the least harassed, sir. I felt the two gentlemen you were expecting took the routine questioning in good part . . . and I hope it did nothing to spoil your game of cards and that they never made good their promise to win all your money.'

Lady Hogg rounded on her son immediately, 'Have you been gambling again, Charles? You promised me you had given it up. I should have known better. I wondered why you were missing for most of the night of the ball. I should have come looking for you . . . or perhaps not. We will discuss this later. For now I believe you wish to tell the superintendent of the money that was stolen from you in the burglary?'

The Honourable Charles had been glaring malevolently at Tom while his mother was talking, but now he turned his attention to Amos. 'That's right, I had more than a hundred pounds stolen, together with a wallet I left on the dressing-table in my room last night. It was gone this morning. One of the rogues must have taken it . . . either that or it was stolen by that scheming little housemaid who let the burglars in and ran off with them. She had probably nosed around the house and knew I kept money in my room. I wouldn't be surprised if she had taken some before, I have missed the odd guinea on more than one occasion, but thought I must have miscalculated the amount I left around. I believe she was recommended to us by one of your policemen . . . ?'

'We have yet to establish Miss Merryn's part in the robbery, sir,' Amos commented easily, ' . . . if indeed she had anything at all to do with it.'

'There can be no doubt about that, surely?' The Honourable Charles queried, scornfully, 'The girl had been carrying on with that young criminal who worked here under false pretences and now she's let him in to rob us and run off with him. Any fool can see what has happened . . . '

'You are being extremely tedious, Charles,' Lady Hogg said sharply. 'I have no doubt there are many things you need to be attending to while Superintendent Hawke and I go around making an inventory of exactly what *has* been stolen.'

When her son had walked off with a final malevolent glare at Tom, Amos spoke to Lady Hogg, 'I would appreciate your help in making such a list, Your Ladyship, but first I would like to speak to my sergeant. I would also be grateful if we might take advantage of Miss Wicks's knowledge of the house and servants for a while longer?'

'You may . . . but I trust you will not keep her from her duties for too long. With this wretched burglary following so closely on the heels of the ball the staff are all at sixes and sevens. You will find me in the pantry, where that poor under-butler was attacked . . . although I fear he brought it upon himself by not locking the door when he went to bed, after all that was the sole reason he was sleeping there in the first place. If I discover he has committed a flagrant breach of his duties he will have to go . . . although trained staff are so hard to come by these days . . . '

* * *

While Amos was giving his instructions to Tom, Flora stopped two passing maids and gave them instructions about cleaning the burgled rooms. Amos set off after Lady Hogg and when Flora returned to Tom, he said to her, 'Superintendent Hawke wants you to show me how you draw the bolts on the kitchen door that was opened on the night of the robbery.'

'That will not take long,' Flora retorted, 'I

can't draw them. The top bolt is too high for me to reach and too stiff even if I could . . .'

Stopping suddenly, her eyes widened as she said, 'Of course . . . If I can't do it then neither could Enid. She is not as tall as I am and so could not have reached it. Superintendent Hawke must have realized that . . . but if Enid did not let them in, then who did . . . and where is Enid now?'

'I can't answer either question,' Tom replied, 'but yes, he has realized that Enid wasn't tall enough to reach up and draw the bolt, but thought she might have used something . . . perhaps a walking-stick from the hall?'

Flora shook her head, 'The bolt is much too stiff for that, it must have been another member of staff . . . probably a man.'

'That brings me to the next thing Superintendent Hawke would like,' Tom said, 'He wants a list of all male members of staff; showing how long they have been working at Laneglos and any comments you might like to make about them. In particular, whether there is anyone *you* consider is perhaps not as trustworthy as he should be.'

Flora began to protest but Tom stopped her immediately. 'He thought you might object and consider you were being disloyal to your staff but, as he pointed out, *someone* opened the door for the thieves and your first loyalty has to be to your employer.'

Her indignation ebbing away, Flora said, 'He is right, of course, and I will try not to allow any personal prejudices to cloud my judgement.

Many of the servants have worked at Laneglos for far longer than I . . . indeed, some have been here all their working lives! I doubt whether they are involved in the burglary, but it *is* a very nasty business and I realize you have a job to do, so we ought to get down to it right away . . . '

* * *

That evening Amos, Tom and Talwyn were talking at the dinner table about the burglary and Talwyn was adamant Enid would never have become involved in anything as dishonest as robbing the house of her employers, saying, 'No, Amos, gullible she most certainly is — and trusting too, even of someone like this young London criminal who was working at the house, but she would not help him do anything remotely dishonest . . . in fact, I am very concerned for her.'

'Flora . . . Miss Wicks, said very much the same thing when she realized Enid *couldn't* have opened the kitchen door to them,' Tom said, 'In fact she became quite upset when she realized something might have happened to her.'

'We are all concerned for Enid,' Amos agreed, 'and now we have established she couldn't have opened the door I believe there is very good reason to be worried. We could end up with something rather more serious on our hands than a burglary. We'll get a search started tomorrow — but without saying a word to anyone that we *don't* believe Enid was involved. We must remember to ask Miss Wicks not to say anything about it for the time being.'

'I have already suggested she should say nothing and she has agreed,' Tom said, 'but won't it be obvious when we start searching for Enid?'

'No,' Amos said, 'There is no need to mention her. As far as everyone involved is concerned we'll be searching the countryside around Laneglos for anything unusual that could lead us to the burglars . . . We'll get Lord Hogg's gamekeepers involved too, they should be able to notice anything that's not right in the woods around the house — and I fear that's where we are going to find the answer to Enid's disappearance . . . '

'What possible motive could anyone have for wanting to harm poor Enid?' A distraught Talwyn asked, 'I doubt if she has ever deliberately done a bad turn to anyone.'

'It's a question that can only be answered when we find her — and perhaps not even then,' Amos replied, grimly. 'Unfortunately, we are dealing with men who don't live by the rules that govern the lives of civilised folk.

19

Thirty hours after the discovery of the burglary at Laneglos, Enid's body was found by one of the estate gamekeepers. It had been hidden beneath branches broken from trees and bushes in a small patch of scrubland at one end of the burial ground beside the church, only a very short distance from the great house.

The body was taken to the mortuary in Bodmin town, where a post mortem would be carried out. However, a preliminary examination was made on behalf of the coroner and from marks found on her neck the surgeon who would be carrying out the post mortem declared there was little doubt that she had been strangled.

The hunt for those responsible for the burglary at Laneglos house had now become a murder investigation.

The surgeon, a Doctor Sullivan, was young and keen and wasted no time in performing the autopsy. He was able to inform Amos that Enid had indeed been strangled — adding the unexpected information that the simple young servant girl had been pregnant at the time of her death.

Amos took on the distressing task of informing Enid's mother of her daughter's death and the manner in which it had occurred, but at this juncture he decided to say nothing about Enid's condition at the time she was killed. He had a nagging suspicion that this and not the burglary might have been the motive for her brutal murder.

Talwyn broke down and cried when Amos returned home and told her of the murder and of Enid's condition at the time of her death. He held her close until, pulling away and looking up at him she said fiercely, 'You *must* catch whoever did this to her, Amos . . . this Jeremy, or Jimmy . . . it's all so *senseless*.'

'We will catch him,' Amos assured her, 'and I admit that right now everything points to young Jimmy Banks being responsible for Enid's murder, but we still have a great many more questions than we do answers.'

'How many more answers do you need?' Talwyn demanded. 'This young man obtained work at Laneglos using a false reference in order to become familiar with the house and all that's in it so he could burgle it when the time was right. Along the way he seduces an innocent young girl and makes her pregnant. I *still* don't believe she would have willingly helped him to rob the house, so it's probable he persuaded her to come out and meet him — perhaps on the pretext that they would run away together and be married. Instead, he kills her and goes on to rob the house. He is a callous and calculating young criminal who *deserves* to be hung for what he has done.'

Releasing her, Amos moved to the sideboard where he poured brandies for each of them. Handing her one of the glasses, he said, 'Your theory — and I am afraid that is all it is — has too many 'probables' and even more 'improbables'. We now know it's very unlikely that Enid could have unbolted the door herself, so whoever burgled the house would have needed the help of another — possibly a *male* servant. That immediately gives us another unknown murder suspect who must still be working in the house. Someone who would be aware that Enid was a very simple girl and under questioning could easily give his identity away — deliberately, or otherwise, and so he killed her in order to avoid being arrested.'

Sipping her drink, Talwyn was silent for a long time before asking, 'What does Flora Wicks think of this latest theory of yours?'

'It is not so much a theory as a possibility,' Amos said, 'and certainly one that could be used by a defending lawyer to put doubt in the minds of a jury should Jimmy Banks stand trial for her murder — and we will only learn what Flora Wicks thinks of it when Tom returns home. He is at Laneglos at this very moment, putting it to her . . . '

* * *

'I have written a list of the Laneglos servants and employees, with all the details I know about their past lives, but I cannot honestly say that any one of them is a likely suspect for either the robbery or the murder of poor Enid.'

Flora and Tom were in the housekeeper's sitting-room and she spoke as she handed him a few sheets of paper covered with her neat handwriting.

'Didn't you tell me that one of the footmen is a known womaniser?' asked Tom as he took the list from her.

'Chester Woods was a womaniser,' Flora agreed, 'but he married Peggy Kelly, the assistant cook, a year ago and to all intents and purposes has been a changed man since then. He's *had* to be. Peggy is a strong no-nonsense Irish girl with a wicked temper. She'd murder *him* if she felt he was playing her up.'

'No doubt a strong no-nonsense Irish girl is equally capable of pulling the bolt on a door and killing a girl she suspects of having an affair with her husband,' Tom pointed out, 'I'll need to have words with her.'

'Of course. Let me know when you wish to speak to her and I will make certain she is available.'

'Oh yes . . . I'll also need to know the names of any family and friends of Lord and Lady Hogg who were in the house on the night of the robbery and Enid's disappearance . . . '

Aware of the housekeeper's consternation at the thought of involving the family in his enquiries, Tom added, 'Any one of them might have seen or heard something, albeit so trivial they might not even realize it has any significance to our investigations.'

Accepting his explanation, Flora said, 'There was only family here with Lord and Lady Hogg. The Honourable Charles Delville, and Lord Hogg's daughter and her husband, Sir Beville Lander. Lord Hogg's son, The Honourable Rupert, Lord Hogg's heir, had intended staying on for a while but I think he left because The Honourable Charles was still in the house, the two of them don't get on and never have.'

'Is there any reason why?'

Flora shrugged, 'They are two very differing personalities. You have met the Honourable Charles and have no doubt formed an opinion of him for yourself. The Honourable Rupert is a very different man. He is quiet and studious and has something to do with the university in Oxford. He will be very upset when he learns what has happened at Laneglos during these last few days — not least because of the effect it could have upon his father.'

Before Tom could ask for further clarification of her statement, Flora explained, 'Lord Hogg has never been a particularly robust man. The Honourable Rupert would be even more concerned if he saw the way His Lordship is today, he is not at all well. He is aware of the robbery, of course, but Lady Hogg has given instructions that he is *not* to be told of Enid's murder, so I am afraid I must ask you to abide by her wishes.'

Tom nodded, 'I am sorry to hear he is unwell and won't involve him unless it's absolutely necessary but I won't be speaking to *anyone* today. I intend going through the list of names you have given to me and taking things from there.'

'Does that mean you will be returning to Laneglos again soon?'

It was an apparently innocent question, but Tom felt — he *hoped* there was more behind the question. 'You are likely to see a great deal of me at Laneglos in the next few days,' he replied, 'Superintendent Hawke feels that you and I get along so well he's quite happy to let me carry on with the investigation here at Laneglos.'

Flora coloured up immediately, 'I am willing to help the police in any way I can,' she replied then, disconcerted by the look Tom was giving her, she added hurriedly, 'We were all very fond of poor Enid and want to see whoever killed her brought to justice as swiftly as possible.'

'He will be,' Tom replied confidently, 'Superintendent Hawke has sent a message out to every police station in Cornwall that young Jimmy Banks and his uncle are to be prevented from escaping from the county at all costs.'

Tom did not repeat the words that Amos had uttered when the message had gone out from his Bodmin headquarters, ' . . . if they have not already left!'

20

At least one of the Banks family was still in Cornwall at the time Enid Merryn's body was found. He was closer to Laneglos than he would have wished to be — but in no condition to worry about it.

Just after dawn broke on the morning after Alfie and Jimmy Banks had burgled the great house they were heading north eastward in the stolen wagonette drawn by the Laneglos pony, travelling in a direction Alfie thought would be most likely to fool the constabulary.

He believed the police would expect them to head eastwards towards Devon, hoping to cross one of the bridges across the Tamar river and so enter the jurisdiction of a police force unlikely to expend too much energy seeking the apprehension of men who had robbed a *Cornish* manor house. Either that, or go south to the coast and take passage in any boat that could take them to safety.

Instead of taking either of these options, he intended they would cross into Devon from the north east corner of Cornwall, where there was no river border to make it difficult for them to cross undetected.

The pony and wagonette stolen from Laneglos was laden with all the items stolen from Laneglos. Pictures; silver; valuable vases and statuettes, all heaped inside the vehicle in a chaotic manner that would have caused the rightful owners to throw up their hands in horror . . . but worse was to come.

The pair were travelling through a heavily-wooded section of country bordering the estate of one of the Cornish landowners who had been to the Laneglos ball, when a deer broke from cover in front of them and bounded across the narrow lane, to disappear in woodland on the other side.

Jimmy Banks was in control of the wagonette at the time and the sudden appearance of the deer startled him and caused him to jerk involuntarily on the reins. The confused pony, already unnerved by the deer, immediately veered off the road . . . taking the wagonette with it.

Before the inexperienced driver could guide it back to safety a stout sapling came between the body of the vehicle and one of its wheels and the wagonette came to an abrupt and lop-sided halt to the accompaniment of the sound of splintering wood, throwing Alfie and Jimmy, together with much of the stolen property, out of the vehicle.

The younger of the two Banks men crashed heavily against a tree, hurting his shoulder so severely that he screamed out in pain . . . but he received no sympathy from his uncle.

Picking himself up from the soft ground where he had landed, Alfie rounded upon his nephew angrily. 'Now look what you've done! You're bloody useless! I should never have trusted you to drive the pony — or even to have come to

Cornwall with the rest of us. Nothing's gone right since you came on the scene, you're a bleedin' disaster.'

Jimmy was in no doubt about his uncle's anger with him but it was not the most important thing in his life at this very moment. Seated on the ground he clutched his shoulder and rocking back and forth in pain, wailed, 'I've broken something, Uncle Alfie. I think it's me collarbone.'

'Oh, so you're a surgeon now, are you? Well, what do you expect me to do about it, run off to the nearest town, wherever that might be, and find a doctor for you? What shall I tell him, 'Come quickly and treat my snivelling, useless nephew who's sitting in the woods in the middle of nowhere with a cartload of swag we've just nicked from a mansion down the road?' Is that what you want me to do?'

'It hurts, Uncle Alfie, it hurts like hell,' Jimmy whined, his face contorted in pain.

'It'll hurt a whole lot more if the local coppers catch up with us and we're thrown in clink. They won't show you any sympathy, so up on your feet and help me get this lot hidden, then we'll need to do the same with the wagonette. Come on, before someone comes along and finds us.'

The young criminal was in excruciating pain . . . but he was aware of what his violent uncle would do to him if he made no attempt to do as he was told. Climbing to his feet, he did his one-handed best to help move the valuables strewn on the woodland ground about them.

It took the two men more than half-an-hour to

carry the stolen items to a spot Alfie found a short distance into the woods, where a broken but still attached branch of a tree formed a canopy over some undergrowth, where the stolen goods could be safely concealed.

Jimmy's half-hearted contribution invoked the wrath of his uncle that intensified when they turned their attentions to the wrecked vehicle. This proved to be far more difficult to move and Jimmy's increasingly feeble assistance provoked a stream of colourful oaths from Alfie.

Even when the wagonette was freed from the sapling that had broken the wheel they were unable to drag it farther in to the woods. Not until Alfie succeeded in securing the still frightened pony to one of the broken shafts were they able to move it, with Alfie staggering and cursing as he struggled to partly support the badly damaged small cart.

The wagonette was eventually tipped into a deep, bramble-filled hollow, where Alfie expressed the hope it would remain unnoticed until they were well on their way to London.

'How are we going to get there?' Jimmy wailed, 'I'm in agony with this shoulder of mine. I can't use the arm and if I don't get something done about it I might be crippled for life.'

'If you get yourself caught by the law that might prove a blessing,' Alfie replied, callously, 'If you're a cripple you can't be put on the treadmill, or made to do any hard graft while you're in jail . . . but *I* don't intend getting caught, so you'd better do as I tell you. You'll stay here with the loot, keeping out of sight of anyone who might come along the road. I'll take the pony and see if I can pinch a cart from somewhere nearby.'

Alarmed, Jimmy said, 'You're not going to leave me here alone? What if you don't come back . . . or come back and can't find me?'

'You'll just have to hope I *do* find you — and that you don't let anyone else find you first. Now, hide yourself in a place where you can keep an eye on the swag. It'll give you a chance to rest that shoulder. It's all that's needed and you'll be fit as a fiddle by the time I get back to you.'

* * *

When Alfie rode off on the pony, Jimmy tried to convince himself that what his uncle had told him would be so and he settled himself to await his return . . . but it was not easy.

The pain in his shoulder showed no sign of easing and he occasionally caught himself moaning aloud. There was another problem . . . he was hungry. He had not eaten for some sixteen or seventeen hours, during which time he and Alfie had expended a great deal of nervous and physical energy.

Jimmy also found the silence and the loneliness of the woods disconcerting. He was used to neither. There was always something noisy happening in Hoxton, by day or by night. The tenement house in which he lived with his mother was occupied by more people than he could count, all of whom were engaged in a wide variety of nefarious activities and one or more of them were always either coming, going, or involved in noisy or violent argument.

Here in the Cornish wood there was an awesome quietness, broken only occasionally by the unfamiliar sound of a breeze, or perhaps a bird, rustling the tree-tops, or the scuffle of some unseen creature somewhere on the woodland floor. These were sounds that disturbed Jimmy far more than the less innocent noises of the London slum that was his home.

However, despite his unfamiliar surroundings, the pain in his shoulder and the increasingly noisy hunger rumblings of his stomach, when the sun reached its highest point in the summer sky and its warmth filtered down through the leafy canopy above him, fatigue, brought on by the events of the past few days proved stronger than his uncle's instructions to guard the stolen Laneglos property and Jimmy fell into an exhausted sleep.

* * *

Jimmy woke with a start, momentarily confused about his whereabouts. Evening was far advanced and it was gloomy here, among the trees. When he tried to sit up his injured shoulder gave him an agonising reminder and he cried out aloud. Breathlessly, he did his best to stifle the sound, only partially succeeding. The pain he felt was excruciating, so much so that by the time he was able to rise to his feet he was sobbing.

Staggering, he felt light-headed and was aware

of his grumbling stomach now. Remembering the events that had led to his shoulder injury gave him a moment of panic, wondering whether Alfie might have returned and, not being able to see him, had carried away the stolen property and left him alone in the wood.

Disconcerted, he looked about him in the gathering gloom with increasing panic. Then, recognizing the sagging branch, he staggered to where it hung over the undergrowth — and there were the valuable items stolen from Laneglos.

Despite the pain of his injured shoulder Jimmy felt tremendous relief at the knowledge that he would not incur his uncle's wrath . . . but it was a fleeting feeling. Where was Alfie, he should have been back by now?

Many thoughts went through Jimmy's mind. Had Alfie been unable to find the spot where he had left his nephew with the loot . . . or had he perhaps been captured? Then another thought came . . . what if Alfie had deliberately made good his own escape and left him here to fend for himself?

To Jimmy, confused by pain, hunger and doubt, this seemed the most likely answer. After all, Alfie had made it very clear what he thought of him. If he had found it difficult to locate a cart of some kind, or if there was a great deal of police activity in the area, Jimmy knew he would not hesitate to make good his own escape and leave his nephew to his fate.

Looking about him in sudden despair, Jimmy sank to his knees and began to cry.

Jimmy was still on his knees when he became

aware of a new sound in the tree-tops above him. He had climbed awkwardly to his feet before he felt the rain upon his face and realized it was this that was causing the noise in the trees.

It was quite dark but the rain was falling harder now. Jimmy needed to find shelter and he stumbled off in the direction of the road. He could bear the pain he was suffering no longer and was desperate to escape from the frightening loneliness of the woods. He would follow the road until he reached the first sign of habitation and give himself up to whoever he found there. A lengthy prison sentence was inevitable . . . but it was preferable to his present dire situation.

Jimmy staggered on for what must have been at least an hour — he could not be absolutely certain because he was having intermittent bouts of delirium. He was soaked through, in constant pain and increasingly aware that he had become hopelessly lost.

He could see nothing in the gloom and needed to walk head down to protect his face from the rain, his useable arm outstretched to detect trees, or wayward branches.

Suddenly, he became aware that the sound he had been hearing for the past few minutes had increased and was too loud to be rain, but it was a moment or two before he realized that what he was hearing was the sound of rushing water tumbling over rocks. There was a river nearby!

Jimmy headed for the sound, hoping the river might indicate the edge of the woodland and bring him closer to habitation. He cursed the rain and the darkness it brought with it. If there was even a glimmer of light he might have been able to see what was on the other side — or even how wide or deep was the river.

He reached the water's edge, but dared go no farther. However, there was a path of sorts here and as the ground sloped away to his left this was the direction he took. He was more concerned about his footing now because the path was muddy and slippery and the river very close, following the slope in a series of unseen but noisy shallow cataracts.

Suddenly, Jimmy saw a faint light in the distance. Yellow and indistinct, he thought it could be coming from the window of a cottage, possibly beyond the edge of the wood.

He had no way of knowing on which side of the river it was, but the glimpse of the light gave him a feeling of indescribable hope that the nightmare in which he had been caught up was almost over.

It was . . . but not in the way he envisaged.

He lost concentration on what he was doing for only a moment, but it was sufficient time for him to collide with the overhanging branch of a tree. It was probably no thicker than his little finger but when it brushed his face he involuntarily stepped back away from it. His foot slipped on the mud and before he could regain his balance he tumbled into the fast-running river.

He cried out from the pain it caused to his injured shoulder, but the next moment his head struck one of the rocks protruding from the water — and Jimmy Banks knew no more.

21

'Why are you asking me these questions? I had nothing to do with the killing of Enid Merryn . . . although on the few occasions I had her working for me in the kitchen she was so slow I might have *felt* like doing it, but it would have been like punishing a baby.'

The pugnacious observation was made by Peggy Woods, the Laneglos assistant cook, in response to the questions being put to her by Tom in the housekeeper's sitting-room.

'In view of what has happened to Enid I don't think that is something that ought to be said, even in jest.' The sharp rejoinder came not from Tom but from Flora, who was present at his interview with the Irish woman.

'I meant nothing by it,' the assistant cook said, 'Why, I'd be saying the same thing to my husband more than once — and for all his faults I wouldn't harm a hair on his darling head.'

'I'm sure he'd be pleased to hear you say that,' Tom said, hoping as soon as the words left his lips that Peggy Woods would not take offence. The assistant cook had the physique of an Amazon and Flora had warned him that she possessed a quick temper, ' . . . but you haven't answered my question,' he added, 'and it's one I need to ask every member of the household staff . . . what were you doing on the night of the robbery . . . the night Enid Merryn went missing

— and was your husband with you?'

'What we were doing is a private matter between a husband and wife,' the assistant cook retorted testily, adding, 'and it's not something I'd be doing by myself.'

'I'm not asking for personal details of your married life,' Tom replied to the touchy Irishwoman, 'Just where you were and whether you and your husband were together all night.'

'I was cuddling him when I went to sleep and still had my arms around him when I woke up, so the answer to your question is 'yes'. I'd been cooking the whole night of the ball for everyone who is anyone in Cornwall, then feeding the family for the rest of the day because cook had taken to her bed, 'suffering from exhaustion' . . . or so she said.'

The last remark was accompanied by a disdainful sniff that indicated quite clearly to Tom that Peggy Woods disagreed with the cook's self-diagnosis . . . but she was still talking, 'Chester . . . that's my husband, had been on his two feet for as long as I'd spent in the kitchen, so once we were both asleep we neither of us so much as twitched for the whole of the night — and there you have it, so can I go off now and get on with what I'm paid for?'

When Peggy Woods had left the housekeeper's sitting-room, Tom said to Flora, 'That's pretty much what Chester Woods told us. Unless we find evidence to the contrary it rules the two of them out . . . certainly as far as the burglary is concerned. There are still one or two servants to be seen, but we are no closer to finding an answer to the question of who opened the kitchen door than we were when I began talking to them. I doubt if we'll find the answer until we pick up Alfie and Jimmy Banks, although getting *any* information from them is likely to prove as easy as squeezing water from a stone.'

'I've been thinking about that,' Flora mused, 'Do you think it possible that Jeremy — Jimmy Banks — could have somehow managed to get inside the house and hide himself until everyone was asleep and opened the door himself to let his uncle in? He would certainly know the house well enough to hide himself away somewhere. He might even have hidden in Enid's room . . . and that could provide a motive for her murder. I always believed her to be a naively honest girl and if she hid him only to find out what he was really up to he might have felt he needed to kill her to stop her from giving him away, or perhaps spoiling the plans he and his uncle had made to burgle the house.'

Flora became increasingly excited as her suggested sequence of events unfolded and Tom thought about it very carefully before saying, 'It's an interesting theory, Flora — very interesting, and one that's entirely feasible but perhaps we ought to have a look in Enid's room before I put it to Superintendent Hawke. We might find something to substantiate it in there.'

'You *could* be lucky,' Flora replied, 'I usually check the maids' rooms every day to ensure they are being kept tidy, but with all that's been happening at Laneglos, it has not been carried out. All I have done with Enid's room is to look in there when she couldn't be found, just in case she had fallen ill and was lying in bed . . . but, of course, she was not there and her bed had not been slept in.'

Thinking of what had really happened to Enid brought Flora close to tears and Tom had a strong urge to take the housekeeper in his arms and comfort her. He refrained only because be felt that their relationship, although improving with every meeting, had not yet reached the point where he might act in such a familiar manner and he wanted to do nothing to jeopardise the closeness they had achieved in a relatively short time.

* * *

The room allocated to the late Laneglos kitchen-maid on the top floor of the house was one of the very smallest. Nevertheless, it was spotlessly clean and comparatively tidy. There was a small, under-the-eaves cupboard in one corner and Tom opened it to disclose a dress, coat and small pile of personal clothing in addition to a clean uniform.

The room contained pitifully few personal possessions but, as Flora pointed out, her home was not far away and she had been allowed to go home for one afternoon a week, so any personal items had probably remained there.

Looking through the pile of personal clothes, he found something wrapped in a towel. It dropped out but Tom managed to catch it before it fell to the floor. It was a small porcelain ash-tray, decorated with an image of Buckingham palace, Queen Victoria's London home.

When Tom showed it to Flora, she said, 'It's most probably a present from Jimmy to Enid, he often bragged about seeing the queen and her great London home. Enid was particularly impressed, he was a man-of-the-world in her eyes.'

'Do you think he would have brought it from London for her when he came back this time?'

Flora shook her head in answer to Tom's question, 'I doubt it very much, it's more likely something he had with him when he came to work here and that he gave it to Enid as a present.'

'If it was a present why did she not have it on show? Why keep it hidden wrapped in a towel?'

'It would have been very much a treasured possession and she would have wanted to keep it safe. Besides, had I or anyone else seen it we would have known where it came from and questions would have been asked about their relationship. It might have caused a great deal of trouble for her.'

Wrapping the ash-tray in the towel once more, Tom said, 'When her things are handed over to her mother perhaps it ought to be explained away as a present from 'one of the other servants', there's no need to mention Jem Banks.'

Once again Flora allowed a side of her nature to show that was not usually seen by the Laneglos servants when she said, 'Poor Enid, she really was a very simple little soul.'

Tom was inclined to agree with her. From his search of the room he had formed an opinion that Enid was a young girl who neither expected, nor received, much from life. She was perhaps ideally suited for the tasks she was employed to perform in the great house of Laneglos.

22

'We think one of the two men you are looking for has been found, sir . . . at least, he fits the description of the younger one, according to the constable from Launceston.'

The news was brought to Amos by a constable employed in Bodmin police station's charge office. A man getting on in years, he had been taken on as a policeman in the Cornwall force only because he had spent many years employed as a parish constable. Too old for the rigours of the beat he was employed on duties that mainly involved cleaning and taking care of any prisoners lodged in the police station cells.

This was exciting news and Amos said. 'That would be Jimmy Banks, but why do you only *think* it's him, won't he say who he is?'

'Seems he hasn't said anything to anyone,' the constable replied, 'He was pulled from the river unconscious according to the Launceston constable, found the night before last by some young lads searching for a lost pig or so they said. They were probably poaching, but they carried him home to their cottage and kept him there all day yesterday, hoping he'd come round. He didn't and by this morning they were so worried about his state that they reported it. The inspector in charge at Launceston realized it might be the young man you wanted and sent a constable here to tell you.'

'Where's this Launceston constable now? Why wasn't he brought straight up here to see me?'

'He's walked all the way from Launceston, sir, wearing a pair of new boots and they've blistered his feet something cruel. I don't think it's *too* serious, but he'll need to put something on his feet before he starts on the walk back. Now, when I used to get blisters as a boy, my old ma used to . . . '

'Damn the man's blisters,' Amos interrupted, 'We have a murder and a major burglary to solve. Send him up here to me . . . Now!'

The constable who limped in to Amos's office was not only suffering from blisters, but had also been caught in a heavy shower during the early part of his 20-mile walk from Launceston to Bodmin. The long spell of hot weather had broken and there had been some awesome storms with thunder, lightning and torrential rain. Water was pouring off the moors and floods were reported from all parts of the county.

Despite his irritation at the delay in being informed about Jimmy Banks being found, Amos felt sorry for the constable standing before him. Cornwall's police authority was reluctant to provide transport for its policemen, except in dire emergencies and walking very long distances was the norm for them. It was a policy Amos was trying to have changed, especially for constables like the man standing before him. He was not one of the youngest of the recruits to the force.

'Sit down and tell me about the man you have found. Where was he detained, and why is there any doubt about his identity?'

Easing himself down into the chair Amos had indicated, the constable said, 'Thank you, sir. He was found by some children caught between rocks in a river at the bottom of a cataract that comes down off Bodmin Moor. He must have slipped in farther up, somewhere in the woods, I reckon. He's lucky to be alive . . . very lucky. If the river hadn't been in full flood and wedged him up between the rocks with his head out of the water he'd have drowned for sure. As it is, he's seriously hurt because he's been some battered about on the way down. He was unconscious when he was found and spent a day and a night in the cottage belonging to the youngsters' parents. The inspector had him brought to the police station cells at Launceston, but he was in a bad way when I set out to come here. The doctor hadn't arrived by the time I left, but I saw him myself and I don't think he'll live long. He's hardly more than a boy, but I'm pretty sure he's the one you're looking for, sir, he's not wearing country clothes and wasn't recognized by any of them who found him.'

Amos was dismayed by the news that Jimmy Banks might not survive. He was probably the only person who could give him any idea of what had happened. If he lived he would most probably hang for killing Enid, but if he died before being brought to trial there would always be a doubt — certainly in Amos's mind — that he was the guilty party. There were also many unanswered questions about the burglary at Laneglos.

'Have you eaten?' He asked the Launceston constable.

'No, sir.'

'Then go back to the charge office and tell the sergeant to get you something while I find Sergeant Churchyard and have my pony and trap made ready. You can return to Launceston with us.'

* * *

When they arrived in Launceston Tom Churchyard was able to confirm that the injured man brought to the police station *was* Jimmy Banks. He had regained consciousness, but was in great pain and seemed confused.

A Launceston town doctor was with him. Having seen the young London criminal earlier, he had returned when a constable took news to him that his patient appeared to be regaining consciousness and now the young doctor was treating some of his many cuts and abrasions.

'I am sorry, he is in no fit state to answer questions,' he said, in answer to Amos when the police superintendent told him he wished to speak to his patient. 'He has a great many injuries . . . including, I suspect, a fractured skull and internal injuries. When I have finished dressing his wounds I intend giving him laudanum to ease the pain and, hopefully, send him to sleep. I fear he may never wake again, but at least we can make his last hours easier.'

'I appreciate your concern, Doctor, but even if your efforts are successful, I fear you may only be saving him for the hangman — and he has the answers to a number of very important questions.'

When the doctor began to protest, Amos cut him short. 'I am sorry, Doctor, but, as you say, he may not survive and if he has not told me what I want to know a young girl's murder may remain unsolved forever. I must talk to him . . . *Now!*'

The young doctor had never been faced with such a situation before and, tight-faced, he said, 'I have given you my opinion, Superintendent . . . a *professional* opinion. I cannot physically restrain you from carrying out what you consider to be your duty, but you can be assured that I will make a report to your superiors . . . '

While the doctor was talking Amos had been looking at Jimmy. He had closed his eyes and to Amos it appeared that his breathing had become weaker. Ignoring the doctor, he bent down and put his mouth close to the young patient's ear.

'Jimmy, can you hear me? I want to talk to you . . . about Enid. Enid Merryn.'

Jimmy's eyes flicked open and although he was looking up at the ceiling of the cell where he was housed and not at Amos, it was evident that he had heard him. Speaking in a barely audible whisper, he said, 'Enid . . . I'm sorry . . . about Enid.'

'You're sorry for what . . . ? For killing her?'

For a few moments Amos thought Jimmy had not heard him. He was about to repeat his questions when Jimmy whispered, ' . . . I wouldn't hurt her . . . never hurt her . . . tell her.'

'Jimmy, don't lie to me, not now. Enid is dead . . . murdered. Did you kill her . . . or was it Alfie?'

Mentioning Alfie had struck a chord in Jimmy's mind and he said in a stronger voice, 'Alfie went off and left me. He didn't come back like he promised — I'd hurt my shoulder . . . '

'Jimmy . . . listen to me! What happened at Laneglos . . . Why was Enid killed? Did she let you and Alfie into the house?'

'Enid didn't know . . . sorry if I got her into trouble and went off . . . and left her.'

Amos wondered whether Jimmy was talking about her involvement with the burglary, or whether it was because he had made her pregnant, but he felt Jimmy was slipping away and he still had no answers to his questions.

'Jimmy, someone killed Enid on the night you and Alfie broke into Laneglos. Was anyone else involved? Tell me, Jimmy . . . for poor Enid's sake.'

'No one . . . killed her.'

Jimmy was definitely tiring now and the doctor was protesting again, but Amos still had no answers.

'Jimmy . . . listen to me . . . for Enid's sake. Was there someone else helping you that night? Did you see anyone . . . anyone at all?'

The reply, when it came, was barely audible and had Amos been any farther away from Jimmy's lips he would not have heard it.

'Only . . . Chester . . . '

With this, Jimmy slipped into unconsciousness and as Amos straightened up the doctor pushed him aside and bent over his patient.

Tom had been standing nearby while Amos was trying to draw some replies from Jimmy Banks and now he asked, 'Did Jimmy answer you when you asked him whether anyone else was around that night.'

'Yes, but I don't know whether it made any sense. He mentioned the name 'Chester'. Does that mean anything to you?'

Excitedly, Tom replied, 'Yes . . . Chester Woods, one of the footmen who's married to Peggy, the assistant cook. He had a reputation as a womaniser before they were married and he's also very fond of his drink. But both he and his wife said they were in bed together all night.'

'Then we'll need to speak to them both again,' Amos said, 'and find out whether Jimmy is telling us the truth.'

The doctor had straightened up from Jimmy in time to hear their exchange and now, tight-lipped, he said, 'Well he certainly isn't going to confirm whether or not it was the truth he told you. He has just died.'

23

Before returning to Bodmin with Tom, Amos visited the spot below the woods where Jimmy had been found. A police search party was already scouring the area in a bid to ascertain where — and if possible *why* — he had gone into the river.

As they arrived the smashed Laneglos wagonette was discovered and only a few minutes later a constable stumbled across the cache where the items burgled from Laneglos had been hidden.

There was some damage to a couple of the pictures but as far as Amos could remember from the list he had compiled with Lady Hogg, the only item of stolen property still missing was the Laneglos pony, and he and Tom were in agreement that Alfie must have ridden off on the animal, leaving an injured Jimmy behind to fend for himself. It seemed the most likely explanation.

As they were travelling back to the police headquarters, Tom said, 'I'm not surprised Alfie deserted Jimmy. He's ruthless enough to sacrifice his own mother if he ever thought it necessary, but it's not like him to abandon so much valuable loot. I would have thought he'd have moved heaven and earth to make money on it. There is some very valuable stuff back there — probably more than he's ever had in his hands before.'

'Perhaps he somehow got word that Enid's body had been found and realized we would be looking for him and Jimmy. He's shrewd enough to realize that no matter how valuable the stolen property might be it would be no good to him if it led to a meeting with the hangman.'

'He certainly seems to have made good his escape,' Tom said, regretfully, 'I was hoping he might have managed to get back to the *Mermaid*, perhaps when it was coaling at Plymouth, then he'd have been picked up when the boat reached London.'

Amos had discussed the question of conspiracy charges with the Cornwall chief constable and it had been decided to bring no charges against the *Mermaid*'s passengers, Amos pointing out it would be difficult to prove exactly what crimes the more sophisticated of the criminals on board had planned to carry out at the Laneglos ball. Besides, those who *had* committed crimes, the Hoxton gang and Conrad Shannon, had been caught and charged with either burglary, or attempted burglary — and in Shannon's case, forgery. Now, with the death of Jimmy, only Alfie remained to be apprehended.

The Chief Constable had agreed that the Laneglos burglary should be regarded as a separate crime but when the body of Enid was discovered, Amos had telegraphed to Scotland Yard with the result that the London river police boarded the *Mermaid* when it sailed into their jurisdiction, searching for the prime murder suspects. But their search for the missing members of the Banks family had proved fruitless.

'Alfie was aware we knew of his association with the *Mermaid*,' Amos pointed out, 'He would have kept well clear of it. I doubt whether he'll return to Hoxton for a while, either. With a murder charge hanging over his head he might even have boarded an emigrant ship bound for Australia or America! If he did, we'll never see him again.'

'If it wasn't for Enid's murder that would be a very welcome state of affairs,' Tom commented. 'The Met police would certainly be happy about it.'

'Unfortunately, his disappearance doesn't make solving Enid's murder any easier,' Amos said, 'Had anyone asked me earlier today, I would have said the death of Jimmy was sufficient for us to close the case, but now I'm not so sure. What Jimmy told us just before he died worries me. He seemed genuinely surprised that Enid was dead — in fact was totally unable to take it in. Then there's what he said about seeing the footman, Chester Woods, on the night of the burglary. I wish he had been able to give us more details about that. When did he see him . . . and where? Was Woods the one who opened the door to Alfie and Jimmy? If Jimmy told us the truth then both Woods and his wife have been lying and both were probably involved in the burglary.'

Flicking the reins over the back of the pony, urging it to greater speed, Amos said, 'We need to speak to Chester and Peggy Woods again — and the rest of the staff at the house too. With Jimmy's information in mind we might learn something we weren't looking for when we spoke to them before. We'll call in at Laneglos before returning to headquarters to tell them we've recovered the stolen property and make arrangements to interview everyone tomorrow.'

* * *

Amos's intention to question the Laneglos staff suffered an unexpected setback. When they arrived at the great house the following day to interview the servants they learned that yet another tragedy had befallen the Hogg family. Earlier that morning, a maid taking early morning tea to Viscount Hogg in his bedroom had found him dead.

Suffering indifferent health for some time, the ageing peer had taken to his bed the day after the Laneglos ball, apparently suffering from a mild stomach disorder. It had been attributed to the amount of rich food and wine available for all and sundry all night long and which he was known to have enjoyed, most probably to excess.

When his condition failed to improve Lady Hogg called in the physician from Bodmin Town Doctor Hollis, who had attended the family for very many years. The ageing doctor agreed that Lord Hogg had not only over-eaten but also over-exerted himself, something he had been warned against in the past.

Prescribing a strong purgative, the doctor instructed Lady Hogg to keep the patient resting in bed for a few days, by which time he declared he should be 'as right as rain'.

Despite this cheerful prognosis and increasingly concerned by her husband's condition, Lady Hogg called the doctor in again on the following day. Whilst accepting that her husband was in the habit of over-indulging in food and drink, she declared she had never seen him in such a feeble state before.

The doctor felt she was worrying unnecessarily but in order to placate a very important member of the community he decided upon an old-fashioned 'cure-all' and resorted to blood-letting. At the same time he pointed out, as tactfully as he could, that Viscount Hogg was an old man and should not expect to be able to maintain the life-style he had enjoyed as a younger man.

Still not reassured, Lady Hogg had telegraphed the son and daughter of her husband's first marriage suggesting that they should return to Laneglos as a matter of urgency.

Unfortunately, both reached Laneglos too late to see their father alive, arriving late in the day of his death. The Honourable Rupert was now the 7th Viscount, he and his sister taking some small comfort from the knowledge that that they had been able to spend time with him on the occasion of the County summer ball.

The news of Viscount Hogg's death was given to Amos and Tom by a very upset Laneglos housekeeper and they knew it would be insensitive to continue investigations at the great house at such a time. Instead, Amos concentrated on collating the remainder of the information that had come to hand concerning the burglary and the murder of Enid Merryn.

He discussed both cases with the Chief Constable who was in favour of closing the murder file in view of the death of their chief suspect, but Amos argued that there were still too many loose ends to be tied up before the young maidservant's death could be brought to a satisfactory conclusion. The Chief Constable eventually conceded the argument — and events were to prove that Amos was right to keep the case open.

* * *

Later that day, Doctor Andrew Sullivan, the young surgeon and pathologist who had carried out the post mortem on Enid Merryn called at the Bodmin police headquarters to personally deliver an autopsy report on a baby born to a single young girl who lived on the moor near the town. She had not reported the baby's birth and the baby had been found dead by a constable, called in by neighbours. The pathologist's report showed the baby had suffered from a serious heart defect and the trauma of the birth had proved too much for its fragile constitution.

His report delivered, Sullivan put his head around the door of Amos's office and, greeting the police superintendent, said, 'I hear that the lad from London you suspect of murdering the young Laneglos housemaid has met his own violent end?'

'That's right,' Amos confirmed, ' . . . but

almost the last words he spoke were a denial that it was his doing.'

'Do you believe he was telling you the truth?' Suddenly interested, the young doctor entered the office and seated himself on a chair on the opposite side of the desk from Amos.

'I wish I knew. I would be a happier man if I could convince myself he was lying.'

'So you *do* believe him! Why? He had both motive and opportunity and was a known criminal — you said so yourself.'

'True,' Amos agreed, 'but he had no history of violence and when he was dying — and I'm convinced he *knew* he was dying — he wanted me to tell Enid he was sorry if his actions had got her into trouble.'

Doctor Sullivan snorted disdainfully, 'If he was apologising for getting her pregnant it was far too late. He should have thought about it four months ago, when he made love to her . . . '

The expression that came to Amos's face brought the doctor's condemnation of Jimmy Banks to an abrupt halt and, leaning forward towards him, Amos demanded, '*What did you say*?'

Startled, by the unexpected intensity of Amos's question, Sullivan began, 'I said it was far too late for . . . '

'No,' Amos said, 'After that. How many months pregnant did you say Enid was?'

'Four months . . . '

'Are you *absolutely* certain of that?'

'Positive,' Sullivan said, emphatically, ' . . . It might even have been slightly more. She wouldn't have been able to keep it a secret for very much longer.'

Amos was silent for so long that the doctor began to feel uncomfortable, but something in the Superintendent's expression stopped him from interrupting his thoughts.

Eventually, Amos said, 'Doctor Sullivan, you have just produced the strongest evidence yet that young Jimmy was telling the truth — and that someone *else* had a motive for killing Enid Merryn.'

'I'm sorry . . . I don't understand. How does anything I have said indicate that this young man did *not* kill Miss Merryn? She was certainly pregnant.'

'Yes, but *not* by Jimmy Banks. I don't doubt he made love to the girl, she was apparently quite besotted with him, but he did not go to work at Laneglos until two months before she was murdered . . . *by which time she was already two months pregnant*! If the *real* prospective father knew of her condition and had a great deal to lose by having his secret found out then there is still a suspect out there. It is possible Jimmy Banks actually saw him on the night. If so, and the new suspect's wife gets to know of it we might well have another murder on our hands!'

* * *

In spite of the latest information that had come into his possession, Amos was unable to pursue his enquiries at Laneglos until after the funeral of Viscount Hogg, the chief constable declaring it would be 'in bad taste' to further upset the Hogg family. He pointed out that no one at the great house was aware that suspicion had shifted from the ex-footman, so if the killer was still working there he would be unlikely to abscond.

The funeral itself was a sombre but impressive event. Not only were representatives of all the Cornish gentry present, but nobility from beyond Cornwall's border came to pay their last respects to the well-known and highly respected peer of the realm.

Amos and a number of uniformed constables were in attendance to ensure there were no untoward incidents and Tom took the opportunity to speak with Flora Wicks about Amos's intention to interview the Laneglos servants once more.

She was surprised by the request but did not question him further after he promised to give her his reasons when he and Amos came to the house. She suggested they should wait until after the reading of the will, which was due to take place the next day. Amos agreed and it was arranged he and Tom would visit Laneglos during the morning of the day after.

* * *

When Amos and Tom arrived at Laneglos they found the house in turmoil, with vans and wagons standing outside the front entrance, being loaded with boxes, trunks and small items of furniture from the house.

Amos was about to ask one of the servants the reason for such activity when Flora Wicks came from the house. When she reached the two policemen, Amos said, 'We seem to have arrived at yet another inconvenient time, what's going on?'

'Some of Lady Hogg's personal belongings are being moved to the dower-house at the far end of the park. The Honourable Rupert is now the seventh viscount. In addition to the title he has also taken over the estate and, of course, Laneglos House.'

'But this is very soon after the late viscount's death! I am aware the new viscount is Lady Hogg's stepson and not her actual son, but surely he is not turning her out only a couple of days after his father's funeral?'

'No, Rupert . . . Lord Hogg, wouldn't do that and she won't actually be leaving Laneglos for some days, but there's been a falling out between him and the Honourable Charles yet again and I think Lady Hogg wants to move away with her son as quickly as possible in the hope that he might calm down.'

'Oh? What's happened between the step-brothers?' This time the query came from Tom.

Flora hesitated for only a moment before replying, 'Well . . . it's no secret that the Honourable Charles and the new Viscount Hogg have never got along with each other, so there's nothing new there, but when the late Lord Hogg's will was read the family learned he had left the Honourable Charles absolutely nothing. Not only that, although he ensured that Lady

Hogg would be well looked after and want for nothing, he left her with no immediate access to capital, which means she is unable to finance the extravagance of her son. I believe he was expecting to be left enough to pay off his debts and then rely on his mother to continue to fund his extravagant London lifestyle.'

Detecting a hint of satisfaction in Flora's explanation, Amos made no comment, instead, he asked, 'Did Lord Hogg make it obvious when he was alive that he disliked his stepson?'

'No, he wasn't the sort of man to do that and wouldn't have wanted to upset Lady Hogg. In fact he was very tolerant and had paid off the Honourable Charles's debts on more than one occasion — as well as making arrangements for his illegitimate children, but he warned him some time ago that he would pay for no more. He had no illusions about his stepson and his will ensures he will be unable to bleed his mother dry.'

'What will happen at Laneglos now? Will you stay on as housekeeper . . . at least, until the old housekeeper returns?'

The question came from Tom and Amos was aware the question was personal and not prompted by professional interest, but Flora had proved very helpful to them in the past and he awaited her reply with some interest.

'The late Lord Hogg left Mrs Hooper, the housekeeper, a very generous sum of money in his will, enough to enable her to live quite comfortably for the rest of her life. As she is still not very well I think she will retire. The new

Lord Hogg is expected to marry next year and with a new mistress in the house Mrs Hooper would need to learn new ways. She is a little too old for that. I have met the future mistress of Laneglos and quite like her — although she has a strong personality which she will no doubt impose upon the household, but Lord Hogg has already asked me if I will stay on if Mrs Hooper *does* retire and I have said I would be very happy to do so . . . but you haven't come here to gossip with me. I believe you wish to speak with Chester and Peggy Woods?'

'Not immediately,' Amos replied. 'Before I do, Tom and I would like to chat with some of the other servants who work with the Woods. Perhaps you would tell us those who are particularly friendly with them — and those who are not.'

When it seemed Flora might protest, Amos said quickly, 'I am not asking you to repeat any gossip about them, Flora. It's just that I want to know who might be biased against them, or who is not likely to say anything to incriminate them, so your knowledge is important to us — and to them too.'

24

The interviews took place in the study of the great house, put at Amos and Tom's disposal by the new Lord Hogg, who also arranged for them to take a midday meal in the housekeeper's dining room.

The 7th Viscount was a very pleasant and easy-going man and he seemed genuinely interested in what they were doing. After thanking Amos for recovering the property stolen from the house by the two Banks men he asked to be kept informed of the progress they were making into both the burglary and the murder of Enid Merryn.

By mid-afternoon, Amos and Tom had spoken with all the Laneglos servants except Chester and Peggy Woods. They had tried to be as discreet as was possible in their questioning, but in such a closely knit community it was inevitable that word should spread among the servants that the two policemen were particularly interested in the activities of the assistant cook and her footman husband.

As a result — and as Amos had anticipated — the few friends the pair possessed tended to give vague replies to any questions that might incriminate them. However, the majority of the servants seemed only too happy to mix gossip and fact in order to discredit the married couple — and Peggy in particular.

Thanks to his briefing by Flora and despite the disparity in the statements made about the two servants, Amos was able to make a fairly accurate assessment of the characters of the two people he suspected of involvement in either the burglary, Enid Merryn's murder — or possibly both.

Nevertheless, the married couple were still able to come up with enough surprises to cast serious doubts upon their involvement in any *criminal* activities.

Peggy was the first of the couple to come to the study and she had lost none of the arrogant self-confidence she had shown during her previous interview with Tom Churchyard. When Amos asked her to tell him what she had been doing on the night of the Laneglos burglary, she inclined her head in Tom's direction and said, 'I've already told *him*.'

'I am aware of that,' Amos retorted sharply, 'but we've been given some new information since then, so I want you to tell *me* what you and your husband were doing — and this time I want the truth.'

Leaning forward in her chair, jaw thrust out aggressively, Peggy Woods said, 'Is it a liar you're saying I am now?'

'*Yes!*' Adopting the same pose across the desk from her, Amos returned her angry scowl, ' . . . that's *exactly* what I'm saying and if you don't start telling me the truth then I'll *know* you're involved in the burglary and perhaps the murder of Enid Merryn too. You'll be taken to Bodmin police station and kept there in a cell until you *do* tell me what you were doing on the night of the robbery.'

For a few moments Peggy Woods maintained her pose, as though hoping to stare him down, but Amos's glare never wavered and suddenly the assistant Laneglos cook's shoulders sagged and she unexpectedly capitulated.

'Alright, so I didn't tell the truth before — and I wish to the Good Lord I didn't have to tell you now — but better to lose me husband and me work here than be blamed for something I had no part in and that might have me sent to gaol for the rest of me life.'

'If you've done nothing criminal you have nothing to worry about, but are you saying you had no part in the robbery or murder . . . ? That it was your husband?'

Startled, Peggy exclaimed, 'Chester? Why, he no more had a part in the robbery than I did — and he hasn't got it in him to murder anyone. Besides, he was sleeping like a babe when I left our room and was still snoring when I came back. The only thing Chester did wrong that night was to pour too much drink down his throat, same as he does all too often . . . '

Remembering to whom she was talking, Peggy added hurriedly, 'Mind you, he's never been the worse for drink while he's working, so I'll thank you not to repeat anything I say to that Miss Wicks. She's a nice enough young woman, to be sure, but she's less understanding of the weaknesses of ordinary folk than Mrs Hooper ever was . . . despite the eyes she has for your sergeant here.'

Hiding a momentary urge to smile at Tom's evident embarrassment, Amos said, 'Anything you say to either me or Sergeant Churchyard will be in strict confidence, Peggy, but let's forget your husband for a few minutes. What were you doing up and about on the night of the robbery. I would have thought you'd have been even more tired than your husband after all the cooking you'd been doing for the ball.'

For a long time Peggy Woods hesitated, as though trying to make up her mind about whether or not to reply and Amos prompted her, 'I have already told you that unless there's something criminal involved anything you will say to me will go no farther, Peggy, but I am investigating a murder and a very serious robbery which has now resulted in someone else dying, so I want the truth from you. You've admitted that you lied to Sergeant Churchyard when he first interviewed you and that immediately throws suspicion upon you. Unless you can satisfy me you *weren't* involved then I have no alternative but to arrest you. If I need to do that I doubt very much whether you will ever come back to Laneglos again, innocent or not.'

Making up her mind, Peggy was no longer the tough aggressive Irishwoman feared by her fellow servants, 'Alright, I'll tell you . . . but I'm trusting you and your sergeant to keep your word and not repeat what I say to anyone else.'

Her glance went to Tom who nodded in uncertain agreement. Satisfied, Peggy began. 'When I first came to Laneglos I was a young, raw Irish girl who knew no one here and found it difficult to make friends because of how I speak and because I didn't know the ways of the people I was working with. I was very lonely, grateful to anyone who was at all kind to me. One of the gamekeepers, Harry Clemo, was kinder to me than anyone and, being a simple Irish girl, I suppose I let him become more familiar with me than I should have done, for all I knew he was married. Eventually people began to talk but I put a stop to it by marrying Chester . . . and I've made him a good wife, he'll tell you that himself, yet I haven't been able to wean him off the drink and sometimes I need someone to talk to . . . can you understand that? Well, Harry has always been there for me, so sometimes I slip away to meet him . . . and it helps.'

'You go out late at night . . . or even in the morning, leaving a drunken husband in bed, just to *talk* to another man?' Amos asked, sceptically.

'I didn't expect you to either understand, or believe me,' Peggy replied with a hint of her earlier spirit, 'That's why I never told your sergeant the truth in the first place.'

'Oh, I think I understand well enough,' Amos said, 'but, tell me, what does Mrs Clemo feel about her husband's role as a comforter of unhappy women?'

'You'll not be telling her?' Peggy said, showing concern once more.

'Not unless I have to,' Amos replied, 'My business is catching criminals, not breaking up marriages. Where did you and gamekeeper Clemo meet and at what time?'

'It must have been soon after eleven. Everyone in the house went to bed early that night, and we met in the hay barn behind the stables.'

'How did he know where and when to meet you?'

Aware that her reply gave the lie to her story that she only turned to the Laneglos gamekeeper in moments of unhappiness, Peggy said, 'We made the arrangement when Harry delivered half-a-dozen rabbits to the kitchen earlier in the day.'

'I presume you used the kitchen door when you left the house to meet with him?'

When the assistant cook nodded in response to his question, Amos said, 'So it was *you* who drew the bolts on the door?'

'No, they were already drawn.'

It was an unexpected reply and Amos said sharply, 'The kitchen door wasn't bolted . . . even though everyone was in bed? The butler has already made a statement saying he personally bolted the door just after ten o'clock.'

'So he might have done,' Peggy retorted, 'but it wasn't bolted when I went out . . . and it's the truth I'm telling you.'

Unsure whether or not to believe her, Amos asked 'Didn't you think it unusual to find the door unbolted when everyone in the house was in bed?'

'Not really. The kitchen door has always been used by house servants with sweethearts among the out-of-house staff, or from the nearby villages. It's probably been used for as long as the house has been here without causing anyone any trouble before this. The servant who unbolts it always makes sure they bolt it again when they return. For that very reason I didn't stay out of the house for very long, just in case whoever unlocked it came back before I did and locked me out. It's happened once or twice to the maids and they've had to shiver outside until the scullery maid came out with ashes from the kitchen fire, first thing in the morning.'

'Are you telling us the butler and Miss Wicks were aware of what went on, but said nothing to us about it?' The question came from Tom.

'I'd say the butler didn't *want* to know. As far as he was concerned he'd done his duty by bolting the door last thing at night.'

' . . . And Miss Wicks?' Tom persisted.

'I doubt she would have known,' Peggy replied, 'Had it come to her notice she would have done something about it, so the servants keep it very much to ourselves. There's little enough freedom for us to enjoy as it is.'

'But your husband would have known about it too?' Amos suggested, 'I believe he once had something of a reputation as a ladies' man. How well did he know Enid Merryn?'

Tight-lipped, Peggy replied, 'Chester was no better, nor no worse than any of the other servants at Laneglos. He knew Enid, of course he did, you can't be living beneath the same roof for months on end without getting to know every one else who's living here, but I'd swear on me mother's life there was never anything going on between the two of 'em . . . and he certainly had nothing to do with the killing of her. Except for the drinking he's behaved himself as well as any husband should since we've been married and I don't let whatever he did before then trouble me. Besides, as I've told you, he was fast asleep in bed when I left him — and he was still there when I got back, no more than fifteen or twenty minutes later.'

'And you saw no one else when you left the house — or when you returned?'

Peggy Woods shook her head emphatically, 'No one.'

When she had been allowed to leave the study, Tom made a gesture of despair, saying to Amos, 'That widens our list of suspects and could even mean that no one in the house deliberately opened the kitchen door to Alfie and Jimmy Banks. Jimmy would have learned of the use made of the kitchen door and he and Alfie could have slipped in when whoever it was went out.'

'Perhaps,' Amos was non-committal, 'but it still doesn't explain what Chester Woods was doing outside the house when Jimmy Banks saw him. It's not only Peggy Woods who has been lying to us. Let's have Chester in and see what he has to say to us now.'

* * *

Amos found it difficult to equate Chester Woods with the man Flora Wicks had described as being a womaniser until his marriage to the ebullient assistant cook. A small, thin man with a tired expression and an ingratiating manner, the word 'weasely' immediately sprang to mind.

When Amos explained to him that, in common with the other Laneglos servants, he had been called to the study in order that the two policemen might go over his statement once again, the footman said, 'Of course, sir, I am as eager as any of the other servants to have those who robbed Laneglos and murdered poor, dear Enid brought to justice, but I really can't think of anything I can add to what I have already told Mr Churchyard.'

'Really?' Amos raised an eyebrow quizzically, 'Sergeant Churchyard and I believe there is a great deal more you are able to tell us. Matters that you not only failed to disclose when you were last interviewed . . . but which you actually lied about.'

Startled out of his urbane manner, Chester Woods protested, 'What do you mean . . . ? I never lied.'

'Don't get deeper into trouble than you already are, Woods. A witness saw you outside the house when you claim to have been sleeping . . . and we have just spoken to your wife who has changed her statement and told us she was *not* in bed with you for the whole of the night. I think you had better give us a true account of what you were doing out and about, otherwise I will arrest both you and your wife and keep you in custody until we have it.'

Deeply unhappy now, Woods said, 'If you've got the truth out of Peggy then you'll know that when she thought she'd got me in a drunken stupor she went off to see that fancy-man of hers, just as she's done many times before.'

'So you know about him?' Amos said.

'I've known for a long time,' Woods admitted, 'She was sweet on him before we were wed and I've often suspected she only married me to prevent a scandal and stay on at Laneglos to be near him. On the night after the ball she was forcing drink on me, telling me as how I'd been working so hard I deserved it. I knew she was wanting me to pass out, so she'd be able to go off and see him. I thought I'd go along with her and pretend to drink far more than I did. Then, when she believed I was sleeping it off and went out to see him I'd follow her and catch them at it.'

'Is that what you did?' Amos queried.

'That's right, I saw them both go into the hay barn behind the stables. I was going to go in after them . . . then I started thinking of what might happen if I did. I mean . . . chances are I'd have taken a beating from Harry Clemo, him being a whole lot bigger than me. I'd certainly have lost Peggy and my job here at Laneglos, and so would Peggy — and Harry. That would mean his wife and kids ending up in the workhouse . . . and they don't deserve that. Dot Clemo is a good woman.'

'Are you saying they were in the hay barn and you knew what they were doing, yet did nothing about it?' Tom's voice revealed his disbelief.

The Laneglos footman nodded miserably, 'It sounded as though they were only talking. I thought of coming back inside the house and bolting the kitchen door after me so Peggy couldn't get back in again, but that would have been the end of us at Laneglos because she wouldn't have been able to explain it away to me, even if she wasn't caught out.'

'It might have caught out more than your wife,' Amos commented. 'She said the bolts were drawn when she went out, so either someone else was having a clandestine meeting — or they'd been drawn to let burglars into the house. By bolting the doors again you might well have lost your wife, but you could also have prevented a burglary and perhaps saved the life of Enid Merryn — which reminds me . . . you once had quite a reputation for seducing young female servants. How well did you know Enid?'

Aware of the implications in Amos's question, Chester became very frightened, 'What are you trying to say, sir . . . that I had something to do with the death of Enid? No! No . . . I never had anything to do with her like that. Not before I was married, nor afterwards, I swear to that!'

'Well somebody did — and *you* are my prime suspect. Unless more evidence comes in to me you will remain under suspicion and are likely to be arrested in the very near future . . . Oh, there's one more thing. How long was it after you returned to the house that Peggy came in.'

'I can't say for certain, sir. It might have been five minutes, or a few minutes more, but it wasn't long. If I'd left it any longer I would hardly have got back to our room and settled in bed before she came in. But I didn't do anything to Enid, on my life I didn't . . . I wouldn't. All right, so I've had a good time with *some* of the maids we've had at Laneglos, but there wasn't one of 'em who wasn't willing . . . and they were all pretty much of a type . . . not *exactly* like Peggy, but built something like her. You know . . . big strong girls. Not at all like poor Enid. No, sir, I felt sorry for her . . . I wouldn't have touched her for worlds.'

'Well, you can leave . . . for now, but we'll be wanting to talk to you again, so if you learn anything that will put you in the clear you had better tell me right away, you understand?'

'Yes, sir. I will, sir . . . '

Chester Woods was halfway to the door before he slowed . . . stopped . . . then turned around and addressed Amos. 'When you were talking about poor Enid you said that *somebody* had certainly touched her . . . does that mean she was expecting when she was killed?'

'You tell me. Do you know something?'

'I don't really *know* anything, but Peggy said some time ago that one of the kitchen-maids had told her Enid had been asking a whole lot of questions about having babies, and that sort of thing.'

'Peggy has never said anything about this and neither have any of the kitchen-maids. How long ago was this . . . during the time Jimmy Banks was working here?'

Chester Woods shook his head, 'No, he hadn't started work here then, so it must have been about three months ago . . . or even more.'

Amos and Tom exchanged glances before the former said, 'What is this kitchen-maid's name?'

Woods needed to think for some moments before saying, 'Connie . . . Connie Dawes.'

Leafing through his pocketbook, Tom looked up and said, 'I've got no Connie Dawes down here. We can't have seen her.'

'You wouldn't have,' Woods replied, 'She left soon after that young London thief came to work here. She'd got herself pregnant and although she managed to hide it for a long time, eventually she couldn't stop it from showing, so Miss Wicks got rid of her.'

Leaning back in his chair, Amos expelled his breath in disbelief, 'What sort of a house is this?! Are there *any* servants at Laneglos who are not either having affairs with each other, or getting themselves pregnant?'

'It's no worse than any other big house, sir,' Woods said, 'and you can't put all the blame on the servants. If a man-servant gets a maid pregnant he's usually made to marry her. When there's no marriage and the maid leaves, then it *might* be that the father is a lad from the village, but it's far more likely to be someone in the family of the house who is responsible. Mind you, when that happens the maid's likely set up for life and won't need to think about going out to work again. The master of the house will see she gets money enough to keep both her and the child — and if there's some man willing to marry her and take responsibility for the both of them the gentry can be very generous. There's more than one publican hereabouts who owes his living to some gentleman's bastard.'

'Do you think that someone in the family, or a family friend, was responsible for getting this kitchen-maid pregnant and where will I find her, is she living locally?'

'I don't know the answer to any of those questions, sir, but you can be sure Miss Wicks does.'

* * *

Flora was able to confirm that Connie Dawes had returned to her former home in a remote cottage close to the village of North Hill, on the eastern fringe of Bodmin Moor where her widowed mother earned a meagre living washing and ironing clothes for a few busy wives of farmers in the area. In reply to Amos's question the Laneglos housekeeper refused to speculate on who might have been responsible for the kitchen-maid's condition.

Amos decided he would pay a visit to Connie Dawes the next day, leaving Tom to return to Laneglos and interview the estate gamekeepers. Tom's main purpose would be to speak to Harry Clemo and confirm that his version of events corroborated the stories told by Peggy and Chester Woods, but he would interview all the gamekeepers. This would not only prevent rumours circulating about Clemo, but might possibly provide new information should any of the men patrolling the vast estate during the night of the robbery have seen or heard anything out of the norm. They were a group of estate employees who had not been questioned in depth at the time the body of Enid Merryn had been discovered.

On the way back to the Bodmin police

headquarters, Tom said to Amos, 'If we believe what Chester and Peggy Woods told us we are no closer to solving either the burglary or the murder of Enid Merryn. In fact it seems that as many of the Laneglos servants were gallivanting around the countryside as were tucked up in their beds!'

'It's certainly given us a fascinating insight into life in the great houses of the country,' Amos agreed, 'but I don't think we've wasted our time. We'll see what our amorous gamekeeper has to tell us — and find out whether Enid Merryn said anything to this Connie Dawes about the father of the baby she was carrying. My hope is that when we have collected all the different bits of the jigsaw puzzle we'll be able to fit them all together and find we have the complete picture.'

25

Amos's journey to North Hill took him across the wide expanse of Bodmin Moor. Here ponies and sheep grazed untended on empty wastes of coarse grassland where two thousand years before men and women had lived out their short lives in the harsh and unrelenting upland landscape.

There were still people living on the moor. Hardy farmers and their families eked out a lonely and precarious existence in the extreme weather conditions which prevailed here in winter. There were miners working here too, although in recent years they had concentrated more and more on the fringes of the moor. Evidence of their present endeavours could be seen in the distance where plumes of smoke rose from tall, but for the most part unseen, engine-house chimneys on mines where men were toiling in shafts and tunnels hundreds of feet beneath the moor, hacking out tin and copper ore for the mine 'adventurers' and speculators who would make or lose fortunes by the labours of the miners.

Following a faint narrow path which skirted weathered granite tors, his horse eventually picked its way down from the high moor and crossed a narrow wooden bridge across a river that had not yet lost the speed it had gathered tumbling over its own rocky path from Bodmin Moor.

North Hill was a small, sleepy village with an impressive church and it was here, in the graveyard, Amos found someone from whom to ask the way to the cottage occupied by Connie Dawes and her mother. A bearded and perspiring gravedigger, only head and shoulders above the ground, looked up at Amos suspiciously and countered his question with, 'What be wanting of they, then?'

'I want to ask Connie about one of her friends, a girl she used to work with.'

'This maid you'm talking about . . . she in trouble?'

Amos knew that in such a small community anything said about the true purpose of his visit to the Dawes house would be repeated, misquoted and start wild rumours circulating within hours, so he said, easily, 'No, her friend has spoken of her and as I happened to be passing close by I thought I'd call in on her.'

It took the gravedigger a while to make up his mind, but then he directed Amos back the way he had come, it seemed the Dawes cottage was in a wooded hollow off the path that led down from the high moor.

Thanking the gravedigger, Amos went back the way he had come but before he was out of sight he glanced back and saw the man still leaning on his long-handled shovel and peering over the edge of the newly-dug grave, watching him ride away. He formed an opinion that his informant had not fully believed his reason for going calling on Connie Dawes.

* * *

The Dawes cottage was in a poor state of repair. Paint was peeling from the door and window frames, and thriving green weed was taking over the ragged thatch of the roof. Despite this, there was a flourishing vegetable garden and it was here Amos found Connie.

The former Laneglos maid looked pale and ill and when she straightened up to see who was visiting the cottage a hand went to the small of her back and she grimaced painfully. It was quite obvious she was no longer pregnant and Amos thought the baby must be inside the house.

At that moment an older woman came to the door of a small outbuilding attached to the cottage, the sleeves of her dress rolled up and strands of damp hair hanging down across her face. A few wisps of steam escaped from the doorway around her and she had a clean and almost colourless copper-stick in her hand.

'Hello, can we help you?' It was the older woman who spoke.

'Thank you, but it's actually Connie I've come to speak to. Let me introduce myself, I am Superintendent Hawke of the Cornwall constabulary.'

At his words, Amos was astonished to see an expression of terror come to Connie's face and she immediately looked to her mother.

'What are you wanting with Connie — she's done nothing wrong?' There was aggression in the expression on the face of Mrs Dawes, but Amos thought he also recognized another emotion there. He believed she too was frightened by his unexpected arrival at the cottage.

Their fear was something he would inquire into later. His immediate concern was with a murder.

'I want to speak to her about poor Enid Merryn . . . you have heard about what happened to her?'

Both women exchanged glances and this time it was Connie who replied. 'I haven't heard anything about her since I left Laneglos, we're too far away to get any news from over there. What's she been and done?'

'Enid hasn't done anything, it's what been done to *her* I've come to see you about. She's dead . . . Murdered.'

Connie's reaction to Amos's blunt statement left him in no doubt that her shock was genuine. Staggering backwards until she was able to lean upon the cob wall of the cottage for support, her mouth opened and closed several times without uttering a sound before disjointed words came forth.

'Murdered . . . ? Someone's killed Enid . . . ? Why . . . ? Enid never did a bad turn to anyone. Who did it?'

'That's what I am trying to find out, Connie. I was hoping you might be able to tell me something that would help.'

'Me?' The fear had returned to her face again, 'What could I possibly know about a murder at Laneglos, the house is miles away from here and

I've been left for nigh on a couple of months?'

Her manner puzzled Amos. She was obviously very shocked about the death of Enid but he did not think it was the murder of the Laneglos scullery-maid that was frightening her.

'Shall we go inside and have a talk about it, Connie? Then you can sit down while I talk, you look as though you've been working too hard in the garden.'

Again there was an exchange of glances between mother and daughter before Mrs Dawes spoke, 'She hasn't been very well just lately. You go on into the cottage and make the gentleman a cup of tea, Connie . . . I think we have enough leaves left from the last pot we had. I'll be in just as soon as I've rinsed this washing and hung it out to dry. I've promised to have it back with Winnie Hodge by tonight.'

Amos needed to stoop to pass in through the doorway of the low-ceilinged cottage. The door opened into a room that obviously served as living-room, kitchen and dining-room. It was sparsely furnished with old and clumsily repaired rustic furniture, but there was a scrubbed slate floor and the room was clean.

A fire was burning in the grate and after attacking it with a poker and adding a couple of small logs which caught immediately, Connie pushed a blackened kettle from the hob farther into the flames where it immediately began making a low, singing sound.

As she began assembling the tea things on the plank-wood table, Amos asked, 'Where's your baby, Connie, is it upstairs? It's wonderfully quiet. That must be a great relief to you.'

'You know about the baby?'

'Of course, that's the reason you left Laneglos, isn't it? It's one of the reasons I've come to see you. I believe Enid was asking you a lot of questions about babies while you were working together. Did you get the impression she believed she might be pregnant too?'

After only a moment's hesitation, Connie said, 'It did just cross my mind, sir, especially with Enid being so simple, it would have been easy for any man to take advantage of her.'

'Especially if it was someone in authority,' Amos said casually, 'Someone she didn't feel she could say 'no' to.'

'Enid felt that *everyone* was more important than she was,' Connie retorted, 'It wouldn't make any difference who told her what to do, she'd do it because she thought she had to.'

'But you were never like that, Connie, from what I hear you were not in the habit of doing anything you didn't really want to do . . . unless, of course, you were being told to do it by someone either *really* important, or who perhaps promised that by doing it you'd be able to live comfortably for the rest of your life and would never have to work again. Was that how it was for you, Connie?'

When she again failed to reply, Amos said, 'I suppose the same man could have made both you and Enid pregnant . . . ?'

'No!'

Connie's vehement denial momentarily startled Amos, but before he could pursue his questioning, Mrs Dawes came into the cottage in time to hear her daughter's outcry.

'What's going on? What you doing upsetting Connie? I knew I shouldn't have left you alone with her.'

'I was merely asking a question about the father of her baby, Mrs Dawes. I believe it might help me with my enquiries into the murder of the Laneglos scullery maid . . . and I am still waiting for Connie's answer.'

'What baby? It was all a silly mistake, the sort that silly young girls are likely to make before they're old enough to understand their own bodies. There never was any baby.'

Amos raised an eye quizzically, 'Now who am I to believe? Your daughter just told me the baby was upstairs . . . asleep?'

'No I didn't!' Connie said, hurriedly, 'It was you who spoke about it being upstairs.'

' . . . And *you* who didn't appear particularly surprised that I knew about the baby.'

'I've just told you, there *is* no baby,' this from Mrs Dawes, after glaring angrily at her daughter.

'I think we could call a great many credible witnesses from Laneglos to prove Connie was pregnant, Mrs Dawes . . . ' Remembering the expression on the face of the North Hill gravedigger when he had asked where he could find Connie, Amos added, 'and if it becomes necessary I might have a serious talk with the sexton at North Hill church.'

From the startled expression on Mrs Dawes face, Amos knew his hunch about the whereabouts of Connie's baby had been correct. 'It would be better for everyone if you were to begin telling me the truth about everything,' he said. 'My coming here today has nothing to do with what *you've* done, Connie but the fate of your baby will be looked into and the proper procedure followed. Mind you, even if it goes to a criminal court, you know yourself that both judge and jury show great leniency to young girls who get into trouble in the way I believe you did and the coroner might not even send you to a criminal court . . . but I came here to enquire into the brutal murder of a young girl who was once a friend of yours, Connie and I need your help.'

Amos believed Connie's baby was dead and had been buried in the North Hill graveyard. It was a common practice for unmarried girls to pay a sympathetic — or mercenary — sexton to bury a dead, unchristened baby in a quiet corner of consecrated ground during the hours of darkness — with no questions asked. If such an illegal act was discovered there would need to be a post mortem and inquest into the cause of the baby's death, but both coroner and the doctor carrying out such post mortems were usually sympathetic towards the unfortunate and usually poverty-stricken mother. A verdict would be given that there was no evidence to show the baby was born alive and the mother would walk free.

'I can't help you. I didn't even know for certain Enid was pregnant. If she was you ought to speak to that London boy who was working there as a footman when I left. He had more to do with Enid than any of the other men servants. Far too much, if you ask me.'

'I believe anything that happened to Enid occurred *before* he arrived at Laneglos, Connie. Besides, he's dead now too. He fell into a river and drowned after being involved in a robbery at the big house.'

Connie was obviously startled by the news, but after a few moments, she said callously, 'Oh well, he wasn't much good to anyone. The only one who would have missed him is Enid . . . and now she's dead.'

'Things have certainly been happening at Laneglos since you left there, Connie. You know your late employer, Lord Hogg is also dead?'

'Mum told me. She was at church on Sunday when they offered up a prayer for him. I was sorry to hear of it, he was a nice man.'

'So I believe — but if you can't tell me anything about Enid perhaps we ought to clear up the business of what happened to your baby, does the father know it's dead?'

The closed down expression that came to Connie's face confirmed Amos's suspicions about the father of her dead baby and he added, meaningly, 'You see, Connie, anything you tell me about the father of your child might help you in the coroner's court.'

'I'm not saying anything. There's some things best kept quiet — and that's what I intend doing.'

'You maintain that attitude to a coroner, Connie, and you are likely to lose any sympathy he might have for you — and that would be disastrous for your future.'

'I'll worry about that when the time comes. You said your main concern is to catch whoever killed Enid. I know nothing at all about that, so you're just wasting your time here with me.'

26

At the Hawke's home that evening Harvey Halloran joined Amos, Talwyn and Tom for supper. He had called at the house with information for Amos, who had been absent from the Bodmin police station all day. When Talwyn saw him she told him he looked as though he needed fattening up and she insisted that he stay for the evening meal.

Each of those at the supper table had contributions to make on the events of the day and of them all Harvey's was possibly the most important. He had received a letter from a friend in London who was aware that Harvey had been making inquiries about Alfie Banks some weeks before.

He wrote to say Alfie had not been seen in Hoxton for some time but although word was going around that he was on his way to America there were few who knew him who believed the rumours. It was felt that he was lying low until the anger of a number of prominent villains who felt Alfie had let them down badly by persuading them to take part in an ill-planned and badly bungled criminal excursion to the south western region of England had cooled.

Those who had taken part in the abortive trip were seriously out of pocket. As a result, Alfie's standing in the Hoxton community was at an all time low. If he returned there in the very near future his life would be in serious danger.

It meant Alfie was not going to be easy for Amos to find but, as he pointed out to the others about the table, unless they were able to find more evidence to use against him, they still had nothing to *prove* his guilt in either the Laneglos robbery or Enid Merryn's murder. In fact, unless some of the men arrested on the night of the county ball for burglary, or attempted burglary, gave evidence against him they had no firm evidence he had ever been in Cornwall!

When Talwyn suggested it might be possible to recover the horse stolen from Laneglos and have the purchaser identify Alfie as the seller, Amos revealed that he had already sent details of the animal to neighbouring police forces but was not optimistic about having success in finding it. The chances were that Alfie had sold the horse to gipsies who would either sell it on again quickly, or change its appearance in order to render it unrecognisable.

Tom's interview with the gamekeeper known to be having an affair with Peggy Woods had proved equally frustrating.

'He is a thoroughly unpleasant man,' he said, 'Although he became worried when I told him we knew of his ongoing affair with Peggy and that he had seen her that night, he confirmed the story that she was with him in the hay barn for only a few minutes. He made a statement about what he'd done but there was no remorse. He seemed almost proud of the affair. It baffles me what any woman would see in him, yet he has a loyal and loving wife, two very nice children — and a mistress!'

'There is no accounting for a woman's taste in men,' Talwyn commented, as she left the room to fetch something from the kitchen, 'it is sometimes the apparently most mismatched couples who seem to have the best marriages, however badly either of them behaves.'

'Did you find out anything of interest from any of the other gamekeepers?' Amos asked Tom.

'Nothing . . . although one of them said he heard a pony and what he believed to be a light cart trotting along the lane to the North of the estate, but he was too far away to get to the lane and find out who it was.'

'That could have been Alfie and Jimmy,' Amos said, 'What time did he hear them?'

'He couldn't say for certain but thought it might have been between one and two o'clock.'

'Then the chances are that it was them — but that brings me to something else we must look into. Jimmy was not working at Laneglos for very long and had little time off to get to know the roads and lanes of Cornwall while he was here. Someone must have supplied him and Alfie with a map and told them how best to leave Cornwall using a route that we wouldn't be expecting them to take.'

'Alfie couldn't have been anticipating having to use that particular route,' Tom pointed out. 'He and the others were expecting to put their loot on board the *Mermaid*, return their hired horses and vans and sail away leaving us wondering how they had made good their escape. Alfie would have had a very short time to change his plans and was unlikely to know how best to get away with the loot . . . but where does Enid Merryn's murder fit in with all this?'

'Perhaps she was just in the wrong place, at the wrong time.' Talwyn had re-entered the room in time to hear Tom's question and put forward the suggestion.

'It's possible,' Amos agreed, 'but I don't think so . . . and I don't believe we will find an answer until we learn who unbolted the door for the burglars. I am convinced it wasn't any of the servants going out to meet a lover who inadvertently allowed the burglars to gain an entrance to the house. In my opinion the robbery at Laneglos was not included in the original plans of the Hoxton gang, but was decided upon at the last moment by someone who knew where to find Alfie and Jimmy — and who probably told them exactly what they should take from the house.'

'What makes you believe that?' Talwyn asked.

'Well, from all we were able to learn about the original plan, it seemed that all the criminal activity was to take place on the night of the summer ball. If we hadn't got wind of it in time the Cornwall constabulary would have been thrown into utter disarray. By the time we pulled ourselves together the *Mermaid* would have reached London with the villains and their ill-gotten gains. No professional burglars would have stayed behind to burgle a house like Laneglos. They would have known the police would be swarming over the county like a swarm of angry bees. No, the decision to rob Laneglos was a desperate and daring attempt to recover something from their abortive journey to Cornwall and it was only made possible because we had been successful in thwarting what had been a cleverly planned and co-ordinated criminal attack against Cornish society.'

'And because there was communication between the two Banks's and someone in Laneglos!' The observation came from Talwyn, who added, 'but how could that be achieved without anyone noticing something out of the ordinary — or seeing strangers about the house or its grounds?'

'That takes us right back to where we started,' Tom said, in frustration, 'One of the Laneglos servants *must* be involved, but we are no closer to knowing who it is.'

'Unless Enid Merrryn saw something and was murdered as a result,' Amos suggested, 'I've been giving it a great deal of thought and I'm not convinced that the person involved is necessarily a *Laneglos* servant. A lot of the guests took servants with them when they went to the ball and some were left behind to help with clearing up and packing the belongings of their employers. We are *told* they had all left by the night of the burglary, but I doubt if anyone can be absolutely certain — after all, no one really knew when Enid was last seen alive. What if one of the visiting servants had been hiding in a maid's room, perhaps with her connivance? Someone might even have been hiding in Enid's room without her knowledge and she found them there? It would provide yet another motive for her murder, to stop her from telling us who it was — but Tom found no evidence of anyone having been there.'

Entering the conversation once again, Talwyn said, 'I thought you believed she had been murdered so she wouldn't reveal the identity of the father of the child she was expecting?'

'I still favour that as a motive,' Amos conceded, 'but until we have something positive to go on we can't rule out anything.'

Shifting his attention to Tom, he said, 'I think you are going to have to return to Laneglos and have another chat with Flora Wicks, Tom . . . but I presume that will be no hardship?'

'I'm glad you have mentioned Flora,' Tom said, 'She has one Sunday off each month and is off duty this coming Sunday. I've been wanting to ask her if she would walk out with me on her next day off . . . perhaps for an hour or two in the afternoon, but I'm not sure she would agree to that. I wondered whether I might say that Talwyn would like to meet her . . . and perhaps invite her back for tea?'

Talwyn realized that her reply was of importance to Tom and she did not have to feign pleasure at his tentative suggestion, she was delighted. 'What a lovely idea, Tom, I *would* like to meet her, she sounds as though she's an extremely bright woman. Invite her to come here to Sunday dinner and I'll cook something special for her.'

Tom had not led an easy life and had learned to hide his feelings, whatever the circumstances, but he was finding it difficult now. 'I'll go to Laneglos first thing in the morning and invite her . . . What I mean is, I will go there and *interview* her and if the opportunity arises I'll ask her to come here to dinner on Sunday. Thank you . . . Thank you very much, Talwyn.'

* * *

Tom left the Hawke house early the next morning and walked to Laneglos to make inquiries about servants of ball guests who might have stayed on at the big house during the night of the burglary.

Flora seemed pleased to see him, greeting him with a warm and welcoming smile and suggesting they hold their conversation in the privacy of the housekeepers' lounge. As they went to the room Tom explained his reason for his visit, but Flora seemed certain no servants from other houses had remained at Laneglos for a second night.

'The house had been put straight by the time the family and the guests who stayed on came back from church. There *might* have been one of them hidden away in a maid's room,' she added, 'It is certainly not unheard of, but it would mean instant dismissal for both of them, so it is unlikely to have happened. I will look into it thoroughly and let you know if I have any doubts. Was that your only reason for coming to Laneglos? If so you have had a very long walk for nothing.'

'There is something else,' Tom said, hesitantly,

'but it's of a more personal nature. Talwyn . . . Mrs Hawke, suggested I should ask you to come to their house for dinner one Sunday . . . This Sunday, if possible.'

The invitation took Flora by surprise. 'Why should she ask me to her house for dinner, we have never even met?'

Trying with difficulty to make it appear that is was no more than a casual invitation, Tom said, 'Talwyn takes a great interest in her husband's work and he and I have mentioned you often — because you have been so helpful to us in our inquiries here, at Laneglos, so I think she would like to meet you. You'd like her, Flora, she is a very pleasant and intelligent woman.'

'All the same . . . '

For a moment Tom thought Flora was about to decline the invitation, but looking directly at him, she unexpectedly asked, 'Will you be there too?'

Realizing that Flora knew very little about his personal life or circumstances, Tom said, 'Yes . . . I am living at the Hawke house until things settle down a bit and I am able to look around for a place of my own.'

Flora thought she now understood the *true* reason why she was being asked to have a meal at the Hawke's home and the knowledge gave her a thrill of pleasure. Although giving the impression of thinking about the invitation, she had already made up her mind and, eventually, she said, 'It is a very kind invitation. Yes, I would love to visit the Hawke's home for dinner.'

If Flora had entertained any doubts about

Tom's part in the invitation the expression on his face now would have dispelled them immediately.

'That's wonderful! . . . I mean, Talwyn will be delighted. Superintendent Hawke has said I can use his pony and trap to come and collect you.'

'That will be an adventure in itself . . . but I would rather not have the servants gossiping about me — not that I have had any private life for them to gossip *about*, so far, but I would prefer it if you met me just up the lane from the lodge. It's not far for me to walk and there's a large oak where I can shelter if it's raining. Shall we say about half-past ten?'

'I'll make sure I arrive early so you will have no need to wait,' Tom said happily, 'and you *will* like Talwyn, she and Amos . . . Superintendent Hawke, are a very close couple. The murder of Enid Merryn has upset her a lot. She once taught Enid when she attended her school — and then, of course, her own father was murdered too. That's how she and Amos met. It happened before Cornwall had a police force and he was sent from Scotland Yard in London to investigate. She was able to help him catch the murderers — and she caught Amos too.'

'It must be very satisfying to be able to help your husband when he's involved in such interesting and worthwhile work,' Flora replied.

Their relationship had hardly begun, but the implications of her statement was not lost on either of them and for a few moments they each avoided meeting the eyes of the other.

At that moment a diversion came in the form

of Lady Hogg's personal maid. After knocking and being told to 'Come in', she entered the room looking distraught. 'I am sorry to trouble you, Miss Wicks but I am very concerned about Lady Hogg, she doesn't seem at all well this morning. I think it might be something to do with all the business of moving to the dower-house. Coming on top of losing Lord Hogg it has all been a great strain for her. You know how strong and determined she usually is, but this morning she says she doesn't feel like getting up and intends staying in bed today.'

'That is certainly *not* like her ladyship,' Flora agreed, 'I'll come and see her right away. Go back and remain with her until I get there.'

When the maid had left the housekeeper's lounge, Tom said, 'You're busy, I'll leave you now . . . '

Interrupting him, Flora said, 'I am always pleased to see you, Tom . . . I think you know that, but Lady Hogg has been off-colour for a day or two. It is hardly surprising with all that's been going on, she ought to rest more. Unfortunately, the Honourable Charles is still at Laneglos and it is not easy for *anyone* to relax when he's around . . . but I must go now. Thank Mrs Hawke for her kind invitation — and thank you for offering to come and fetch me. It is exciting to think of getting away from Laneglos for a few hours, I don't know when I last had any time away from the house and it has been particularly busy lately with one thing after another.'

Tom was delighted that she had accepted

Talwyn's invitation. He had learned nothing new about Enid's murder, or the Laneglos burglary, but he left the great house a happy man, remembering Flora's obvious delight at being asked out for the day.

27

Although the days until the week-end seemed to pass exceedingly slowly, Sunday eventually came around and when Tom took Amos's pony and trap to pick up Flora, he found her waiting anxiously at the appointed place.

Helping her into the trap, he gave her an admiring look. Her dark hair, which she usually kept pinned up, was now drawn back and allowed to hang beneath the back of a dark blue spoon bonnet. She also wore a dark blue velvet cloak beneath which he caught a glimpse of a pale blue poplin dress.

It was very different from the grey, rather austere garb she wore during her duty hours as housekeeper at Laneglos and he was aware she had dressed in her best clothes for the visit to the home of Amos and Talwyn.

It soon became evident that Flora was feeling nervous at the prospect of the meeting with her hosts but when she was seated and Tom set the pony off at a sharp trot, he said, 'You look very, very smart, Flora.'

'Thank you. To be honest this is the first time I have left Laneglos for the whole day and I am feeling nervous about meeting with Superintendent Hawke's wife. What is she like?'

'I think you will both get on very well. Talwyn is not dissimilar to you, she is intelligent, straightforward and attractive . . . you'll like her,

I'm quite sure of it.'

As he spoke Tom was guiding the pony past a farm labourer who was leading three cart-horses along the narrow lane, the youngest of which was unused to a bridle and behaving in a skittish manner. As a result, Tom needed to maintain tight control of the pony and he was unaware he had inadvertently revealed more of his feelings for Flora than he might have done had he been thinking about what he was saying.

Flora was about to make a flippant response but stopped herself. Secretly delighted that Tom found her attractive, she was aware that by comparing her with Talwyn he had paid her a great — and sincere — compliment.

'Where was Mrs Hawke teaching school when she taught Enid — and when she and Superintendent Hawke met?'

'In Charlestown, on the south coast — but I know she would want you to call her Talwyn, as I do. I also call Superintendent Hawke 'Amos' at home. It was in Charlestown where Talwyn met with Enid, but I don't think she was able to teach her very much, apparently she was rather backward.'

'She was, that's why she would probably have never been more than a scullery-maid — or a kitchen-maid, at best, but she was a pleasant and willing girl. She certainly did not deserve what happened to her. But don't let's talk of dreadful things like that . . . not today. Tell me all you know about Mr and . . . about Talwyn and Amos.'

Much of the journey from Laneglos was spent in talking about the married couple with whom

Flora would spend the day. For the remainder of the time Tom persuaded her to tell him of her childhood in a West Cornwall manor house where her mother had been housekeeper to an elderly relative of Lady Hogg and where, as a child, she had lessons with the relative's grandchildren.

By the time her mother died Flora was already familiar with life in a large house and had come to work at Laneglos, where she swiftly rose through the servant ranks until she became assistant to the ailing housekeeper. When the housekeeper became too ill to continue Flora took over her duties and was still fulfilling that task.

Despite his earlier assurances to Flora about the welcome she would be given by Talwyn, Tom was apprehensive about their first meeting. He need not have worried, the two women took an instant liking to each other and when they discovered that Flora had read a number of the books that stood on Talwyn's bookshelf they chatted happily about the merits and demerits of the various authors.

When Flora left the room with Talwyn to look at some chicks that had been hatched by a hen kept in a coop in the back garden Amos commented to Tom, 'To listen to the two of them talking you would think they had known each other for years!'

'It's a great relief,' Tom admitted, 'I was concerned they might not get along — and I feel Flora needs someone she can talk to as a friend. She is in a very difficult position at Laneglos. As an employee, she could never confide in the family, yet, as housekeeper, she can't become too friendly with any of the servants. In addition, she is exceptionally young to be a housekeeper and I sense there's a certain amount of resentment of her among senior servants such as the butler and the cook.'

In a similar situation, being considered by some to be too young to be holding the rank of the most senior superintendent in the Cornwall constabulary, Amos gave his companion a wry smile, 'I do know the feeling, Tom.'

'Yes, of course, you must . . . but you have Talwyn to talk things over with. Flora has no one.'

Conceding the truth of Tom's observation, Amos said, 'That's quite true, Tom, but are you hoping to rectify that situation for her?'

'I would very much like to,' Tom replied, 'but I couldn't ask her to give up the life she has at Laneglos in order to become the wife of a police sergeant.'

'You can't be certain of how she would feel about that until you know her well enough to ask her,' Amos said, 'and, of course, whether it's what you really want. Besides, you are not going to remain a sergeant for very long, especially if we can find the murderer of Enid Merryn and get to the bottom of who is responsible for the burglary at Laneglos.'

* * *

In the garden, Talwyn and Flora were having a conversation on the same subject . . . and with equally inconclusive results.

As Flora stood by the small chicken run with a nervously cheeping three-day old chick cupped in her hand and expressing delight with the appealing little creature, Talwyn said, 'You'll obviously not be allowed to have pets in the big house?'

'No . . . although the family keep two dogs and a bitch and she regularly has pups, so there is quite often something small to cuddle . . . ' Holding the chick up close to her face, she added, ' . . . but they are far more troublesome than this little fellow . . . or is it a girl?'

'It is still too early to tell,' Talwyn replied, before adding, casually, 'Do you ever wish you had a place of your own, where you could have a few pets . . . and a garden?'

Giving Talwyn an open smile that dispelled her fear that she might have offended her guest, Flora replied, 'If you are asking whether I am ever likely to get married . . . it's a question I sometimes ask myself.'

'I used to do the same,' Talwyn admitted, 'I would spend my days teaching other people's children and getting involved with their problems and wondering whether I would ever have a family life of my own . . . but then I met Amos.'

'Tom has told me that Amos came to Cornwall and caught the murderers of your father but did you know right away that he was the man for you?'

Talwyn gave an amused laugh. 'On the contrary, when we first met each other the horse he was riding was startled by a dog and knocked me on my backside on a muddy grass verge, ruining my favourite cloak and scattering my shopping over the ground. I was not amused — and told him so in no uncertain manner! What's more, it took me a long time to forgive him.'

'But you did eventually,' Flora said, adding thoughtfully, 'What's more, you are still working at something you enjoy doing.'

'I am — but there had to be a compromise. Fortunately, the chief constable is a very understanding man who has great faith in Amos and is not afraid to justify his decisions with considerable firmness should the police committee call them into question. He did that when Amos took on Tom, even though he was suffering from a broken wrist at the time. Fortunately, his decisions concerning both Amos and Tom have proved right and Amos says Tom has a great future in the Cornwall constabulary — if he decides to stay with us.'

'Tom's not thinking of leaving?' Flora's dismay was genuine — and Talwyn was delighted.

'Amos wants him to stay and I think he has told Tom that if he does he will receive rapid promotion, but he knows that Tom enjoys the work he does and although he has had plenty of excitement during the time he has been here there is far more actual police work to be done in London.'

Looking directly at Flora, she said, 'I suppose it really depends on how much incentive there is for him to stay in Cornwall.'

It was such a pointed remark that Flora felt

herself colour up and she replied, simply, 'I hope he decides to stay here.'

It was enough to satisfy Talwyn. She felt she could now safely report to Amos that the Laneglos housekeeper would do everything in her power to keep Tom happy in Cornwall.

28

'Have you enjoyed your day? You and Talwyn seemed to get on well together.'

'I like Talwyn very much and, yes, I have had a lovely day, Tom. Thank you.'

They were driving back to Laneglos in the pony and trap and Tom beamed at her, 'I'm glad because I can't remember when *I've* had a happier day.'

It was quite true. Amos and Talwyn had gone out of their way to make Flora feel welcome and Amos had made it quite clear that despite the disparity of their respective ranks within the Cornwall constabulary, behind the doors of the Hawke household they were two very good friends.

'I wish I could show my appreciation by inviting you, Talwyn and Amos to dinner with me, Tom, but it is just not possible,' Flora spoke with a real regret.

'We all realize that and, as Talwyn said to you when you left, you must come to the house again soon. She really did enjoy your company, Flora. I think she left all her close friends behind in the Charlestown area where she was living when she had the school there and first met Amos.'

'Yes, she was telling me about her first meeting with him . . . ' Remembering the conversation that had taken place in the Hawke's garden, she added, 'She thinks you have an assured future with the Cornwall constabulary. It seems Amos has told her that you will be given rapid promotion.'

'It would be very satisfying to think so.' Tom was pleased at such a prospect and was grateful to Talwyn for pointing it out to Flora.

'When you are promoted will it mean that you will be moved away from this area?' Flora broke into his thoughts.

'It's always possible, but now the force is almost up to strength Amos is talking of having a proper headquarters staff, with an inspector in charge. He has promised to recommend me for the post. I would also act as his second-in-command — which would basically mean doing very much what I am doing now, but with more responsibility and, of course, more money.'

'Will you still live with Talwyn and Amos when you are promoted?'

'No. It was originally intended there would be accommodation over the station for an inspector, but the building isn't spacious enough to house a police station, offices *and* quarters for an inspector. I, or whoever becomes the inspector, might need to find somewhere else to live, not too far away — although there is a suggestion of an annexe being built on to the headquarters.'

Giving Flora a quick glance, Tom hoped to see something to indicate there was more to her questioning than mere curiosity, but her expression gave nothing away.

After a few minutes of silence between them, he asked, 'Would you come out with me again, Flora?'

'You mean, to the Hawke's home? Talwyn made me promise I would visit them again, soon.'

'I'm glad . . . but I wondered whether we could perhaps meet up and go for a walk somewhere . . . along the river bank, perhaps, or better still take a train ride! Yes, that would be fun, we could go to Plymouth over the new bridge and have a look around the city together.'

It had not been easy for Flora to arrange to take a whole day off from her duties at Laneglos. Despite her status as the most senior servant in the household, she *was* still a servant and as such was expected to be absent from the house for no more than a half-day each week. Nevertheless, she was delighted that Tom wanted to see her again and was equally eager for their blossoming relationship to move forward.

'I may not be able to take another whole day off so soon, Tom, especially as Lady Hogg is unwell and still at the big house, so we may have to put off thinking about a train ride to Plymouth for a while . . . but we could certainly take a walk. On my afternoons off I sometimes used to go down to the River Fowey and walk along the bank. It is beautifully quiet there and you can occasionally see a kingfisher. They are beautiful little birds, have you ever seen one?'

Tom's knowledge of river life had been gained from the commercially busy Thames, running through the heart of London and he confessed that the only water birds that had come to his attention were the noisy scavenging gulls that abounded on and around the London river's heavily polluted waters.

Flora gave him a description of the brightly plumaged kingfisher, but she repeated on her earlier precautionary note, 'You would enjoy a walk along the river bank, Tom but, as I said earlier, my being able to take an afternoon off at all will depend on how well Lady Hogg is. If she becomes any worse I probably won't even be able to leave the house.'

'What exactly is wrong with her?'

'That's the most puzzling problem of all,' Flora replied. 'Doctor Hollis says it's something she's eaten that is upsetting her and he has prescribed various medicines but nothing seems to be helping. He said much the same about Lord Hogg yet none of the medicines that were prescribed helped him either. To be perfectly honest, I think he has been practising medicine for too long. The medical profession has improved rapidly since the Crimean War but Doctor Hollis has not kept up with the various advances and is still treating his patients using methods he learned fifty years ago.'

'That's a pretty alarming state of affairs for his patients,' Tom said, 'Especially as there's a new and very keen young doctor in Bodmin right now. Doctor Sullivan was trained in London and is the surgeon who carried out the post mortem on Enid. He is up-to-date with all that's new in his profession. We get on quite well because he was once a surgeon at the hospital where my fractured wrist was treated and I am due to see him this week when he has promised to take the plaster cast off my arm and check that it has healed. I'll speak to him about Lady Hogg. If he feels he might be able to help, you can ask Lady Hogg or her son, if they will allow him to examine her. What are her symptoms?'

'They are very similar to those Lord Hogg showed shortly before he died. He complained of severe pain in his stomach and it was tender to the touch. He had a sore throat and towards the end he could hardly speak. He was very sick and once when I was in his room he had convulsions too. When I helped to hold him down I noticed his skin was a peculiar mottled colour, he was sweating heavily and didn't seem to know what was going on around him.'

'And you say Lady Hogg is showing the very same symptoms?'

'Yes. Doctor Hollis thinks that something might have found its way into the water supply to the house and is upsetting their stomachs, but if that was the case we should all be suffering, shouldn't we?'

'I would have thought so,' Tom agreed. 'I'll have a word with Doctor Sullivan first thing in the morning and see what he thinks.'

For the remainder of the journey to Laneglos they spoke of more pleasant matters and, when they parted company, Tom kissed Flora for the first time and not only did she raise no objection, but responded in a manner that left him in no doubt that their relationship had moved on to an exciting new level.

* * *

Despite Tom's happy state of mind as he drove back to the Hawke home, it did not prevent him from thinking of what Flora had told him about Lady Hogg's illness and the similarity of its symptoms to those of Lord Hogg before his death.

When he reached the house Talwyn enthused about the Laneglos housekeeper and it was a while before she left the room to go to the kitchen and Tom had a few minutes alone with Amos to inform him of his conversation with Flora.

'What are you suggesting, Tom?' Amos asked, adding bluntly, 'Do you think someone is trying to poison Lady Hogg — and possibly killed Lord Hogg too?'

Reluctant to commit himself, even though Amos had put his own suspicions into words, Tom replied, 'I am no expert, Amos, but in my early days as a constable in a richer part of London than Hoxton, I went with an inspector to a house where there was a woman with the same symptoms as Lady Hogg is showing. The inspector had been called in by the woman's doctor, who suspected she was being poisoned with arsenic by her husband. He was right, even though we were too late to save the life of the wife. I found a chemist who had sold arsenic to the husband 'to kill rats in the cellar'. There were no rats and it turned out that the husband was having an affair with their maid-of-all-work. He eventually confessed to what he had done and was hanged.'

'So you do think someone is poisoning Lady Hogg and probably did the same to her late husband?'

Amos put the question to Tom, fully aware of the consequences to himself — and the Cornwall constabulary — if Tom's suspicions were investigated and proved to be unfounded.

Aware of Amos's dilemma, Tom said, 'We know there is someone at Laneglos who is prepared to kill — and if he's done it once and got away with it I doubt if he would hesitate to do it again . . . especially if he stood to gain enough by his actions.'

'Or . . . in the case of Enid Merryn, *lose* a great deal by *not* killing.' Amos mused.

Both men looked at each other without saying anything for long moments until Amos broke the silence by saying, 'Are we both thinking of the same suspect, Tom? Someone who fits the bill for all that has happened at the house? Who has motive and opportunity — and is probably desperate enough to commit murder?'

Tom nodded, 'I believe we are, Amos. The doctor who dealt with the case in London that I mentioned referred to arsenic as 'inheritance powder' — but we would be walking a tightrope trying to prove it. One false move and we would both be out of a job and as Chief Constable Gilbert will be aware, he would go down with us.'

Amos nodded his agreement, 'There's no doubt about it . . . I think the Honourable Charles Delville might be our man but the most important thing is to see that Lady Hogg gets no worse. It's too late in the day to do anything now. We will go and speak to Doctor Sullivan first thing in the morning.'

29

In the darkened main bedroom of the Hawke home that night, Amos and Talwyn were discussing Tom's theory and he told her who both he and Tom suspected of being responsible for two deaths, attempting the murder of a third, and who they believed of planning a robbery and the appearance in Cornwall of a small multi-talented criminal army.

'It beggars belief,' Talwyn said, incredulously, 'Such a theory can't possibly be right, surely?'

'I can't be *absolutely* certain, not until we gather some real evidence against him but we do have a strong circumstantial case. We know he is desperately short of money and deeply in debt and whoever drew up plans for the London villains to descend upon Cornwall with the Laneglos ball as their main target had an intimate knowledge of Cornish society. He could have obtained a ticket for the ball in order for Conrad Shannon to make excellent forgeries, knowing that if he used genuine tickets for the number of men involved it would not only cost a great deal of money, but purchasing such a quantity would immediately call attention to him. He probably also provided Jimmy Banks with a forged letter of recommendation enabling him to gain employment to Laneglos. When I questioned Flora about accepting it without making inquiries about its authenticity she said that Delville was present, with his mother, and it was he who persuaded them that the reference should be accepted. The Hoxton men who came with the Banks's also knew which mansions to burgle while the owners were at the ball — and when Laneglos was burgled only items of the greatest value were taken — and they knew exactly where to find them. Jimmy Banks knew where each particular room was, of course, but he lacked the knowledge to identify which items were of most value.'

Talwyn thought over what her husband had said before saying, 'You have made a *circumstantial* case against Delville, but even if he *did* have something to do with the robberies, why should he want to murder poor Edith?'

'There are a couple of possible reasons. We know Alfie and Jimmy Banks had been skulking around the Laneglos gardens, Enid could have seen them talking with Delville — and he couldn't afford to have her pass that on to anyone. There is another possible motive too. Enid was four months pregnant when she was killed and it's likely Delville was responsible. She might have threatened to make known what he had done and the robbery gave him an opportunity to put her out of the way. He would know that suspicion was bound to fall on the burglars — and he probably believed they would never be caught.'

'But why should he murder Enid even if he *had* made her pregnant? From all I have heard, he has fathered children born to more than one

Laneglos servant girl and none of them have ended up dead.'

'That's because Lord Hogg always took care of them — but it seems he had declared he was not going to pay for any more. Not only that, Delville was aware that if he didn't change his ways he was likely to be banned from Laneglos and receive no more money to finance his irresponsible way of life. He couldn't allow that to happen, especially after the elaborate plans he had made with Alfie Banks and his accomplices were foiled. He is deeply in debt and desperate for money. If Enid had said she was going to report her pregnancy to someone, or had seen him talking to the Banks's then you have a couple of motives for murdering her.'

Still not entirely convinced, Talwyn asked, 'But why kill Lord Hogg and — if what you believe to be true — now be trying to kill his own mother?'

Talwyn had great faith in Amos's ability as a policeman but she was finding it hard to accept his theories about the Honourable Charles Delville.

Building on his theory, Amos said patiently, 'Lord Hogg was a sick man and probably didn't have too long to live anyway. Delville might even have convinced himself he was being kind to the old man . . . but Delville's reasoning doesn't matter. What is more certain is that he expected to gain financially by Lord Hogg's death. If not directly he would have expected money to be left to his mother and she would have got him out of the deep financial trouble he is in. Instead,

Delville was cut out of Lord Hogg's will entirely and the money left to Lady Hogg was very cleverly tied up to *prevent* her from squandering it on her son. The only way Delville can get at her money and property now is if she dies!'

'But . . . killing his own mother! It's unbelievable.'

'Perhaps, but it is certainly not unheard of and as a result of Alfie Banks and his friends having had a wasted journey to Cornwall, the Honourable Charles has made some very dangerous enemies, he will be desperate to get money in order to pay them off.'

There was silence in the bedroom for a very long time before Talwyn asked, 'Even if all this is true, Amos, could you prove it in court?'

'Not at the moment. If young Jimmy Banks had lived we might have been able to prove Delville's involvement in the burglary — and that could have given us some helpful information about Enid's murder. But Jimmy is dead and Alfie Banks has probably fled the country, so I will need to look elsewhere for answers — and I think I'll begin by following Tom's suggestion and have Doctor Sullivan take a look at Lady Hogg.'

* * *

Having Andrew Sullivan examine Lady Hogg proved simpler than Amos had anticipated. He called at the surgeon's home on his way to the Bodmin police headquarters and, although it was early in the day, he found him putting medicines and instruments into a leather bag.

When Amos told Doctor Sullivan of his reason for calling at such an early hour, the surgeon said, 'You are not the only one to be concerned about Lady Hogg's condition, Superintendent. I had supper with Doctor Hollis yesterday evening and we were discussing her case. When he described the symptoms I asked him whether he had considered the possibility of arsenic poisoning. He dismissed the idea out of hand immediately but later in the evening he came back to it, recalling a case where a number of miners were poisoned as a result of arsenic finding its way into the drinking water on a moorland tin mine. He agreed the symptoms were similar. As I have up-to-date knowledge of both diagnosis and treatment for such a condition, he has asked me to accompany him today on a visit to Laneglos. I am packing my bag right now with medication that will be useful if it *is* arsenic poisoning . . . but that brings me to an obvious question, Superintendent. What is the police interest in the case and, if it turns out to be arsenic poisoning, do you have a particular suspect in mind?'

'No one I am in a position to name as such,' Amos replied, circumspectly, 'but you might be able to help if you can learn how it is being administered — if in fact it is arsenic poisoning.'

'It all sounds quite intriguing.' Closing his bag and preparing to leave the house, Doctor Sullivan said, 'I have to carry out a post mortem in Lostwithiel after seeing Lady Hogg, but will you be in your office all day?'

'As far as I know.'

'Then I will call in and see you sometime later today and give you my diagnosis.'

30

When Amos arrived at the Bodmin police headquarters he found his late arrival had caused some consternation. A relieved station sergeant explained, 'A woman arrived on the overnight train from London and came here asking after her son. She'd been told he had been arrested here, in Cornwall, and had come here to see him. She got quite angry when I wouldn't tell her anything, but I managed to quieten her down and put her in the interview room until you were able to speak to her.'

Slightly annoyed, Amos said, 'We have no one in the police cells at the moment, you should have sent her to Bodmin jail, they probably have him there.'

'I was going to, sir . . . until she mentioned the name of her son. I thought you'd want to speak to her before anyone else did. She's the mother of Jimmy Banks.'

The news took Amos by surprise, but he said, 'You did the right thing, sergeant. I'll go and speak to her now. In the meantime, find Sergeant Churchyard, or Sergeant Halloran — better still, both of them. Send them to the interview room right away . . . and have some tea sent there, I think we are all going to need it.'

Entering the interview room Amos saw a tired, lank-haired woman wearing cheap clothing. He guessed she was probably in her mid-thirties, although she had the weary expression of a woman whose hard life had aged her beyond her years. He had seen many such women in the East End of London during his police service there.

When she raised her glance to him, he said, 'Hello, Mrs Banks, I am sorry you've been kept waiting. I am Superintendent Hawke. I understand you have travelled overnight from London? It's a long journey and I've asked for some tea to be brought for you . . . but have you eaten since leaving London?'

Looking at him scornfully, the woman said, 'Don't try the old 'I'm your friend, you 'elp me and I'll 'elp you' malarky with me, I've 'ad dealings with far too many coppers to be sucked in by that. All I'm 'ere for is to find out where my Jimmy is and what it is 'e's supposed to have done.'

'What makes you think he's done anything, Mrs Banks . . . and who told you he was here?'

'Like I told you, I'm not answering any of your questions . . . '

At that moment the door opened and the powerful figure of Harvey Halloran filled the doorway. Seeing the woman he said, 'Hello, Mary.' Then, a pained expression taking over his face, he added, 'I'm sorry to see you here.'

'Harvey Halloran!' She pronounced it 'arvey 'alloran . . . 'What the 'ell you doing so far away from 'oxton . . . and wearing a rozzer's uniform?'

'I came here because Mr Hawke is here, Mary. He was my captain when I was in the Royal Marines.'

Mary glanced at Amos once more but there was no scorn in her look this time and he seized the opportunity to speak to her again. Grave faced, he said, 'I especially asked Harvey to join us, Mrs Banks, because I have bad news for you . . . *very* bad news, I'm afraid.'

As he spoke Mary Banks's expression changed to one of consternation, 'Is it about Jimmy? What's he done . . . and where is he?'

Amos looked at Harvey and it was the big sergeant who replied bluntly to her question. 'I'm afraid Jimmy is dead, Mary.'

A strangled scream escaped from Mary and, looking from Harvey, she said, 'No . . . It can't be true, you're trying to trick me for some reason. Alfie said Jimmy had been arrested, that's all . . . '

Amos's interest quickened immediately. Her words meant that Mary must have seen Alfie since the robbery. He was about to ask her where and when she had spoken to the wanted man, but he checked himself in time. Instead, he said, 'Alfie was lying to you, Mary . . . and for a very good reason. He and Jimmy burgled a large manor house near here and got away with the proceeds in a wagonette they stole from the stables. When they were some distance from the house they had an accident and it seems Jimmy was hurt . . . he broke a collarbone. Instead of staying with Jimmy and looking after him, Alfie took the pony and rode off, leaving Jimmy hurt and alone in a wood. He was there all that day and into the night and we believe he got hopelessly lost in the rain and fell into a river that flowed down off the moor. He was battered against rocks and was found the following day by some children. A doctor was eventually called but there was nothing he could do for him.'

While he was talking Tom Churchyard had entered the interview room quietly and stood just inside the doorway. Now, speaking for the first time, he said, 'That's right, Mary. Superintendent Hawke and me were with Jimmy when he died.'

Fighting back her tears, Mary Banks looked from Tom to Harvey and in a strained voice said, 'You wouldn't lie to me . . . not you, Harvey? This isn't a cruel trick to get me to tell you something you want to know?'

Harvey shook his head, sorrowfully, 'No one is lying to you, Mary, I wish I could say we were. We *know* Jimmy was involved with Alfie in the burglary, but he didn't deserve to die for it. Certainly not in the way he did, alone and hurt and lost in surroundings that would have been terrifying for a Hoxton boy. Alfie shouldn't have done that . . . not to a young lad who was a blood relative.'

Fighting hard to keep control of herself, Mary said, 'Did he . . . did Jimmy say anything before he died?'

This time it was Amos who replied, 'It was as much as he could do to say anything, but just before he died he managed to whisper to me that I was to tell Enid he was sorry. Enid was a scullery-maid in the house where Jimmy worked for a while . . . the house that he and Alfie burgled.'

Almost in control of herself now, Mary said, 'Jimmy told me about Enid. I think 'e liked 'er a lot. I'd like to meet 'er while I'm 'ere. I'd like to see Jimmy too.'

The three policemen exchanged glances and once again it was Amos who spoke, 'Enid is dead too, Mary. She was murdered on the night of the robbery . . . we believe by Alfie.'

The expression of mistrust returned to Mary's face once more and she said, 'Why would Alfie want to kill a young scullery-maid? Jimmy said she was a bit simple, but was one of the kindest people you could wish to meet.'

'That's a question we were hoping Jimmy would be able to help us with,' Amos said, 'It could have been because she'd seen something she wasn't supposed to see — and we know someone from inside the big house helped Jimmy and Alfie with the burglary. In fact, whoever it is probably planned the whole thing. If Enid found out about it they might have felt it necessary to silence her.'

Mary shook her head vigorously, 'Jimmy wouldn't have 'ad anything to do with that, 'e might 'ave got in trouble with the law once or twice, but 'e wouldn't 'ave 'armed no girl — 'e wouldn't 'arm anyone, Jimmy wasn't like that.'

'That's what I told Superintendent Hawke,' Harvey agreed, 'but the same couldn't be said for Alfie. He's a bad one, Mary, for all that he's your brother-in-law.'

'Don't I know it? I told Jimmy so more than once, but 'e wouldn't listen to me. Alfie was an uncle, 'is dad's brother, and Jimmy looked up to him . . . but can I see Jimmy now?'

Once again it was left to Amos to reply to her, 'I'm sorry, Mary, Jimmy has already been buried. He was given a proper funeral a couple of days ago and is in the Bodmin graveyard. I'll let Harvey take you there when you've finished your tea and had something to eat. You've had a long journey and it's ended very unhappily for you.'

* * *

Walking towards the church with Harvey, Mary Banks asked, 'Was that superintendent telling the truth about what happened to my Jimmy, or was 'e just trying to get me to say something against Alfie?'

'He told you as much as we know about what happened, Mary. Amos Hawke is a straightforward bloke. I've known him for many years. He was my captain when we served in the Marines together in the Crimean war and he got me this job in the police here. We both feel sorry for Jimmy. He did wrong and he'd have been punished for it had he lived, but he didn't deserve to be left to die, the way he was.'

After a thoughtful silence, Mary said, 'Tell me *exactly* what 'appened, there's a few things I need to get sorted out in me 'ead.'

Harvey told Mary Banks everything, from the forged reference which had gained Jimmy employment at Laneglos; the abortive plan to cause mayhem at the Cornwall summer ball and the subsequent arrest of all the Hoxton gang with the exception of Jimmy and Alfie. He concluded by telling her of the burglary at Laneglos, the finding of the wrecked wagonette and the hidden stolen property and the finding of Jimmy by the local children.

'What makes you think Jimmy was badly 'urt when Alfie rode off and left 'im? Couldn't 'is injuries 'ave been caused by falling in the river?'

'According to the doctor who carried out the . . . who examined him after he'd died, he'd had the broken collarbone long before he got the other injuries. It would have caused him a lot of pain and probably made him delirious. It might even have been the reason why he fell into the river, especially as it must have happened sometime in the night.'

Mary Banks tried hard to control her emotions as she conjured up a picture of her son wandering alone in the woods in the darkness, suffering from a broken collarbone, but her face contorted as a tear escaped from her tightly closed eyelids. It was followed by another and a third.

Seeing them, Harvey said, 'I'm sorry, Mary . . . but you wanted to know the truth about what happened.'

Mary nodded vigorously and speaking between clenched teeth, she said, 'I'm glad you told me, 'arvey, it means I've been right to detest Alfie so much for so long. It was 'im who was the cause of my old man — Jimmy's dad — being transported all those years ago — and now 'e's taken Jimmy from me and probably robbed another mother of 'er daughter. 'e should have been given the drop years ago.'

'Alfie might meet the hangman yet, especially now we know he's in London again. We thought he must have left the country.'

'He probably 'as by now,' Mary spoke unaware of the effect her words would have on Harvey. 'Alfie was saying 'goodbye' to 'is ma yesterday, just before I left London. Then 'e went off to catch a ship to Australia.'

'What was the name of the ship, Mary, do you know?'

'Alfie did say but all I can remember is that it's *James* . . . something or another. It's a Scottish name.'

'Where is it sailing from . . . and when?'

Mary shrugged, 'It'll be from one of the London docks, but I don't know when it was due to leave.'

They had arrived at the Bodmin graveyard now. Hurriedly showing Mary the mound of newly dug earth beneath which lay the body of her son, Harvey said he would leave her alone for a few minutes before returning for her.

Leaving the graveyard, he ran all the way to the police headquarters to tell Amos what Mary had revealed.

31

An urgent telegraph from Amos to Scotland Yard received a prompt reply with the news that a sailing ship named *James Macintyre* had sailed from London on the night tide carrying emigrants bound for Adelaide in South Australia.

It would appear that Mary Banks's information had come too late to enable Amos to arrest the man he believed held the key to the two most serious crimes to have taken place in Cornwall since the formation of the county's constabulary — and Amos was furious!

Pacing the floor of his office he was castigating the Metropolitan Police to an equally frustrated Tom Churchyard.

'I sent details of Alfie Banks to Scotland Yard and stressed that he was wanted urgently here in Cornwall for questioning about murder and burglary. Why did no one pick him up when he returned to Hoxton? Surely the Division would have got news of his return? You would have known had you still been in London, especially after all the information we have given them about what has been going on here.'

'They *should* have known,' Tom agreed, 'but we know who is in charge of 'K' Division and Dyson wouldn't have put himself out to help us.'

Ceasing his pacing, Amos said, 'You are right, of course, Tom. We should both have been aware of that when I sent the original details to London, but it's frustrating, to say the very least. Send another telegraph right away requesting details of the ship's planned movements, the ports it will be calling at and the approximate date of its arrival in Adelaide. We'll try to have Alfie picked up there and returned to us. The problem is going to be that the voyage will take so long that the Australian police will have forgotten all about it by the time it arrives. Even if they do remember he'll probably be using a different name and nobody there will be able to identify him. I am furious about the whole business but I suppose we must accept what has happened and try to solve both the murder and the robbery without his help. I will need to tell the Chief Constable what is happening.'

An hour later Amos was in Chief Constable Gilbert's office telling him all that had happened that morning when there came a heavy hammering on the door. Before the Chief Constable had time to respond, the door was flung open and an excited Tom Churchyard appeared in the doorway.

Addressing Amos, he said, 'I sent a telegraph message to London, sir, asking if they had any information about the *James Macintyre's* ports of call on the way to Australia. They have come straight back to say the ship is due to put into Falmouth — today! It's expected to sail again at dawn tomorrow. If we hurry we might be able to get down there and arrest him . . . '

* * *

Following Tom's dramatic news, there was great activity at the Bodmin police headquarters. The information about the emigrant ship had come from the London river police, who were an extremely efficient organisation that had been operating for far longer than the Metropolitan Police itself.

Amos's message requesting details of the ship's movements had been passed to them and, although the vessel had already left their jurisdiction they immediately contacted the ship's owners, who informed them that the *James Macintyre* was scheduled to call at Falmouth to embark Cornish miners who were emigrating to Australia seeking a more secure future than was to be found in Cornish mining. While in the port the ship would also take on board foodstuffs which were cheaper here than in the metropolis.

Amos swiftly learned that if they hurried, it would be possible to reach the railway station at Bodmin Road in time to catch a train that would carry them westwards as far as Truro. While they were on their way instructions would be telegraphed from the Bodmin police station to have a carriage and four Truro based policemen waiting to accompany them on to Falmouth and hopefully succeed in the arrest of Alfie Banks.

Amos took Tom and Harvey with him in order to make a positive identification of the wanted Hoxton criminal as it was almost certain he would have assumed a new identity.

The three policemen reached the Bodmin Road railway station only minutes before the train and were grateful to climb on board and relax on the hour-long journey to Truro.

* * *

An inspector was waiting in the Truro station yard for them, excited at the prospect of assisting in the capture of the man who was currently the most wanted criminal in the short history of the Cornwall constabulary.

As the hired carriage bowled along the twisting, undulating and wood-fringed road that led to the busy port of Falmouth, Amos was pleased to discover that the inspector was a keen young policeman who had only recently transferred on promotion, from the longer established Bristol City constabulary. He was eager to prove his worth to the most senior superintendent in his new force.

The inspector had sent a constable ahead of them to locate the Australian bound vessel and seek the aid of the Falmouth revenue men. Awaiting them on the outskirts of the town this constable was able to inform Amos that the *James Macintyre* was anchored in the Carrick Roads, a large, deepwater natural harbour that had brought past prosperity to the South coast Cornish town.

'There have been a great many boats going out to the ship carrying stores,' the constable reported, 'and I have seen about fifty or so emigrating miners going out to it too, but I was talking to one of the ship's officers who was checking stores on the jetty. Claiming I had a friend on board, I asked if he might be allowed to come ashore and see me before the ship left. The officer told me the captain would not allow either passengers or crew to leave the ship before it sailed, so if Banks is on board he'll be kept there and we'll find him.'

It was what Amos wanted to hear, but he was aware that Alfie Banks was a very resourceful man — and he was not *yet* a prisoner.

Taking stock of all that was going on around the ship, he said, 'Have the boats taking stores out to the *James Macintyre* detained and kept here as they return, I don't want any more of them going out to the ship until our search is over.'

It was another thirty minutes before the last of the port's boats pulled away from the side of the emigrant ship and Amos and his men set off to board the vessel. They were accompanied by a party of revenue men. Familiar with ship searches they would be aware of likely hiding places that the policemen might miss.

When Amos climbed the ladder to the deck of the *James Macintyre* he was confronted by the vessel's furious captain who demanded to know what was happening.

'Who are you . . . and why has the victualling of my ship been halted?' The furious mariner demanded. 'Do you realize I am setting off on a three-month voyage and every ounce of food that has been ordered is vital to the well-being of my passengers and crew?'

'You'll get your victuals, Captain, and I and my men will delay you no longer than is absolutely necessary, but I have received information that one of your passengers is a wanted man. As soon as he is found and arrested the boats will be allowed to come out to you again.'

Unappeased, the angry sailor said, 'I am in charge of this ship, sir, and the passengers are *my* responsibility. Who is it you are seeking — and what is he supposed to have done that is serious enough to cause such unforgivable inconvenience to me, my ship and a couple of hundred passengers?'

'His name is Alfie Banks — although he is unlikely to have booked a passage under that name. He is known to have carried out an audacious burglary against one of the most important homes in Cornwall, during the course of which a man died. He is also wanted for questioning about the murder of a young girl who was a servant at the house.'

Only slightly less belligerently, the captain asked, 'How long is this search of yours likely to take?'

'With your co-operation not too long, I hope, although I doubt he will make his arrest easy for us.'

'I am not happy about the disruption you are causing on my ship, sir, and will be submitting a complaint through the ship's owners, but if it is likely to speed things up you may look through my passenger list and I will make men available to conduct you around the ship . . . but I trust you will waste as little of my time as is possible. All the signs are of bad weather coming in from the east. I want to stay ahead of it if at all possible.'

'We'll take up no more of your time than is necessary, Captain, but Banks is a desperate man and well aware of the fate that awaits him if he's taken. I don't intend allowing him an opportunity to evade capture yet again.'

'If you hadn't given him the opportunity in the first place you wouldn't be here disrupting my ship's routine today . . . but just get on with your job, so that I might get on with mine.'

With this the captain turned on his heel and stalked off to his cabin, leaving his first mate to assist Amos with the search of the emigrant ship.

The first search was carried out in the hold which had been fitted out to accommodate the majority of the emigrating men. Many had only just boarded the ship and the hold was in chaos.

It took a while to check the identity of every man in the hold but Harvey and Tom confirmed that Alfie Banks was not among their number.

Leaving two constables to ensure nobody either entered or left the hold until they had completed their search, Amos and the others moved on to the accommodation provided for emigrants travelling as families, or married couples, but here again they drew a blank.

A full hour later the captain was pacing the deck of his ship, muttering darkly about the incompetence of the Cornwall constabulary, his anger fuelled by a liberal helping of the fine cognac he kept in a locked cupboard in his cabin, the fumes of which assailed Amos when he reported on the lack of success of his search.

'We have searched everywhere except the hold for unaccompanied women — and they are refusing to allow us in there. It seems one who is on her way to join her husband is giving birth and they say it's no place for a man, whether he's a policeman or a criminal.'

'A woman giving birth on my ship?!' The captain's complexion took on an even deeper hue as he found another subject for his anger. 'The mate has orders not to allow any heavily pregnant women to take passage on the *James Macintyre*. If they give birth on the voyage the brat invariably dies. That not only brings bad luck, but it casts a pall of gloom on passengers and crew for the remainder of the voyage. I'd as soon cast mother and baby over the side *before* it's born. If there's a woman giving birth I want her off my ship . . . *now*! You come with me, mister . . . and bring some of your constables with you. You're paid to deal with trouble . . . my duty is to get this ship to Australia without it. You can take the woman and her brat ashore with you.'

A canvas-hooded hatchway sheltered a make-shift companionway leading down to the womens' quarters in the ship's forward hold and here a small crowd of women blocked the path of the captain, Amos and the policemen.

'Get out of the way!' The captain commanded, 'Your quarters need to be searched.'

'It's no place for any man down there,' said a woman in an accent that Amos immediately recognized as originating from the East End of

London. 'Someone's giving birth and it ain't a pretty sight.'

'Then she can take her *un*pretty sight somewhere else,' declared the captain, 'She's not having it on board *my* ship — and if you don't get out my way *you'll* go ashore with her.'

The women were in no doubt that the ship's captain meant what he said and, albeit reluctantly, complied with his order.

It was gloomy in the hold, but light from the sheltered hatchway was sufficient for Amos to see the rows of tiered beds filling the space, allowing only a narrow walkway between them.

There were many women down here and a number were gathered around a bunk that occupied a dark corner.

'Get some light over here!'

The captain's order was immediately obeyed by one of the two seamen who had followed the party down the companionway. He reached down a lamp that hung from an iron hook in a crossbeam. Fumbling clumsily, he eventually succeeded in lighting it and the impatient captain called, 'Bring it over here, I want to see what's going on.' Pushing his way between the crowding women, he advanced upon a bunk where a figure lay hidden beneath a blanket.

'She's had a bad time,' called a voice from the group of women, 'We've left her there to get some rest.'

Wasting no time with a reply the irate captain seized the blanket and, pulling it off sharply paused for a second before exclaiming, 'Oh! So it's the bearded lady from some circus who's giving birth, is it . . . ?'

Before he could say any more, the fully clothed 'lady' in question leaped free of the bunk on the side farthest from the captain and sprinted in the direction of the companionway, only to have his path blocked by one of the constables.

Veering to his left, the 'bearded lady' pounced upon a young girl of about nine or ten years of age. She screamed with alarm but the sound was cut off by her captor who, holding her about the neck, forced her head back — and suddenly there was a knife in his other hand and the point of it was pressing against the girl's throat.

'Stay back . . . all of you, or I'll slit her throat.'

The voice was certainly not that of a woman and Tom Churchyard said, 'Don't make things any worse for yourself than they are right now, Alfie.'

Without lessening his grip on the girl, her captor peered into the gloom beyond the light thrown from the lamp held aloft by the seaman. 'Who's that . . . do I know you?'

'You know me very well, Alfie . . . and I know you. It's Tom Churchyard of Hackney police station, on 'K' division. The last time we met you stamped on my arm and broke my wrist, remember?'

Tom was doing his best to distract the wanted man's attention, hoping someone would creep up behind him and secure him before he did any harm to the girl. Unfortunately, the only man who might have been able to do this was Harvey and he had remained on deck.

'I remember you . . . and since you know me you'll know I mean what I say. Come anywhere near — any of you — and I'll cut her throat from ear to ear . . . ' In order to emphasise his threat he forced the girl's chin higher and she began choking.

'Let the girl go, Alfie, you're not going anywhere so it's a choice between prison and the hangman.'

'I'd rather meet the hangman than spend the rest of my life banged-up,' came the reply, 'So that's no deal at all. If you want her to live you'll let me take her up on deck and we'll go ashore in a boat while all of you stay on board. Once we're ashore and I can see none of you following me I'll let her go, all safe and sound. If you don't do as I want . . . '

He pricked the point of the knife into the girl's throat and she let out a strangled cry as blood escaped from the small wound and trickled down the pale skin of her neck.

The girl's mother screamed and would have rushed at Alfie but Amos caught her and, despite her struggles held on to her until she went limp and began sobbing in his arms. Meanwhile, Alfie had inspected his handiwork and, looking up, said, 'She's a right little bleeder, ain't she . . . ? But there's plenty more where that came from, so if you don't want to see it you'd better do exactly what I tell you. Get everyone away from those steps up to the deck. I'll go up backwards very, very slowly and be holding the girl and watching you every inch of the way. You seem to be the man everyone takes notice of, Captain, so you shout out for everyone on deck to keep well clear of the hatch. Once I'm up there you'll all stay down here until someone from up top tells you we're in a boat and on our way to the shore.'

On Amos's prompting the captain did as he was instructed and Alfie began going up the companionway in the manner he had described while those in the hold could only look on helplessly.

When he reached the deck Alfie turned slowly, then glanced back into the hold to make certain no one had tried to follow him up the companionway. Still sheltered by the canvas arch which was placed over the hatchway to deflect any water coming over the bow when the ship dipped into a wave, Alfie could see a number of policemen in front of him, standing well back in order not to alarm him, but the Hoxton man was aware others could be using the canvas hood to hide from his view so he took a quick glance around it in order to check no one was here.

It was fortunate for the girl he was holding that Alfie chose to look first on the side farthest away from where Harvey was hiding. As he was in the act of turning to ensure the other side was clear, the wrist of the hand holding the knife was suddenly seized and held tight in a vice-like grip. He tried to fight against it but another powerful arm came around to take him into an identical grip to the one he had on the young girl.

At the same time a deep voice that he immediately recognized said, 'Hello, Alfie, it's been a long time but I'm sure you'll remember me, Harvey Halloran . . . ?'

32

Amos went to great lengths to ensure that Alfie Banks did not escape from custody on the journey from Falmouth to the headquarters police station at Bodmin. He was taken ashore from the *James Macintyre* handcuffed and wearing heavy leg irons, the latter provided by the ship's captain from the stock kept on board for use in the event of a mutiny.

Alfie refused to say anything on the short boat trip from the ship and once on shore he was transferred to a closed police van with four constables riding on the outside of the van as guards. He was then subjected to a bone shaking forty-mile drive to the Bodmin police station where he would be held for questioning.

It was after dark when the party arrived and Alfie shuffled awkwardly from the van to be locked in a cell. Unused to remaining silent for such a long period of time, it was here he spoke for the first time since his arrest, directing a question at Tom.

'I thought your days as a rozzer were over after you'd been taught a lesson in Hoxton but perhaps they aren't as fussy in these parts who they take on. All the same, there can't be too many one-handed rozzers here.'

'You're right, Alfie, I don't think there are any.' Stretching out the arm from which the plaster had only recently been removed, Tom wriggled his fingers, 'See . . . ? It's as good as new. You must be losing your touch, but we'll no doubt be throwing in a charge against you of causing grevious bodily harm, just for the record — not that it really matters, you'll hang anyway.'

Startled, despite his earlier assertion that he would rather hang than face the prospect of spending a lifetime in prison, Alfie said, 'What d'you mean, I'll hang? Even if I'm found guilty of . . . '

Realizing he had almost admitted to carrying out the burglary at Laneglos, which had not yet been mentioned, Alfie caught himself in time, ' . . . whatever it is you think I've done — which I ain't — it won't be anything I'll be given the drop for.'

Amos had been listening to the conversation and now he said, 'I'm afraid you're wrong there, Alfie. You didn't give me an opportunity back on the ship to tell you exactly *why* you were being arrested, but let me enlighten you now. As well as the burglary at Laneglos and conspiracy with your Hoxton pals to commit various other burglaries, you'll be charged with wounding the little girl on the *James Macintyre* and causing grevious bodily harm to Sergeant Churchyard. But all these crimes are just for the record, by far the most serious crime of all is the one you're going to be hung for . . . the murder of Enid Merryn.'

'Murder?'

Alfie's bewilderment was either genuine, or very cleverly feigned — and Amos was quite aware the London criminal was cunning enough to put on a thoroughly convincing act, especially with his life at stake.

'I don't know no Enid . . . whatever her name is!'

'Oh, you know her well enough, Alfie, you and young Jimmy met her only a couple of weeks before the robbery at Laneglos, remember? She met up with you in the grounds of the house . . . in fact you spoke to her and told her you and Jimmy had come back to explain how he was going to repay the money he'd borrowed from her. The trouble was, once she'd seen you she was sure to recognize you when next you met, especially if at the time you happened to be robbing the house where she worked! She was a simple little soul, wasn't she? Certainly not bright enough to be relied upon to keep it to herself that she'd witnessed you and Jimmy robbing her employers. A villain like you would need to kill her in order to save your own worthless skin. I doubt if a jury will even need to leave the courtroom in order to find you guilty, Alfie, and even the most tender-hearted judge will delight in donning the black cap and sending you to the gallows.'

As Amos's words struck home much of the bravado and aggression left Alfie, 'Now, that ain't right, Mr Hawke . . . none of it. All right, so I met up with this girl when I came down to Cornwall with young Jimmy, but it was like you said, he owed her money and I told him he was to see her right and pay it back to her. On my oath, I wouldn't have hurt a hair on her head, Mr Hawke. You don't do harm to those who help you and your family. She was one of us — looked down on by them as lives in houses like the one where she was working. No, I never so much as said a harsh word to her, you ask our Jimmy. No doubt you've nicked him as well?'

'No, Alfie, we don't have Jimmy in custody, by now he'll have been tried by a much higher court than any we have here on earth — but his last thoughts before he died were of Enid. He said he was sorry — no doubt you know exactly what he was sorry about.'

This time there could be no doubting Alfie's look of bewilderment, 'Jimmy's dead . . . ? What happened to him?'

'You tell us, Alfie, after all, you were the one who went off and left him alone in the woods, badly hurt.'

It was no more than a guess based on the pathologist's report, but it worked.

'I didn't know he was hurt that badly or I would never have gone and left him there by himself, but he was always a bit of a namby-pamby. If he so much as scratched himself he was convinced he was going to bleed to death. All the same, he was my brother's boy and I wouldn't have just gone off and left him to die on his own in a place like that.'

Suddenly aware of what he was admitting, he looked at Amos suspiciously, 'Is Jimmy *really* dead, or are you just saying he is to trick me into admitting I burgled that big house? If you are I shall deny I ever said anything about it.'

'I am not particularly concerned about the burglary right at this moment, Alfie, although I'll want to speak to you about that and the other charges at some time in the future. As for Jimmy, his mother came down to Cornwall overnight only last night, expecting to find her son in police custody . . . an idea I think she got from you. She was grief-stricken to learn he was dead and already buried. Harvey took her along to see Jimmy's grave and I think he's fixed up for her to stay at the Town Arms tonight, here in Bodmin. If she's still there in the morning we can arrange for her to come along and see you. It would probably be the last time you will ever see each other, but I'll leave you for now. You can spend the night thinking about it — and about poor Enid's murder, of course. I think that's quite enough to tax your brain for now.'

'I don't want to see Mary,' Alfie declared, 'We've never had much to say to one another in the past and no amount of talking now is going to bring Jimmy back to her.'

'That's true, Alfie, and I can quite see why you wouldn't want to meet with her face-to-face. I just thought that if you two were to meet again, now she's been told how her son died she might just be inclined to tell us a few things about you we'd be interested in knowing . . . and that she probably wouldn't have mentioned before today. It's something else to think about while you're lying in your cell tonight, trying to sleep.'

33

The morning after Alfie's capture, Amos arrived at the Bodmin police headquarters to find he was in great demand. Doctor Sullivan had called in the previous day wanting to speak to him on what he had said was 'A matter of considerable urgency.' He had left a message with the station sergeant to say he would call again this morning.

There was also a message from Conrad Shannon, the forger and fraudsman awaiting trial in Bodmin jail, expressing a wish to speak with Amos, this too was claimed to be 'urgent'.

Shannon was due to appear at the Assize court which was in session the following week and Amos guessed he was worried about the result of his trial. Amos might have put off speaking with him until he had more time to spare, but there was a possibility he might be able to throw some light on whoever was behind Alfie's elaborate plan to plunder the guests at the Laneglos ball and, in so doing, reveal who had assisted Alfie and Jimmy by opening the kitchen door for them.

It was doubtful whether Shannon even knew of the murder of Enid Merryn yet, but Amos felt that by insinuating that both murder and robbery were probably connected he might be able to frighten him enough to reveal all he knew of the whole ambitious affair, so he decided he would go to see him and, hopefully, be able to return to the headquarters before the chief constable put in an appearance at about nine o'clock.

Amos's belief that Shannon was concerned about his pending appearance before the Assize court judge proved correct. Incarceration in a Bodmin jail cell awaiting trial had done nothing for Shannon's former debonair appearance. His clothing was creased and the linen grubby, he had not shaved for several days and his hair was lank and greasy.

Remembering how he had appeared upon his arrival at Bodmin road railway station posing as Sir Richard Donahue, Amos felt almost sorry for him.

'I understand you wish to speak to me, Shannon?' Amos said, by way of greeting.

'That's right, sir, I want to have a word with you about the charges you've brought against me, and what's likely to happen if I'm found guilty.' Shannon's manner was almost humble.

'There is no 'if' about it, Shannon. You came to Cornwall using a forged railway ticket, had a forged invitation to the county ball in your pocket and a number of forged share certificates in your luggage. I might also have thrown in a charge of conspiracy to defraud and one or two other charges I could think of — such as forging a false reference for Jimmy Banks, for instance — but I don't think that is really necessary. With the charges you are already facing in court, coupled with your past record, you are facing a life sentence anyway. Any more charges would only make extra work for us without making any difference to the time you'll spend inside prison.'

Shannon winced at Amos's bald statement before saying, 'Can't we talk about this, Mr Hawke? At the end of the day the only one who has been a loser is Alfie Banks! After what's happened to his grand scheme of making a fortune for everyone taking part in it he'll be the laughing stock of Hoxton and have lost all the authority he once had there.'

'He's lost more than authority,' Amos said, 'We arrested him yesterday so you might well meet up with him here, in prison, before he keeps an appointment with the hangman.'

Startled, Shannon said, 'You've got Alfie? Well, that goes to show that what I've said is true. It's always been his boast that he'd be able to live out his time in Hoxton because everyone there would protect him with their lives if it ever became necessary . . . but what's this about meeting up with the hangman? Alfie's a hard man and more dishonest than anyone I've ever met with, but I've never heard it said that he's killed anyone.'

'You tell that to the mother of Jimmy Banks. She's in Bodmin right now and came here to see Jimmy, believing he'd been arrested, only to learn that he'd been badly hurt when he and Alfie burgled Laneglos House and then left alone to die while Alfie rode off and made his way back to London. He was concerned for his own life because, in spite of what you say, it's highly likely he was involved in a murder. A young scullery maid was found dead soon after the burglary at Laneglos . . . but I haven't come here to fill you in on all the latest news of what's been happening in the criminal world while you've been locked away. I thought you had something you wanted to tell me . . . something important.'

'And so I have,' Shannon said, hurriedly, 'but if I'm going to be locked away for the rest of my life I might just as well keep it to myself and persuade a certain gentleman to contribute a little something to make life inside a bit more comfortable if I keep quiet about what I know about him.'

'You're talking in riddles, Shannon, what is it that's so important to this 'gentleman' that he'll pay you to keep quiet about it . . . and who is he?'

'As I said, Mr Hawke, if I'm going to have to spend the rest of my life in jail I'll need someone on the outside to pay for those little extras that are important to anyone doing time. On the other hand, if you were to drop some of the charges against me and have a word in the judge's ear, I could look forward to a time when I'd be out of jail and you'd be in possession of information that a London detective would give his right arm for, especially if Alfie Banks had intended carrying out such a raid on his patch.'

'You'll pardon me if I seem cynical about this 'important information' that's in your possession, Shannon, it's probably worth no more than those forged bonds we found in your possession when you were arrested.'

'Oh no, Mr Hawke, I wouldn't even think of wasting your time about something like this. It's important to you . . . and even more important to me, because it's the rest of my life we're talking about. This information is real *kosher*, I promise you.'

Amos was aware that Conrad Shannon was a clever and experienced confidence trickster, someone quite capable of deceiving the most cynical of his victims. But Shannon was right, if he had some really useful information to impart then it *could* mean a lighter sentence for him and provide the breakthrough Amos was seeking. Besides, he had nothing to lose by listening to him.

'What is it you have to tell me that's so important it's going to change both our lives, Shannon.'

'Well . . . it must have crossed your mind that Alfie doesn't have the brains to think out all the details of what was meant to happen at the ball we had come from London to attend. I mean, the only reason he's top man in Hoxton is because he has brawn — and the family — to back him up in whatever he gets up to. He could never have thought of something on that sort of scale! No, that took a man who knew what he was talking about . . . an educated man.'

Looking more sure of himself now, Shannon said, 'I *could* tell you who he is . . . but I am going to need some guarantees about my future before I do.'

34

When Amos returned to the Cornwall police headquarters in Bodmin, he found the chief constable waiting in his office with Doctor Sullivan for his arrival. Chief Constable Gilbert was more agitated than Amos had ever seen him and he wasted no time in informing Amos of the cause.

'You were right about Lady Hogg's illness,' he said, 'Doctor Sullivan has confirmed that Lady Hogg is suffering from arsenic poisoning. Furthermore, having examined all the facts, he believes it to have been deliberately administered. He also believes Lord Hogg's death can be attributed to the same cause. He wants me to have Lord Hogg's body removed from the family vault in order that he may carry out an autopsy to ascertain whether arsenic poisoning was the cause of his death . . . '

Shaking his head, Chief Constable Gilbert added, unhappily, 'It puts me in a very difficult situation, Amos . . . very difficult indeed. If we go ahead with having the body of the late Lord Hogg removed from the family vault we are going to meet with considerable resistance from the family. Should a post mortem show that arsenic is not the cause of death, I will undoubtedly be forced to resign — and you with me, Amos.'

'On the other hand, if we do nothing and Lady

Hogg dies, who is to say the killer will stop there. Before we know it we could have one of the oldest families in Cornwall wiped out!' Turning his attention to Sullivan, Amos asked, 'How certain are you that Lady Hogg *is* suffering from arsenic poisoning, Doctor?'

'Certain enough to say that if we do nothing she will be dead within a week,' the young doctor replied bluntly. 'I never saw Lord Hogg during his illness, but Doctor Hollis attended him and has admitted that his symptoms were identical with those of Lady Hogg. He is so concerned that he has spoken to the present Lord Hogg and arranged for a nurse to be in constant attendance on her. She will supervise all food and drink prepared for her patient and be present when she has a visit from anyone, whether it be family or servants.'

Amos looked at the chief constable without saying anything and after a few moments, Gilbert said, 'It would seem that Lord Hogg appreciates the seriousness of the situation. Very well, Doctor Sullivan, we will seek permission for a post mortem to be carried out on his late father. Such permission is not really required, but it will make it more pleasant for everyone concerned if we have it. Superintendent Hawke and I will go to Laneglos and speak to Lord Hogg today.'

When the doctor had left his office, Chief Constable Gilbert said to Amos, 'What do we do if Sullivan's post mortem *does* prove Lord Hogg was poisoned, Amos? Will it help us to find who is responsible?'

'That's what I wanted to talk to you about *before* we took any action on having an autopsy on the late Lord Hogg,' Amos said, 'There has been a great deal happening in and around Laneglos and I have my suspicions about who is responsible for at least *some* of what has been going on there. Now we have Alfie Banks in custody I feel I will be able to fill in a few of the gaps in my knowledge . . . and then there is what Conrad Shannon had to say to me this morning . . . '

Amos repeated the conversation that had taken place with the imprisoned forger and Gilbert listened with great interest. When Amos ended, he asked, 'Is Shannon telling the truth . . . and even if he is, is it likely to have any bearing on the attempt to poison Lady Hogg and the death of her husband?'

'I think it most unlikely that the two are *not* connected,' Amos replied, 'and I have my own theories, but theories are not acceptable to a judge and jury. I need to establish facts.'

'Do you think that anything Shannon has to tell us might do that?' Chief Constable Gilbert was sceptical.

'If anything he has to say is sufficient to put pressure on Banks, I think it could . . . but Shannon is going to want an assurance that we are going to drop at least some of the charges against him before he tells me what he knows.'

The police chief thought for some moments before saying, 'Well you have far more experience with this sort of thing than I do, Amos, and you know just how much trust we can put in this man Shannon, but if he can offer us anything to put an end to the mayhem involving Laneglos you can promise him the earth . . . and I will help you get it for him.'

* * *

Armed with the chief constable's promise, Amos left the headquarters building to return to Bodmin jail. Before leaving he sent Tom to Laneglos to arrange a meeting between Lord Hogg, Amos and the Chief Constable Gilbert for later that day.

At the grim Cornish prison, Amos arranged for Conrad Shannon to be brought to see him in one of the administration offices. Pen, ink and paper had been provided and when Shannon had been brought to the room and was seated facing Amos across a desk, Amos pointed to them and said, 'There is the ticket to the rest of your life, Shannon. Pick up the pen and make a true and honest statement and you'll see life beyond these prison walls once more. Try to lie your way out of trouble and I promise you'll never see it again.'

'You mean . . . you'll drop some of the charges against me.' Shannon's pale, haggard expression changed dramatically.

'If what you tell me enables me to arrest whoever planned the burglary at Laneglos . . . and who is possibly guilty of murder, I might even persuade my chief constable to drop *all* the charges against you.'

Excited now, Shannon said, 'Can I have that in

writing, Mr Hawke? Give me that and I'll tell you everything I know.'

'You are in no position to dictate terms,' Amos retorted. 'For all I know what you tell me could turn out to be a pack of lies. Besides, I am not going to promise what might not be possible. All I can do is tell you that if you give me something that proves to be of real help then I, and my chief constable, will do our utmost to help you. I give you my word on that — but you are going to have to take it on trust.'

Some of the animation left Shannon's face, but after thinking it over, he shrugged, 'I don't have very much alternative, do I? All right, but why do you want *me* to write it down? Why can't you do it?'

Leaning across the desk towards him, Amos said, 'Because if what you have to say is true, then you're likely to have to repeat it in court . . . and I don't want you getting up in the witness box and saying it isn't what you told me. You can tell me what you have to say first and *then* we'll see whether it's anything worth putting into writing.'

Amos thought for a moment that Shannon was about to change his mind about telling what he knew. Instead, he shrugged once more and began to talk . . .

'Dolly came to see me before she went back to London, she told me you had heard about the boat coming from London and so were able to put paid to the plans that had been made for the ball at Laneglos?'

'That's right. No doubt you've also managed

to speak to some of the Hoxton gang who are locked up in here, so you'll know we also managed to scotch their plans to rob some of the Cornish mansions while their owners were at the ball? We foiled all the gang except Alfie and Jimmy. They managed to burgle Laneglos the night after the ball, but crashed the cart carrying all their loot. Jimmy died of his injuries and Alfie got away and was on his way to Australia when we picked him up.'

'You were lucky to take him. He's always sworn he'd die before being taken — and would take a great many of your lot with him.'

'He didn't put up much of a fight against my men . . . although he did take a ten year-old girl hostage and threaten to kill her unless we allowed him to get away. Fortunately, Harvey Halloran was there to sort him out. You know Harvey?'

'I've heard of him and I believe I saw him once, but not to speak to. I thought he was still living in Hoxton.'

'No, he's a sergeant in my force . . . but you were going to tell me about the man behind the jaunt you and the others made to Cornwall. How is it that you knew when nobody else did?'

'Because I'm not comfortable working with anyone else unless I know all about them. Alfie came to see me and asked me to do a couple of things he said were for 'someone big', then he let me in on what was going to happen here, in Cornwall. I asked him who was setting it all up and when he wouldn't tell me I decided to find out for myself.'

'How did you do that?'

Before replying, Shannon said, 'I'm not writing down *everything* that I'm going to tell you.'

'I'll decide what I want you to write down when I've learned how much you know. Carry on talking.'

'Well, Alfie said I'd be given some things to copy — tickets for the Laneglos ball, as it turned out — as well as one or two other things, false identifications mainly — oh, and stock certificates. I also had to write a reference for young Jimmy Banks, but using a different name. I knew Alfie can neither read nor write, but I asked why the man behind the whole idea couldn't write the reference himself and Alfie said it was because his handwriting might be recognized and that made me curious. It meant this man must be well known to the family the reference was intended for. Alfie himself didn't give me any of the things that needed copying, they were brought to me by a smart-looking bloke who let it slip when we were talking that he was a valet, working for the man who wanted these things copied. He wouldn't tell me who employed him, but after one of his visits to me I followed him to a posh house in Kensington and by talking to a maid who came out of the house next door I learned who was living there. She also told me there were always tradesmen calling, trying to get money he owed them. I went back to the house once or twice, hoping to see this man for myself and one day when he came out I followed him to a pub in Liverpool Street where he met up with Alfie. I knew then I'd found the right bloke.'

'You never told Alfie that you knew who this man was?'

'Of course not! The less I had to do with the Hoxton crowd the better I liked it. That's why I didn't travel down to Cornwall on the boat with them. Alfie wanted me to but I gave the same excuse to him as did Dolly. I said I would never travel on the sea. That's how it happened he introduced me to Dolly. I don't think he entirely trusted me and wanted her to keep an eye on me. Why did you never charge her, by the way?'

'Because it was you who had the forged railway and ball tickets and a conspiracy case against her would never have stood up in court — but now we come to the point of this whole conversation . . . the name of the man who did all the planning for this whole debacle. I think I know who it is, but I want to hear you tell me.'

'You'll keep your promise . . . about trying to make things easier for me in court?'

'As I said earlier, if you give me enough to get him into court — especially if it helps solve the various suspicious deaths we've had connected with Laneglos — it's possible I might be able to have all the charges against you dropped. What is his name?'

Aware that he might be taking a gamble that would never come off, Shannon decided he had no alternative. He had to trust Amos.

'It's the son of the Lady of the manor up at Laneglos and stepson to Lord Hogg . . . The Honourable Charles Delville.'

* * *

As Amos was leaving the prison a police van pulled into the yard and among three prisoners alighting from the vehicle Amos was surprised to see Connie Dawes, the young ex-Laneglos servant girl who had concealed the birth of her illegitimate baby and had it buried in the North Hill graveyard.

Hurrying across to her he said, 'Hello, Connie . . . What are you doing here, is it because of what you did with your baby?'

'You ought to know,' she replied bitterly, 'It was you who found out about it.'

'True, but I was told the inquest decided it had been dead when it was born and that you were being charged only with concealing its birth?'

'What difference does it make? I'm being locked up in prison now and no doubt when I see the judge next week he'll send me back here.'

'He probably will,' Amos agreed, 'Unless you can come up with some extenuating circumstances . . . '

As soon as he had spoken, Amos realized that Connie would not know what he meant, but the gaoler in charge of the prisoners was becoming impatient and Amos said to him, 'I'd like to talk to her for a few minutes on a matter of some importance. Take the other prisoners inside. I'll be responsible for this one until you return.'

When the others had shuffled away, their leg-irons clanking noisily, Amos returned his attention to Connie. 'I thought the father of your baby was going to look after you. He could have paid for a lawyer to arrange bail which would have meant you could remain at home, at least until the trial.'

'He promised to look after me, but when ma went to speak to him, he said he didn't know what she was talking about and, anyway, with the baby dead I had no need for help and could go back to work.'

'Did you expect any more from him, Connie? You shouldn't have done, you'd been working at Laneglos long enough to know what he was like.'

Looking at him uncertainly, Connie said, 'You know who he is?'

'Unless I'm mistaken it was Lady Hogg's son, Charles Delville . . . the same man I believe got Enid Merryn pregnant.'

'That's who Enid told Peggy and me it was. No doubt he threatened her that if she didn't do what he wanted he'd have her thrown out of Laneglos and make sure she never worked anywhere again. She'd have believed him, I didn't. But I *did* believe him when he said I'd be looked after if he got me in trouble. After all, there are enough girls around Laneglos who don't *have* to work any more because they've had his babies. Lord Hogg saw they were taken care of.'

'Unfortunately, Lord Hogg told Delville he wasn't going to give money to any more of them — or to *him* if he carried on seducing Laneglos servants. Delville must have been satisfied he could rely on you saying nothing, but he would have been very worried about poor Enid. I don't think she was capable of keeping a secret like that.'

'She wasn't,' Connie agreed, 'but surely you don't think it was him who killed her . . . to keep her quiet?'

'That's what I need to find out. If she was killed for that reason then she died unnecessarily, because Delville was cut out of Lord Hogg's will anyway, although, of course, he didn't know that until his stepfather died.'

At that moment the gaoler emerged from the main prison building and, reaching into his pocket Amos drew out a half-crown and passed it to her. 'Here, it's not much, but it will help you get some extra food while you are in here awaiting trial. In the meantime I'll have a word with the inspector who is giving evidence in your case and make sure he tells the court you were seduced by a man who had considerable power over your future and that he let you down.'

'Why would you do that — and why have you given me this money?' Connie asked suspiciously.

'Because I think you have been the victim of a thoroughly unscrupulous man — and you have helped me move a step forward in my hunt for the killer of Enid Merryn.'

35

Back at the Bodmin headquarters once more, Amos paid a visit to Alfie Banks in the police cells before returning to the chief constable. He found the Hoxton criminal in a sullen mood.

'Have you thought any more of what I was speaking to you about last night, Alfie, the murder of Enid Merryn?'

'Why should I, it's got nothing to do with me?'

'Now why doesn't it surprise me that you'd say that? The problem is that I've now learned a great deal more about what went on that night. I've also learned the name of the man who planned what was meant to be the biggest criminal attack on a single target in the history of this county . . . possibly in the history of the whole country. Now, if a simple little servant girl who meant nothing to anyone, except perhaps her mother, threatened the success of such an ambitious plan, what would those involved in it do, especially if their leader was a gang leader from Hoxton with a record of violence? Think about it, Alfie, and at the same time think about the fact that the two suspects in this poor girl's murder are you . . . and the son of a noble family who probably mixes socially with the judge and might even be a close friend of him. Now, when the case comes to court and the jury — men of some standing in the community — have a choice of which of you they convict of murder, who do you think they are going to choose?'

'I've already told you, I haven't killed anyone.'

'I'm almost inclined to believe you, Alfie . . . but I am a realist. Guilty or not, we both know that juries don't always get it right. Suppose you tell me *exactly* what happened on the night you and Jimmy burgled Laneglos . . . '

* * *

Amos travelled to Laneglos with the chief constable, in the latter's carriage, and Tom Churchyard went with them. Along the way Amos related to Gilbert much of what he had learned that morning and said he had brought Tom along with him in case they decided to arrest the Honourable Charles Delville.

'Do you really believe we have enough evidence to link him with the Merryn murder?' Gilbert queried, thinking of the furore it would cause in the county if he not only had the late Lord Hogg removed from the family vault — but had his stepson arrested at the same time!

'No, but if we can persuade Delville's valet to corroborate Shannon's written statement we will be able to put a case together involving him in the burglary at Laneglos.'

'Surely a valet's loyalty is to his employer? A jury of Delville's peers will certainly think so. Besides, he's hardly likely to say anything to convict Delville? Quite apart from any other consideration he would be out of work and never be employed as a valet again.'

'I think the valet is ready to quit his job with

Delville anyway, sir,' This from Tom, 'Delville is always threatening to dismiss him because he can't afford to keep him on and I don't believe he has received any pay for quite some time.'

'Then why on earth does the valet stay with him?'

'I think he's been hoping that Delville will one day have enough money to pay him what he's owed. If he left he'd have nothing and never be able to get his back pay. At least by staying with Delville he gets board and lodging and if he's not called to give evidence against him should have no difficulty in finding another post. A valet who stays with an employer who can't afford to pay him could be considered more loyal than most.'

'That's true,' mused Gilbert, 'By all means sound him out . . . but be discreet. We need to concentrate on persuading Lord Hogg that a post mortem on his late father is to everyone's advantage. We don't want to antagonise him by arresting his step-brother at this point. If it is proved the late Lord Hogg *was* poisoned it will be to everyone's advantage to have his murderer dealt with according to the law . . . but we will not speculate on that until we are in possession of all the facts.'

When the party reached Laneglos, Tom was sent off to seek out Flora and make inquiries about the Honourable Charles Delville's valet, while Amos and Chief Constable Gilbert met with Lord Hogg in the peer's study. The meeting went very much as both policemen thought it might.

At first, Lord Hogg was horrified that they should even consider removing the body of his father from the family vault and carry out a post mortem on it. He objected very strongly to such a procedure, but eventually Amos and Gilbert were able to convince him that however distasteful such a course of action was, if a poisoner remained at large in the Laneglos household there were likely to be other victims — even the present Lord Hogg himself.

It was finally agreed that the body of the late Lord Hogg could be removed from the vault in the family's church but with as much secrecy as was possible and it was to be returned to its resting place when the result of the autopsy was known, but this time with the family's chaplain present to lay him to rest once more in accordance with the rites of the Church.

It seemed the object of their visit had been achieved, however Amos still feared the Laneglos viscount might change his mind. As they were leaving, he asked after Lady Hogg and her stepson replied that her health seemed to have improved, adding, 'No doubt it has something to do with the nurse that Doctor Hollis obtained to take care of her. She is frighteningly efficient and has taken complete charge of the sick room and all that goes on there. I understand she learned her business with Florence Nightingale, nursing in the hospital at Scutari during the Crimean War.'

Amos was interested immediately, 'I wonder if I have met her? I was in the hospital there for a while, when I was wounded'

'I'll send for her and we can find out . . . if I can persuade her to leave the sick room for a few minutes.'

The nurse, Priscilla Goodman, was a small, brisk woman, who exuded confident efficiency. She *thought* she could recollect seeing Amos at Scutari, but in view of the many thousands of soldiers who passed through the hospital, she could not be certain.

However they spoke of a number of doctors and nurses who were known to them both . . . and then Amos mentioned Harvey Halloran. The nurse became suddenly animated. 'You know Harvey? How is he, did he make a full recovery from his wounds? We never thought he would live when he first arrived at Scutari, but he was a determined and strong man and when he was up and about again he became one of the hospital's stalwarts. He was a wonderful man!'

'He still is,' Amos said, 'For a while he was my second-in-command in the Crimea and is now one of the stalwarts of the Cornwall constabulary, stationed very close to here, in Bodmin as the force's sergeant major. Perhaps Lord Hogg will allow him to visit you while you are here?'

'Of course!' Lord Hogg had been listening to the conversation between Amos and Priscilla Goodman with great interest. 'I am fascinated with all aspects of the war. I had two cousins who fought there, one was sadly killed. The other, a Lancer, was in the famous charge of the Light Brigade, at Balaclava. Fortunately he was one of those who survived. He occasionally visits Laneglos. You must come here and meet him, Superintendent. In the meantime, please inform Sergeant Major Halloran he is welcome to call on Miss Goodman whenever he wishes.'

When they left the great House, Chief Constable Gilbert said to Amos, 'Talking of the Crimea certainly thawed our relations with Lord Hogg. Until then I was still unsure that we would be able to go ahead with the autopsy on his father without him raising some objection. Well done, Amos.'

'I think we succeeded in doing more than thaw relations, sir,' Amos said. 'By visiting the efficient Miss Goodman, Halloran will be able to find out about the household routine and who had access to Lady Hogg and the food and drink that came to the room. It could prove important to our investigations — especially if Doctor Sullivan finds that the late Lord Hogg *was* poisoned.'

They had left the house now and coming around one of the wings of the house they saw Tom and Flora coming towards them talking so intently to each other that they did not immediately notice the two senior policemen standing outside the front entrance.

'Who is that with Churchyard,' the chief constable queried.

'It's Flora Wicks, the Laneglos housekeeper.' Amos replied.

'She is rather an attractive girl — and very young to have such a responsibility. She and Churchyard seem to be getting along very well.'

Amos smiled, 'Yes, my wife has high hopes for the two of them.'

'Good, they could both do far worse. Churchyard has a future in the force and I like my senior officers to be happily married . . . like you and Mrs Hawke.'

36

While the two senior policemen were being received by Lord Hogg, Tom had found Flora. Her expression of delight when she saw him was a fleeting one, but it gave him an unexpected thrill of pleasure.

'What are you doing at Laneglos?' she queried, 'None of the maids told me you were here.'

'I came with Amos and the chief constable,' he explained, 'They are here for a meeting with Lord Hogg. Amos asked me to find you and ask some questions about the Honourable Charles Delville's valet.'

'Why, what has he done?'

'I don't think he's done anything wrong . . . unless you know of something that we don't.'

'I don't, in fact he has always been politeness itself in my dealings with him, but to be perfectly honest I wouldn't be surprised at anything that was done by someone associated with the Honourable Charles.'

'I know you don't like him, Flora, but has he done anything in particular lately to upset you?'

They were talking in a passageway that led to the kitchen and a maid wielding a feather duster on the end of a long bamboo pole was within hearing. Glancing towards her, Flora said, 'Everyone seems to have upset me today, but come along to my lounge, we can talk there.'

Once in the housekeeper's lounge, Flora

motioned for Tom to sit in an armchair, then sitting down heavily on another, she asked. 'Now, what is it you want to know about Robson Chalmers, the Honourable Charles's valet?'

'I'd like to speak to him . . . but, first, what's troubling you, Flora? Who's been upsetting you.'

'Well, actually it's my employer, Lord Hogg . . . or, to be more accurate the future Lady Hogg.'

'Is she here at Laneglos already?'

'No, but she is beginning to make her future status felt. I suppose I have always known that I *am* very young to be housekeeper of a grand home like this, but I feel I have carried out my duties quite as well as my predecessor.'

'You mean . . . she is having you dismissed?' Tom was dismayed at the thought of Flora going away from the area.

'Not exactly, but she wants to appoint her long-term lady's maid as housekeeper at Laneglos. Lord Hogg was very nice about it, he said there was no question of my being dismissed. I would simply revert to being the assistant housekeeper but retaining the salary I am being paid now.'

'Will you accept that?'

Flora shook her head. 'However generous the offer might be, I could not remain here as assistant to someone who has taken my place. It would not only be humiliating, but very difficult. As housekeeper I have needed to be firm with some of the servants on occasions, that is what the position calls for. With that authority taken away I would become one of them and I don't think I would have a happy time.'

'If . . . if you leave, when will you go?'

'Not immediately, Lord Hogg will not be marrying until sometime early next year. A date has not been fixed yet.'

'But . . . what will you do if you leave Laneglos?' Tom was still stunned by her revelation. There were so many plans he had begun to formulate in recent weeks . . . and all of them included Flora. But she was speaking again.

' . . . Lord Hogg said I must think about it and not decide immediately. He said he will understand if I feel I must leave and that I will go with excellent references. He said there was also an opportunity of going to the dower house as the Dowager Lady Hogg's housekeeper but I don't think I could bear the thought of seeing more of the Honourable Charles.'

'I don't know what to say, Flora. I was hoping . . . ' Tom broke off, unable to find words for what he wanted to say.

'What were you hoping, Tom?' Flora urged.

'Well . . . you and me . . . We have been getting along so well . . . I thought . . . ' Words failed him but Flora came to his rescue.

'It's something I have been thinking a lot about too, Tom . . . but we haven't known each other for very long. Perhaps when we have known each other for a little longer . . . '

'Hopefully we *will* by the time you need to make up your mind about leaving Laneglos.'

'I think we might, Tom. I hope so.' Aware of where their conversation was going and that the housekeeper's lounge at Laneglos was not the right place to take the conversation any farther, she said, ' . . . but we came here to talk about Robson Chalmers — and it's fortunate that you came to see him today. He will be leaving Laneglos tomorrow and I don't think we will be seeing him again. The Honourable Charles has told him he cannot afford to keep him on and he is packing up Charles's things and taking them up to London tomorrow, where he will be paid off. Charles has already gone there.'

Realising that Amos would not know this news, Tom asked, 'Was going to London a sudden decision by the Honourable Charles?'

'Probably, there was certainly another big argument yesterday between him and Lord Hogg. No doubt that had something to do with it.'

'Do you know what the argument was about this time?'

'I do, but I seem to be doing what I tell the servants they must never do . . . gossip about their employers.'

'You know we are investigating a murder and a burglary, Flora. Any scrap of information we can get about what goes on at Laneglos helps us build up a picture of life here — and one day something is going to fit in with what we already know and enable us to arrest whoever is responsible for one, or both crimes.'

'I am aware of that, Tom, and I wish I could tell you something about the Honourable Charles that would mean he would never be seen at Laneglos again, life here would be much easier. Unfortunately, although what he has done is quite despicable, he has not broken the law — but Lord Hogg has told him he will never be a welcome guest here again, so I suppose that is something.'

'What *has* he done?' Tom prompted.

'He persuaded Lady Hogg to part with some of her jewellery in order that he can sell it to pay of some of his many debts. We all know she has been so ill that she probably doesn't fully realize what she's done, but she has confirmed she *did* give them to him. The trouble was caused because a number of the pieces are considered by Lord Hogg to be family heirlooms — including the tiara worn by all Hogg viscountesses at their weddings since the title first came into the family. Lord Hogg was furious and I think the two step-brothers came very close to blows. Anyway, Charles has gone now and if he ever comes back it will be to the dower-house that Lady Hogg is moving to, and not to Laneglos.'

'How is Lady Hogg?' Tom asked, aware of the reason for the visit of the chief constable and Amos to the house, something of which Flora would not be aware.

'She seemed to be much brighter this morning — it might have something to do with the very efficient nurse who has been brought in to take care of her while she is ill. She has already stamped her authority on the servants and made it clear to them — and to me — that she is in sole charge of the sick room and what she says goes. If there is something she needs then there is to be no argument, it must be provided.'

'Perhaps that's another reason why the Honourable Charles decided to leave Laneglos,' Tom was only half-joking about it, 'They would probably have clashed head-on — and it sounds as though she might have won.'

Shortly afterwards, the two were walking from the house towards the Chief Constable's carriage. There was silence between them for a few moments before Flora asked, 'What we were talking about a little earlier. About you and me. Did you mean . . . what I thought you meant when you spoke of the future?'

'Yes, Flora . . . about a future together.'

'I'm glad, Tom . . . there is still a lot we need to know about each other before we can take any decisions, but I am glad we are both thinking along the same lines. Will I see you on Sunday?'

'I hope so . . . especially now we have had this little talk together.'

Looking up at him happily, she said, 'Good, now I have something pleasant to look forward to . . . and thank you for making this turn out to be a nice day after all.'

At that moment Tom looked up and saw Amos and the chief constable looking at them and their moment was lost . . . at least, for that day.

37

When the autopsy on the late Lord Hogg was carried out two days later, Doctor Sullivan found proof that the peer *had* died of arsenic poisoning. Not only had he apparently been poisoned over a period which Sullivan felt was days rather than weeks, but on the final day of his life he must have been given a massive dose which was sufficient to cause a rapid death.

The chief constable called Amos to his office for a meeting to discuss the case and their future course of action. It was agreed that Lady Hogg had been the victim of arsenic poisoning too because, since the family doctor had brought in a nurse to remain with her night and day and supervise her food and the visitors she received, the widowed peeress had shown a marked improvement in her health.

Amos also agreed with Gilbert that the overwhelming evidence pointed to only one suspect . . . the Honourable Charles Delville. He had motive, access to both Lord and Lady Hogg and was known to have been involved in the burglary of Laneglos by Alfie and Jimmy Banks.

Nevertheless, Amos felt they should apply for a warrant only on a burglary and conspiracy to burgle charge, arguing that they had a much stronger case against him for this, while there were still a number of weaknesses in the murder and attempted murder investigations that a clever defence barrister would seize upon.

'What about the evidence of the valet?' queried the chief constable, 'He told Churchyard he had seen arsenic-based rat poison in Delville's London home, surely that strengthens the evidence against him?'

Robson Chalmers had come to the Bodmin police station before catching a train to London with Delville's personal belongings and had given a great deal of damning evidence against his employer, including seeing rat poison in the basement of his London home — and of finding mud on his shoes when he cleaned them on the morning after the robbery, indicating that he had been out somewhere between the time the valet went to bed and when he commenced his duties in the morning.

'Not necessarily,' Amos said, 'Chalmers is very, very bitter about the way Delville has behaved towards him and a good barrister would make a great deal of that. If Delville has got rid of the rat poison it is his word against that of an aggrieved servant that there was any arsenic in his possession in the first place. If, when he is arrested, we search his house and find the poison we can re-assess the evidence against him. If we feel there is sufficient to convict him of the murder of Lord Hogg and the attempted murder of Lady Hogg we can go ahead and charge him, but that would still leave the murder of Enid Merryn outstanding . . . and I don't like unsolved crimes.'

'Very well, Amos, we will take it one step at a time. Obtain a warrant for Delville's arrest on the burglary charge and arrange for you and Churchyard to go to London. I will telegraph Scotland Yard and have you met on your arrival, taken before a justice there to swear out a warrant and given all the assistance you require to arrest Delville and bring him back to Cornwall.'

* * *

Amos and Tom travelled to London early on the following Monday morning.

The previous day Tom had met with Flora and on a long walk together along the banks of the River Fowey they continued the conversation they had held on Tom's last visit to Laneglos.

Here, in a quiet, secluded spot where willows overhung the gently flowing river Flora was able to point out the brilliant colours of a kingfisher on a hunting foray flying upstream, its brilliant hues mirrored in the unruffled water.

It was here too that a previously undiscovered passion entered their relationship and they were aware it marked the beginning of a new and exciting chapter in their lives. Perhaps for the first time, they both realized they had discovered something special that would last and grow with the years ahead. It was a happy day and they parted with an unspoken understanding that they faced a future together.

However, their work meant they would not see as much of each other as they wished and, today, in London, Tom knew that he and Amos had a difficult task on their hands.

The two Cornish policemen were met at Paddington railway station by a uniformed Metropolitan Police inspector named Anthony Winter, whom Amos had known as a sergeant during his own early service in the Metropolitan Police.

On their ride to the Bow Street magistrates court, where the inspector would obtain a warrant for the arrest of the Honourable Charles Delville, Amos gave him the background to the case against the peer's son.

The warrant was obtained with a minimum of fuss and accompanied by two uniformed constables from the adjoining police station they took a police carriage to the house occupied by Delville, in nearby Holborn.

The door of the elegant terraced house was opened to them by a young maid-of-all-work who appeared terrified at the sight of five men, three of them in the uniform of policemen asking for her master and it took her some time to find her voice and indicate that Delville was in a room at the back of the house.

Ordered to take them to the room, the frightened maid led them to a door at the end of the passageway which led from the front door. She knocked timidly on the door, but Inspector Winter brushed past her and, turning the brass door knob, opened the door and entered the room with the others close at his heels.

Delville was seated at a writing desk in the room and spread out on the surface in front of him were a number of pieces of jewellery, prominent among them being a sparkling tiara that Tom took to be the one the present Lord Hogg considered a family heirloom.

Taken by surprise at their uninvited entry, Delville sprang to his feet, 'What the . . . ?'

Wasting no time on a full explanation, Inspector Winter, said, 'Charles Delville, I have here a warrant for your arrest issued by a magistrate in Cornwall and endorsed by the stipendiary magistrate at Bow Street. I am hereby arresting you as directed by that endorsement and handing you into the custody of Superintendent Hawke of the Cornwall constabulary, who will return you to that county to face charges that have been made against you there. He will tell you all about those charges on the way back to Cornwall.'

Pointing to the jewellery scattered over the face of the desk, he said, 'Before he takes you away I would like to know something about all this . . . where has it come from?'

'I think I can tell you about that,' Tom said, 'Believe it or not, he came by it legally — although I think his step-brother, Lord Hogg, might disagree. They are Hogg family heirlooms given to Delville by his mother to help pay off his many debts. Lord Hogg feels very strongly that they should remain in the family.'

'I think we had better take them back to Cornwall with us,' Amos said, 'We certainly can't leave them here. Perhaps you would like to make a list of them and keep it, Inspector Winter. I'll have another made out when we hand it in at the police station in Cornwall with Delville's personal property. That way he will be unable to claim that anything has gone missing. Now, if you would tell your constables to take him off and lodge him in the Bow Street cells for a couple of hours, Sergeant Churchyard and I will carry out a search of the house then get something to eat before taking Delville back to Cornwall on the night train.'

'You will all find yourselves in very deep trouble over this,' Delville blustered, 'My family has very powerful friends both here in London and in Cornwall, they will not allow your treatment of me to go unpunished.'

'I think anyone of note, wherever they may be, will not want to be involved with you in any way once the details of the charges against you are made known,' Amos retorted, 'but we will talk more about them once we are on the train. Have him taken away please, inspector.'

When Delville had been removed from the house, Amos, Tom and Inspector Winter began their search of the house. In a cupboard in a basement room that was obviously being used as a storeroom, Tom found what they were looking for, an apothecary's jar containing a white powder which the label proclaimed in large capital letters to be 'ARSENIC'.

'Here we are!' he exclaimed, 'Exactly where Chalmers said it was kept. Let's see if Delville can explain this away.'

38

At Paddington railway station, Delville was driven on to the platform in a police van and then, handcuffed to Tom, bundled on board the night train bound for Cornwall and into a compartment which had been reserved for them. Here, Amos pulled down the blinds to hide them from the view of the other passengers and as they settled down for the ten-hours journey, Delville said, 'Will you remove these handcuffs now?' It was not so much a request as a command.

'No,' Amos replied, 'You will remain handcuffed to Sergeant Churchyard for half the night while I relax, then be handcuffed to me for the remainder of the journey.'

When Delville began to protest, Tom said, 'I suggest you make the most of it, the seats on the train are a whole lot more comfortable than anything you'll find in the police cells, or Bodmin Jail.'

'This whole thing is absolutely ridiculous,' Delville protested, 'Exactly *what* am I supposed to have done?'

'There is no 'supposed' about it,' Amos replied, 'We know you planned and took part in the burglary at Laneglos, you conspired with others to burgle a number of other houses on the night of the ball, and you also conspired with convicted criminals to carry out a series of other crimes on the night of the ball at Laneglos.'

'You are going to have to prove all these crimes you allege I have committed,' Delville pointed out scornfully.

'We will,' Amos said matter-of-factly, 'Now, I suggest you try to get some sleep — as I am. You, in particular, are going to have a very busy day tomorrow.'

Amos managed to snatch no more than a few brief dozes for the first half of the night and midnight was still a half-hour away when he exchanged places with Tom and ordered him to try to gain an hour or two's sleep.

The Honourable Charles made no attempt to even close his eyes. He sat next to Amos, their handcuff-linked hands close together on the seat between them, his chin resting on his chest, apparently deep in morose thought.

They had been travelling in this fashion for almost an hour before Delville broke the silence. In the slurred voice of a man who has not spoken for some time, he said, 'All these crimes I am supposed to have committed . . . where did you pick up your information . . . or perhaps I would be more accurate in referring to it as *mis*information?'

'From a great many sources,' Amos replied, 'Some of them quite surprising. There is supposed to be honour among thieves, but it doesn't apply when they have time to think things out and realize what lies ahead for them if they can't shift some of the blame for their misdoings onto someone else. Mind you, not all those who have been willing to tell me what they know of you are criminals. Some are very decent people who have been unfortunate enough to come under your influence.'

Delville's response was a look charged with malevolence, but Amos felt that the peer's son was thinking about what had just been said . . . and his next words confirmed this.

'You still have to prove my guilt in court and I do not think you will be able to do that.'

'You can think what you like,' Amos retorted, 'When I produce a note from you giving instructions to a convicted forger to forge a reference for a convicted young criminal to obtain a post at Laneglos — and another on forging ball tickets, plus a witness who saw you talking to Alfie Banks in a London pub; a map drawn by yourself giving positions and details of houses to be robbed — together with information that could only have come from someone familiar with the contents and occupants of these houses — and proof that you left the house on the night of the burglary at Laneglos, I think a jury will sit up and take notice. These are just a few of the things I will be able to prove in court.'

Shaken now, but still defiant, Delville said, 'Do you seriously believe that when the time comes these so-called 'witnesses' of yours will stand up in court and give evidence against me?'

'I have no doubts at all, because it isn't only thieving and deception we are talking about. There are also two murders and an attempted murder tied in with the events at Laneglos and when murder is mentioned even the most hardened criminal undergoes something of a metamorphosis and self-preservation becomes his sole aim.'

'Two murders?'

In any other circumstances Amos would have accepted the bewilderment of the man he was questioning as genuine, but he knew he was dealing with a particularly clever criminal, 'That's right. Poor Enid Merryn, Lord Hogg . . . and the attempted murder of your mother.'

'What are you talking about . . . ? I know the servant girl was strangled, but my stepfather died of natural causes . . . and what is this nonsense about my mother?'

'I'm surprised your valet didn't tell you when he brought your things to London . . . but he probably didn't feel inclined to tell you *anything* after the way he has been treated. Anyway, new information was received that caused us to have the body of the late Lord Hogg removed from the family vault and a post mortem carried out. It revealed the cause of his death to be arsenic poisoning. Your mother's symptoms were so similar to his that special steps were taken to monitor her food and drink. As a result I am pleased to say she appears to be making a full recovery.'

'Good God! It's unbelievable . . . but even if it's true, what does their poisoning have to do with the strangulation of a scullery-maid — and more to the point, what does any of this have to do with me?'

'I was hoping you would tell me. All I have at the moment is a purely circumstantial case against you . . . although hard evidence is beginning to emerge. I have spoken to Connie Dawes, the young kitchen maid who was pregnant by you — she has been arrested in connection with the death of her baby and will be naming you as the father of her child in court. I believe you had an arrangement to take care of her if she said nothing, but went back on your word. It has made her very angry, so it is unfortunate that she was one of two people to whom poor Enid confided that she too was expecting a baby by you. I know you promised to take care of her too, but she was so simple that the whole business of having your baby was too much for her . . . she just couldn't keep it to herself. She was going to tell the housekeeper.'

'I didn't know anything of this,' Delville said, but Amos thought he was less confident now, 'Even if I did, it's hardly a reason for murdering the girl. She wouldn't be the first servant girl to find herself pregnant.'

'*I* don't believe there are any circumstances in which coldblooded murder is justified,' Amos replied, 'but there is also a suggestion that she might have seen you talking with Alfie Banks, whom she had once met in company with the young servant for whom you had a reference forged. Now, tying you in with the burglary *would* have been a motive for murder. I happen to know that Lord Hogg had threatened to cut off all monies to you if you made any more servant girls pregnant. It is common knowledge you were desperate for money to pay your ever-mounting debts — so desperate that you could even be deemed capable of poisoning your stepfather in anticipation of benefiting from his will.'

'This is absolute nonsense!' Delville declared, 'And as for the preposterous insinuation that I would try to poison my own mother . . . '

'You would not be the first son guilty of matricide . . . and because of the wording of Lord Hogg's will, only her death would give you access to the amount of money you so desperately needed.'

'All this is no more than the product of a warped mind . . . a policeman's mind. You have no actual *evidence* whatsoever.'

'Wrong again,' Amos said, 'Arsenic is the poison that was used to murder Lord Hogg . . . and we found a quantity of arsenic in a basement cupboard in your London home, enough to kill quite a number of people . . . and more than enough to convict you.'

'That poison . . . the house was occupied by a doctor before I moved in. He must have left it there.'

'I don't think that where the arsenic came from would concern a jury too much. Their interest would be solely in what it was used for . . . and I think they will arrive at the right answer.'

Far less arrogant and confident now, Delville said nothing for a while, then, 'Do you really think I killed my stepfather and was trying to poison my mother?'

'I think that within a few days I will have gathered enough evidence to convince a jury . . . and then it won't matter what *I* think.'

Delville was silent for almost twenty minutes, during which time the train stopped at Bristol station where there was the sound of porters calling to one another and the slamming of carriage doors for some minutes before it set off on its way once more.

As the train pulled away from the station and began to gather speed, Delville looked sideways at Amos and had obviously arrived at a decision. With a resigned expression, he said, 'I think I had better tell you my version of events, Superintendent Hawke . . . '

39

On the arrival of the two policemen and their prisoner at the Bodmin police headquarters, Delville was taken down to the cells and Amos and Tom were able to enjoy a leisurely breakfast provided for them by a local hotel, at the same time deciding how much of what Delville had told them should be passed on to the chief constable who was soon due to arrive at his office. Amos felt there were still a number of points to be cleared up.

It had not been necessary for Amos to tell Tom what Delville had told him on the train because, although he had given the impression of being asleep during Delville's version of events, Tom had actually heard every word of the conversation between superintendent and prisoner.

By the time a constable put his head around the door of Amos's office to say the chief constable had arrived, they had agreed he should be told of Delville's confession to the burglary, but that they should make no mention of what he had said about the murders.

Chief Constable Gilbert was greatly relieved to learn of Delville's confession to involvement with the burglary. Had he not done so, the chief constable felt a conviction would not have been a foregone conclusion given the influence the gentry — especially *titled* gentry — had in the county.

'You have both done very well,' he said, 'but do you think you will be able to secure a murder conviction against him now you have found arsenic in his possession?'

'I hope to be able to give you a full answer to that later in the day, sir,' Amos said enigmatically. 'I would rather not commit myself until I and Churchyard have made a few more inquiries at Laneglos and at the same time inform Lord Hogg that we have arrested his step-brother. However, before going there I feel we should go home to tidy ourselves up a little, having spent more than twenty-four hours travelling back and forth, without a wash or shave.'

'Of course. I will await your return with the greatest interest — but tread lightly, Amos, it still remains a very delicate situation.'

* * *

Before he and Tom went home to clean up and change their clothing, Amos took the files containing all the statements taken from the Laneglos servants in connection with the burglary and murder and while Tom drove the pony and trap he went through them, selecting some for special study and comparison.

When they pulled up at the Hawke cottage, Tom asked, 'Did you find anything of particular interest in the statements, Amos?'

'Yes, in the light of what we now know, of *great* interest, but I would like you to read them while I clean up, then have Talwyn read through them. She has a very quick and analytical brain and I want to see if she picks up on a couple of anomalies we have not noticed before — and I might not have noticed them now had it not been for what Delville told us last night on the train.'

Talwyn was pleased to see Amos home again and thrilled that his trip to London had proved so successful. She readily agreed to his suggestion about the statements and when he left to wash and shave she and Tom were seated at the kitchen table, poring over them.

By the time Amos returned to the kitchen an excited Talwyn was able to tell him there were three of the statements that appeared to contradict each other, adding, 'I will not say which three until Tom has finished going through them, but I can see he has already found two of them.'

When Tom separated a third statement, Amos picked them up and, showing them to Talwyn, asked, 'Are these the same three which caught your attention?'

'Yes . . . and you?'

He nodded. 'Go and clean up, Tom, then we'll go to Laneglos. I have an idea that by the time we return to Bodmin we will have solved the murders of Enid Merryn . . . and Lord Hogg.'

* * *

Lord Hogg listened to Amos in disbelief when told of the arrest of his step-brother in connection with the burglary at Laneglos.

Shaking his head, he said, 'I find it difficult to believe . . . are you quite certain about this, Superintendent?'

'There is no doubt about it, sir, he actually planned the whole thing and admitted it to Sergeant Churchyard and myself last night when we were bringing him back to Cornwall from London on the train.'

'Well . . . it is no secret that he and I never got along together, but I never dreamed he would do something like this . . . ' Struck by a sudden thought he said, hesitantly, 'I don't suppose . . . no, I cannot believe he had anything to do with the murders of my father and the young servant girl . . . did he?'

Avoiding giving a direct reply to the question, Amos said, 'I hope to be able to give you an answer to that question when we have questioned three of your servants again . . . actually, it is two servants and a gamekeeper. I wonder whether we might speak with your housekeeper and make arrangements to interview them.'

'Of course. Interview them in my study, I will have the housekeeper sent to you there.'

As Amos and Tom were about to follow the servant who was to show them to the study, Amos turned back, 'By the way, when the Honourable Charles was arrested he had a quantity of jewellery in his possession. I think he came by it honestly, but I believe some of the pieces are family heirlooms. If you would prefer to have them here in the house for safekeeping rather than in the police station, I am sure it might be arranged, if your step-brother agrees, of course.'

The frown that Lord Hogg had worn since receiving the disturbing news of his step-brother's arrest disappeared for a moment and he gave Amos a searching look before saying. 'Thank you very much, Superintendent, that is very thoughtful of you. I will be visiting Charles, of course, and will discuss their safekeeping with him.'

* * *

Flora was obviously delighted to see Tom and had Amos entertained any doubts about their relationship it would have been instantly dispelled. When they told her the purpose of their visit and the order in which they wished to see the three Laneglos employees, she immediately asked, 'Is one of them suspected of Enid's murder?'

'It's possible,' Amos replied, 'but until we have questioned them all, we can't say anything . . . but I think we owe it to you to tell you that Tom and I went to London and arrested the Honourable Charles in connection with the burglary here at the house.'

She seemed less shocked than she might have been, 'I am not surprised by anything *he* does, but it is a good thing that Lady Hogg's health is improving. Had she been given the news a few days ago the shock would probably have killed her . . . but I will have Harry Clemo sent for. He was on night patrol last night, so he should be available at his cottage. In the meantime you can be talking with Chester Woods. I'll tell Peggy you want to talk to her too, but I don't know if you'll get much sense out of her, she seems to have been behaving in a peculiar manner lately, I've been thinking of talking to Doctor Hollis about her when he next comes to see Lady Hogg.'

40

Once again Amos marvelled that Chester Woods could have gained a reputation as a womaniser. A small and insignificant man, he also had a nervous sniff, which Amos decided was due to his discomfiture at being subjected to yet another interrogation by police — and the Laneglos footman had good reason to feel insecure.

'Hello, Woods . . . I think you probably know why we have come to see you again.'

The footman shook his head, 'I have no idea. I told you everything I knew the last time I spoke to you.'

'You certainly told us what had happened on the night of the burglary . . . but that doesn't mean you told us the truth. For instance, how long were you outside the house on that night?'

'I told you, no more than five or ten minutes, then I came back in for fear that Peggy Woods might come back and catch me out.'

'Are you sure you didn't stay outside for long enough to see Peggy leave the hayloft, before going back inside and up to your room?'

'No, I've told you what happened. I couldn't see her come out from the kitchen door, I'd have had to be much closer to the barn and then she might have caught me out.'

'Right . . . I will remind you that as well as the burglary there was a murder that night . . . the murder of a young servant girl who you knew. If I catch you out on a lie I will have you arrested and the chances are you will be charged in connection with that murder. Do you understand?'

Licking dry lips, Woods nodded.

'Good! You said you went up to your bed and pretended to be asleep when she returned. *How long was it before she came up to bed*?'

'I told you that the last time you interviewed me,' Chester replied.

'You did and before I ask you again I want to remind you of what I have just told you about telling me a lie. Now, how long was it before Peggy came back to your room.'

Woods licked his lips again, then, the words being uttered with apparent difficulty, he said, 'I don't know . . . I'm not very good at guessing time.'

'Try again, Woods.'

'About twenty minutes.' He sounded as though he was being strangled as he spoke.

'That's better than the time you gave us in your last statement, but I'm still not satisfied. How long . . . ?'

'It might have been half-an-hour . . . I can't do better than that. Tell me what it is you want me to say and I will.'

'I want you to tell the truth. That will do for now . . . but I am afraid you are not going to be allowed to return to work just yet, Woods.'

To Tom, he said, 'We should have brought more men with us, sergeant, but as we didn't I would like you to handcuff Woods and have him locked in a secure outbuilding until we have finished here.'

'What for? I've done nothing . . . ' Woods was still protesting when, handcuffed, he was led outside by Tom.

Tom had returned to the study, having locked Chester Woods in the woodshed, situated close to the kitchen door, when a bleary-eyed Harry Clemo was shown into the study. The game-keeper had been on anti-poacher patrol all night and had been summoned from his bed to be questioned by the two policemen.

As taciturn as when Tom had interviewed him previously, he was also almost as nervous at being questioned by the police for a second time as Woods had been.

With Clemo, Amos wasted no time in preliminaries, but came to the point immediately.

'When my sergeant questioned you about your movements on the night that Laneglos was burgled, you gave him a statement that you had met with Peggy Woods in the hay barn, but that you did nothing more than talk.'

'That's right, and that's *all* we did.'

'I'm not questioning that, Clemo, what I want to know now is what you talked about.'

'I think that's our business, not . . . '

'I don't give a damn what you *think*, Clemo. I'm conducting a murder investigation and if you don't co-operate now I'll have you taken to Bodmin police station and locked up in a cell until you do . . . is that clear?'

Visibly shaken by Amos's vehemence, Clemo nodded vigorously.

'Good! What did you talk about?'

Gulping, Clemo said, 'She didn't make a whole lot of sense . . . she spoke of having enough of Chester and said we should go away together. She was all het-up, and excited and . . . I don't know, she just didn't seem normal, somehow. I said we couldn't possibly go away together because we had no money . . . I only said that to try to calm her down, I never had any intention of going away with her, money or not, but it didn't work. She said she'd be getting some money soon . . . enough to last us until we'd found work together somewhere. I would never have gone away with her, but because she was so agitated I was worried about what she might do if I told her, so instead I said I'd think it over.'

'How long were you in the hay barn talking to her?'

'Couldn't have been longer than ten minutes at the most. As I said, she didn't seem normal, somehow, so I said I had to get back to patrolling the woods the other side of the estate before someone found out I wasn't there. I left the hay barn then and I suppose she must have gone back to the house.'

'You suppose? You didn't see her go?'

'No . . .'

It seemed that Clemo was about to say more. When he did not, Amos prompted him, 'I think you have something more to tell us, what is it?'

'Probably nothing at all, but, like I said, she was behaving a bit peculiar. She was even worse when I met her a few days later. She was waiting for me near my cottage when I set off on my usual night patrol and was so excited I thought she'd had a brainstorm, or something. She said that things had got even better and that when we went away together now she'd have enough money for us to start a proper new life together. That we'd be able to have our own public-house far away from Laneglos. Somewhere where we weren't known.'

'Did she say where this money was coming from?'

'No, and I didn't ask her. When Peggy gets like that, as she does sometimes, it's better to humour her and wait until she gets back to normal again.'

Amos exchanged glances with Tom before speaking to Clemo again, 'When you say Peggy sometimes acts in a peculiar manner, what exactly do you mean?'

'It's difficult to explain, really. She just doesn't somehow seem *normal*. I used to put it down to her being a bit hot-tempered and thought perhaps all Irish women were like that, but just lately she's gone all . . . oh, I don't know, but the way she behaves worries me sometimes . . . she just doesn't act normal!'

'Tell me, does Peggy have any possible access to arsenic?'

Clemo seemed taken aback by Amos's question, but he replied. 'It would be easy enough for her to get hold of some if she wanted it. It's refined at the mines up around Caradon, on Bodmin moor and we buy a fair amount to poison foxes when they get troublesome and also use it to keep down rats. It's kept in the gamekeepers' store room. Peggy knows it's there.'

Amos was about to question Clemo further when there was the sound of raised voices from the passageway outside the study. A few moments later the door was flung open and a highly agitated and still handcuffed Chester Woods stumbled into the room.

'Quick . . . you must stop Peggy!' Looking at Harry Clemo, he said, 'It's all your fault.' Turning towards Amos, he cried, 'She had the kitchen key to the wood shed and came and let me out. After asking why they'd locked me up she wanted to know what questions you'd been asking me. When I told her and said you'd got Harry in here she went berserk. She said if she couldn't have him then no one else was going to. When she left me she said she was going to the kitchen for a kitchen knife . . . I think she's gone after Dot and the kids.'

41

Amos, Tom and Harry Clemo sprinted for the gamekeeper's cottage as fast as they could, with a still handcuffed Chester Woods lumbering after them and gradually receding into the distance.

The gamekeeper's cottage was at the edge of a wood and although there was no sign of anyone there, the front door was standing open. Although he was short of breath, Amos said, 'Begin shouting . . . It doesn't matter *what* you shout . . . but make it loud!'

The three men began shouting, Harry Clemo making the most noise of them all. When they arrived at the cottage Amos went in first but the others were not far behind him. All the inner doors were open downstairs, although there did not appear to be anyone here. Then they heard the sound of a child crying . . . and it came from upstairs.

This time it was Harry Clemo who led the way. Two of the three doors on the small landing were open. The third was closed — and the sound of crying came from behind it.

Clemo tried the door, but there appeared to be something against it on the inside, preventing it from opening.'

'Dot! Dot, are you there . . . it's Harry!'

'Oh . . . Thank God.' It was a woman's voice and the next moment there was the sound of a piece of furniture being moved and the door opened to reveal an ashen-faced woman and, behind her were two children with grubby, tear-stained cheeks.

Trying to hug his wife and the two children all at the same time, Harry Clemo, said, 'Are you all right . . . ? What's happened?'

'Peggy Woods has been here — I think she's gone mad! I saw her coming when I was looking out of the window, she was brandishing a kitchen knife and shouting something that I couldn't make out. I grabbed the children and took them upstairs to our bedroom. They helped me shift the bed and then that old chest of drawers against the door. We were only just in time. We heard Peggy crashing around downstairs, then she came up here and tried to get into the bedroom. She was shouting that she was going to kill us all. The girls were terrified — so was I. What's happened to make her like that?'

Ignoring the question, Amos asked, 'Do you know where she went?'

Dot Clemo shook her head, 'If you didn't see her when you came in the front she must have gone out the back door when she heard you coming. She could be anywhere.'

'You have a gun in the house?' This to the gamekeeper.

'Yes.'

'Then get it, load it, lock all the doors and stay inside until I get word to you that Peggy Woods has been caught. We'll head back to the house.'

Amos and Tom met a breathless Chester Woods when he was still some distance from the gamekeeper's cottage and Amos ordered him to turn back and hurry to Laneglos as fast as he was able, explaining briefly, 'Peggy has probably gone back there . . . and she's dangerous. Get there as quickly as you can.'

Fast as they were, Peggy had beaten them to it. Amos thought the house resembled a disturbed wasp's nest, with servants, stable-hands and even gardeners hurrying in and out seemingly aimlessly.

They were met at the main entrance by Lord Hogg who was at a loss to know what was happening in his house. 'The butler tells me the assistant cook has gone berserk, do you know what is going on?'

'Where is she now? Amos asked.

'She has shut herself in the dairy armed with a kitchen knife and is threatening to kill anyone who dares to go in there.'

'Will you take me there, please?'

The dairy was off the kitchen, beside the scullery and there were a great many excited servants coming and going in the kitchen. Ordering everyone outside except Tom and Lord Hogg, Amos advanced to the door of the dairy and knocked heavily upon it.

'Peggy, it's Superintendent Hawke, can you hear me? I want to speak to you.'

When there was no reply he repeated the knock and call and this time put his ear against the door.

Straightening up, he said, 'I think I can hear her being sick.' Thumbing the latch, he flung the door open and the three men saw Peggy Woods seated on the floor, slumped against the wall.

Beside her was a pint measuring jug and a stoneware jar resting on its side, in which was a small quantity of white powder. There was more white powder scattered around the jug . . . and there was evidence nearby that she had recently been sick.

As the three men cautiously entered the dairy, Peggy let out an open-mouthed scream of pain and Amos said, 'She has poisoned herself . . . Tom, send one of the servants to fetch a doctor . . . as quickly as you can.'

Clutching her stomach and gasping with pain, Peggy said, 'A doctor won't be able to do anything. I've taken enough arsenic to kill a horse . . . '

Her statement ended abruptly as she doubled up with pain once more. When she raised her head again, she looked up at Amos and said hoarsely, 'I'd rather it ended here, like this. I've watched men and women die at the end of a rope, in Ireland and there's no dignity in it. This way is better.'

'We'll see about that when the doctor gets here, Peggy. In the meantime, are you able to tell me exactly what it is you've done . . . ?'

42

Peggy Woods died before the Bodmin doctor could be found and brought to Laneglos. It would be later confirmed that she had taken a massive dose of arsenic from the stock she kept hidden on a high shelf in the dairy behind some old pans and pots that were no longer in use and where none of the much smaller dairymaids could even see it, let alone reach it down.

Her death and the events that had brought it about horrified the whole of the servant staff at the great Cornish house. She had never been popular with anyone and in recent weeks her increasingly erratic behaviour had meant she was even more isolated than ever, but the manner of her self-inflicted death affected them all deeply.

Lord Hogg was equally shocked, but he found time to thank Amos and Tom for their diligence in the investigation which had resulted in the removal of the self-confessed murderer from his household.

At the Hawke home later that evening, when Talwyn brought in the last of the dishes to be placed on the table for their meal, she said, 'There, that's everything, so now I don't have to keep jumping up to go out into the kitchen you can both tell me what happened at Laneglos today, instead of sitting here looking smug.'

'I don't think smug is the right word, Talwyn. We've solved the murders of Enid and Lord

Hogg, certainly, but there has been too much tragedy involved for it to be a cause for celebration.' Amos went on to tell Talwyn of the traumatic events of the day, his narrative occasionally helped by Tom.

After hearing their story of the various happenings that day, Talwyn asked, 'When did you finally realize the murders had been committed by Peggy Woods?

'She became an immediate suspect after I spoke to the Honourable Charles Delville on our night journey back from London. As you know, he had been our main suspect until then, especially after we confirmed his valet's story of seeing a quantity of arsenic in Delville's London house — even though the arsenic container was full and didn't seem to have ever been opened. However, he told us that Peggy had approached him saying she knew Enid was pregnant by him and that Lord Hogg had threatened to strike him out of his will and refuse to pay any more of his debts if he got any more of the Laneglos servant girls pregnant. She threatened to tell Lord Hogg about Enid unless Delville paid for her silence. He agreed to give her the sum she asked for, although he told her he didn't have it immediately to hand. Tom and I later learned from Clemo, the Laneglos gamekeeper who had been having a long affair with Peggy, that it was about this time she wanted him to leave his wife and family and go away with her, saying she would soon have enough money to keep them both until they could find work.'

'You already knew about the affair, of course,

because Clemo had admitted it to you in his statement.'

'That's right, but it *was* no more than a casual, albeit long-standing affair as far as Clemo was concerned, he had no intention of ever taking it any farther, but Peggy didn't know this. She was totally obsessed with him and had been ever since she came to Laneglos. In fact, the only reason she married Chester Woods was to divert attention away from her relationship with him. So, when Enid became so upset about her condition and told Peggy she was going to report what had happened with Delville, Peggy could see her misplaced dream of running away with Clemo disappearing. On the evening of the night raid on the house, she lured Enid to the Laneglos church on the pretext of accompanying her to collect the candlesticks and altar crosses for cleaning. She murdered Enid and hid her body beneath the altar. There was a great deal of confusion at the house in the aftermath of the ball and everyone was tired, so Enid simply wasn't missed.'

'Poor Enid,' Talwyn said, emotionally, 'She was so trusting of everyone that she would have been delighted to think someone was willing to help with one of her chores. This Peggy Woods must have been insane!'

'Not so insane that she couldn't seize an advantage when she saw it. Later that night when she expected everyone at Laneglos — including her own husband — to be asleep, she slipped out of the house to meet up with Clemo, who should have been on gamekeeper patrol in a different part of the estate. She also used the opportunity to take Enid's body from the church and hide it in the rough ground at the far end of the cemetery. It was while she was on her way back from this that she happened to come across Delville talking to Alfie and Jimmy Banks. They didn't see her and she didn't know what they were up to, but when morning came and the burglary was discovered she put two-and-two together and came up with an answer she felt was going to secure her and Clemo for life. She tackled Delville yet again and told him what she knew, but this time she wasn't talking about just a few pounds. She demanded that he give her enough to enable her and Clemo to buy a public house, far away from Laneglos, and live happily ever after.'

'And we all noticed the discrepancy in the three statements about the length of time Peggy was out of the house that night . . . but surely she was aware Delville was a spendthrift and deeply in debt. How did she expect him to raise such an amount?'

'I think Delville pointed out that he had no money, but she told him he would have it from the proceeds of the robbery. When the stolen property was found and returned, he apparently saw her to say the situation had changed and she would need to wait longer for her money, until he inherited some from Lord Hogg. By now she was obsessed with the thought of going off with Clemo and the pair of them owning a pub and just couldn't bear the thought of having to wait for however long it might be. That's when the idea came to her of speeding up the Honourable Charles's inheritance . . . or what they both *thought* he was going to inherit. As we all know now, although she succeeded in poisoning Lord Hogg, he had already cut Delville out of his will. He had made over a large sum to Lady Hogg, but ensured it couldn't be touched by anyone else until *she* died . . . and so we come to the mysterious illness that she was suffering when Doctor Sullivan came upon the scene.'

'But how did Peggy manage to poison Lord and Lady Hogg without anyone suspecting her?'

'When no one realized that anyone was being poisoned it was easy for her. She was assistant cook at Laneglos and the head cook was a drunkard. In actual fact Peggy did most of the cooking and was able to take 'special care' with the food she prepared for her sick employers.'

Talwyn shuddered, 'It must be horrible to be living in a house where all that has been going on, what does Flora think about it all?'

'I haven't been able to speak to her about it yet,' Tom confessed, 'Too many things happened at Laneglos today for us to be able to say more than 'hello' to each other, but we'll be meeting up on Sunday and able to have a long talk about it then. I must confess that I'm hoping she will feel she wants to leave the house as soon as she possibly can.'

'What will happen if she decides she wants to leave?' Talwyn asked, although she felt she already knew what the answer would be.

'I will ask Flora to marry me,'

It was the reply Talwyn had been anticipating.

43

Before Tom's meeting with Flora, other events occurred which would unexpectedly affect the future of the two lovers and a number of others around them.

Three days after the death of Peggy Woods, the solicitor representing the Honourable Charles Delville succeeded in obtaining bail for his client, on the surety of Lord Hogg.

That afternoon the Laneglos peer sent for Chief Constable Gilbert and when he returned to police headquarters, Gilbert sent for Amos and Tom.

When they were both present in his office, the Cornwall police chief said, 'The information I have to tell you was originally intended only for you, Amos, but in view of all the work that Sergeant Churchyard has put into the arrest of Charles Delville, I feel he has a right to hear what I have to say.'

After telling them that he had just returned from Laneglos, he explained that he had met with both Lord Hogg and Delville's barrister, who told him that bail had been granted to Delville. The chief constable then gave his two listeners the astonishing news that the charge of burglary against the peer's step-brother was to be dropped.

When Amos began to protest, Gilbert held up his hand to silence him. 'I know exactly how you feel about it, Amos, and I admit that was my own immediate reaction, but Lady Hogg has employed one of the finest barristers in the country to represent her son and he has found a loop-hole in our case against Delville that I fear we can do absolutely nothing about. You see, at the time of the burglary, the property taken from Laneglos belonged to the late Lord Hogg, Delville's stepfather. He is now dead and therefore unable to prosecute. The present Lord Hogg had not yet come into the title, or the property at the time of the burglary, so he *cannot* prosecute and Lady Hogg has declared that if a prosecution is brought against her son she will go into the dock and declare that he had *her* permission to take whatever property from the house that he wished!'

Amos looked at the chief constable in stunned disbelief as he held up his hands in a gesture of resignation, 'So what can I do about it?' Then, answering his own question, he added, 'Nothing! The fact that the property was removed in the dead of night by known criminals should be sufficient in itself to prove that this was a nefarious act, but there is no law that dictates when property can be lawfully removed from a house, or who is employed to carry out the removal. So, you see, as far as the burglary is concerned, we have no case to present to the court.'

'Then . . . if there was no burglary, what happens to Alfie Banks? If there was no burglary, we have no case against him either!'

'I must admit I had never even thought about

Banks's part in all this,' admitted Gilbert. 'Will we be able to charge him with breaking Churchyard's wrist?'

Tom shook his head, 'It didn't happen here in Cornwall and I doubt if the Metropolitan Police will want to do anything about it. Even if they did it would be my word against his . . . and I have no doubt he could produce a dozen Hoxton witnesses to prove he was somewhere else at the time. No, it looks as though he'll get away scot free. We can't even charge him with hurting that little girl on the ship at Falmouth, because he would come straight back at us for making an illegal arrest.'

'Well, we will think about that later,' the chief constable said, philosophically, 'The only piece of good news I have to give you is that Lord Hogg has entered into an agreement with his stepbrother that he will buy the family heirlooms back from him at a very good price on condition that Delville uses the money to go out of the country — and never return.'

'Has he agreed?' Amos asked the question.

'Yes. I understand that arrangements are being made at this very moment for him to go to Canada where Lady Hogg inherited a considerable piece of land from her first husband . . . Delville's father. He will go out there and see what he can make of it.'

'Then I suppose there is nothing more we can do,' Tom said, despondently, 'After all the work we put into the case the two people who most deserve to be put away are going to get away scot free.'

'Your hard work was certainly not wasted,' Chief Constable Gilbert said emphatically. 'You have solved two murders, captured a number of burglars and thwarted an attempt to carry out one of the most audacious attacks on society I have ever come across. I think you should both be very proud of yourselves.'

'We have also got rid of a thoroughly obnoxious man in Charles Delville,' said Amos, thoughtfully, ' . . . and I think I might be able to rid ourselves of Alfie Banks too. He was going to Australia not only to avoid being arrested for burglary, but also because he knew he would no longer be looked upon as the top villain in Hoxton. He also said that he'd always had a yen to go to Australia . . . especially as a number of his close relatives are there . . . transported at the government's expense. I could say that we would forget about any conspiracy charges . . . which we couldn't make stick anyway, if he decided to carry out his original plan and go to Australia.'

'I think that would be a very satisfactory conclusion to an extremely difficult situation, Amos . . . oh, and am I mistaken, Churchyard, or is there a possibility you might be marrying in the not-too-distant future?'

The chief constable's question took Tom by surprise, especially as at that very moment he had been thinking how the latest developments in the cases he and Amos had been pursuing would affect his plans for him and Flora. He doubted very much whether Lady Hogg would take her on as a housekeeper if she knew her prospective husband was the policeman who had arrested her son and been partly responsible for him leaving the country never to return . . . but the chief constable was awaiting his reply.

'I hope to, sir . . . but I haven't asked her yet.'

'Well do so . . . and quickly,' the chief constable said, 'There will soon be a flat available here, in the headquarters annexe, to be occupied by an inspector responsible for training, recruitment, headquarters affairs and also, I suspect, carrying out the plain-clothes duties that Superintendent Hawke is so keen on, but which need to be carried out without the knowledge of the Police Committee. However, the flat needs to be occupied by a married man with a wife of whom I can approve, so I suggest you propose to this young lady, Churchyard, if you want to take advantage of the opportunity.'

Books by E. V. Thompson
Published by The House of Ulverscroft:

THE DREAM TRADERS
CRY ONCE ALONE
BECKY
GOD'S HIGHLANDER
THE MUSIC MAKERS
CASSIE
WYCHWOOD
BLUE DRESS GIRL
MISTRESS OF POLRUDDEN
THE TOLPUDDLE WOMAN
LEWIN'S MEAD
MOONTIDE
CAST NO SHADOWS
MUD HUTS AND MISSIONARIES
SOMEWHERE A BIRD IS SINGING
SEEK A NEW DAWN
WINDS OF FORTUNE
THE LOST YEARS
HERE, THERE AND YESTERDAY
PATHS OF DESTINY
TOMORROW IS FOR EVER
THE VAGRANT KING
NO LESS THAN THE JOURNEY
BEYOND THE STORM
THE BONDS OF EARTH

THE RETALLICK SAGA:
BEN RETALLICK

CHASE THE WIND
HARVEST OF THE SUN
SINGING SPEARS
THE STRICKEN LAND
LOTTIE TRAGO
RUDDLEMOOR
FIRES OF EVENING
BROTHERS IN WAR

THE JAGOS OF CORNWALL:
THE RESTLESS SEA
POLRUDDEN
MISTRESS OF POLRUDDEN

AMOS HAWKE:
THOUGH THE HEAVENS MAY FALL
HAWKE'S TOR

Other titles published by
The House of Ulverscroft:

THE BONDS OF EARTH

E. V. Thompson

1837. When rich deposits of copper ore are discovered near Bodmin Moor, a huge influx of out-of-work miners flock to the area from Cornwall's far west, bringing with them problems alien to the hard-working but easy-going countrymen. Young Goran Trebartha, whose working life is divided between two farms, finds himself caught between the seemingly incompatible cultures when he meets and gets to know the daughters of a mine captain who settles nearby. Avarice and intrigue, the vicissitudes of farming life and the sheer desperation of hungry miners all add to the bewildering changes that will irrevocably alter the course of Goran's life.

HAWKE'S TOR

E. V. Thompson

It's the nineteenth century. In a tiny moorland village in Cornwall, where the residents harbour dark secrets, two policemen investigate the brutal murder of a promiscuous young wife and the disappearance of her baby. Superintendent Amos Hawke and Sergeant Tom Churchyard believe the murderer will be found within the isolated and insular community, but unravelling the tangled web of lies and deceit proves frustrating. A young gypsy girl's appearance on the scene has disturbing ramifications for Tom Churchyard — but is she the answer to the mystery?

BEYOND THE STORM

E. V. Thompson

The fiercest storm in living memory pounds the shores of nineteenth century Cornwall, wrecking ships and bringing death and destruction to seafarers and coastal communities. When a young girl is found, washed up among the rocks of a remote North Cornish cove, she is barely alive. However her arrival, and the mystery surrounding her background, will affect the lives of those who come to know her — and, for Alice Kilpeck in particular, nothing will ever be the same again.

NO LESS THAN THE JOURNEY

E. V. Thompson

Wesley Curnow, a young Cornish miner, arrives in the United States to seek an uncle who is working on the mines in Missouri. Taking passage on a boat from New York, bound for New Orleans, he meets up with a charismatic US marshal who is *en route* to the western territories to bring law to the area. After a gun-fight with pirates on the Mississippi River and an encounter with an attractive half-Mexican croupier, Wes parts company with his companions only to find his uncle has been forced to move away. Wes faces a serious altercation with German miners, meets an old 'Mountainman' who teaches him proficiency with a revolver, and then faces a journey overland through inhospitable country. But can he survive the journey?

THOUGH THE HEAVENS MAY FALL

E. V. Thompson

It is 1856. Cornish schoolteacher Talwyn is grief-stricken when her father's body is discovered on the rocks at the foot of cliffs near their home. But his death was no accident. He was murdered. And Talwyn's father is not the only murder victim — there have been two other unsolved killings in recent months. Local magistrate Sir Joseph Sawle is convinced that the killings are connected. When Sir Joseph asks for assistance from London's Scotland Yard, Cornish-born detective Amos Hawke is sent to investigate. Amos's relationship with Tawlyn gets off to a disastrous start but as he works hard to break through the veil of fear and silence in order to bring her father's killer to justice, Talwyn's help becomes indispensable.